~~

ALOHA

~~

REVIEWS of the prequel...

"The Parrot Talks in Chocolate"

(amazon.com)

Magical, Whimsical Tour, September 1, 2010
By   **Mark Hettermann**
This review is from: The Parrot Talks in Chocolate: The Life and Times of a Hawaiian TIKI Bar (Paperback)
A whimsical tale of island life so vividly captured one would swear it is autobiographical. The sounds, colors, and personalities of the islands, specifically the Hawaiian Islands, are captured in a manner that transports the reader from everyday life to a "bar stool" surrounded by a cast of characters headed by a chocoholic parrot named Tiwaka. The peaceful, welcoming culture of the Hawaiian Islands, specifically propagated by the culture of the native Hawaiians, is subtly infused in every page...a must for the nightstand to free oneself of the realities of life while reading this "bed-time story" for adults.

A vacation without leaving home., April 7, 2010
By Dave Hazlett____ (Austin, Tx)
This review is from: The Parrot Talks in Chocolate: The Life and Times of a Hawaiian TIKI Bar (Paperback)
I bought this book on a recommendation from a friend and started reading it before going to bed one evening after a long stressful day. It captured my interest immediately and took me to colorful jungles and breathtaking beaches through the eyes of a modern islander with a good heart. I would read a chapter and fall peacefully asleep rather than caught up in the days worries. The next night I did the same chuckling and pondering the simple and fun lives of the Maui island characters. My wife observed this so I offered to read it to her and started the book all over again in the same fashion. Each evening we found ourselves enjoying the adventures and landscape through the written words of Everett. It became a nightly ritual. We took our time savoring it and fell asleep each night with a smile on our face.

I highly endorse reading this book... but don't keep it to yourself. Share it with someone you love.

Maui-licious-ness, March 23, 2010

By T.Redes
"yankee77"   ____ (CH, NC)

This review is from: The Parrot Talks in Chocolate: The Life and Times of a Hawaiian TIKI Bar (Paperback)
I just finished reading The Parrot Talks in Chocolate and I feel like I haven't quite woken up from the dreamy-state it put me in. I tried to stretch it out for as long as possible because I didn't want it to end. It brought me to a place full of interesting & quirky people, protective banyan trees, and fabulous drinks. I loved the stories and the feelings that it evoked and I love that it transported me to Maui... without even getting on a plane. This author is a very talented writer and I adore how his brain works- I can't wait for more works of his to be released so I can dive right back in!

I want a Parrot like Tiwaka!, December 2, 2009

By

(Fort Lauderdale, Florida) -

Christopher Pinto "Tiki Chris Pinto"

This review is from: The Parrot Talks in Chocolate: The Life and Times of a Hawaiian TIKI Bar (Paperback)

Once in a while I come across a book that is well written, fun to read, and interesting enough to keep me turning the pages. The Parrot Talks In Chocolate is one of those gems, and if you like Tiki and Hawaiian culture, this book should go to the top of your list.

This story has the perfect balance of fact and fantasy, describing life in Hawaii in picturesque detail touched with a bit of magic. It's light reading and fun, and really will make you wish you were there.

Happiness Takes Effort, February 12, 2010

By Jennifer Sopranzi "JenReader" (CA USA)

This review is from: The Parrot Talks in Chocolate: The Life and Times of a Hawaiian TIKI Bar (Paperback)

The Parrot Talks in Chocolate is a magical tale woven around the characters and events in a Hawaiian Tiki bar. The bar is run by a young man who, along with a wise parrot named Tiwaka and an ancient dog named Ococ, has found the true key to happiness. My favorite quote from the book: "Happiness takes effort. You have to make yourself available to happiness. That is probably the best definition of faith that I can come up with."

Happiness is an act of faith and faith takes courage-not superhero, beat-up the bad guy kind of courage, but the courage to be vulnerable and accept what the universe offers. Each of the characters in the book has his or her own kind of courage and wisdom, and so they are drawn to the Tiki bar, itself a magic sort of place.

The story is told with a simplicity that is beautiful and pure. I highly recommend The Parrot Talks in Chocolate.

In the Middle
of the Third Planet's
Most Wonderful
of
Oceans

by

Everett Peacock

visit

TiwakaTiki.com

or drop by on Facebook

No part of this publication may be reproduced, or stored in a
retrieval system, or transmitted in any form or by any means,
electronic, mechanical, photocopying, recording or otherwise,
without written permission of the author. For information
regarding permission, email to everett@peacock.com

ISBN 1453807233

EAN-13 9781453807231

cover design by: John Giordani

JohnGDesign.com

also available for Kindle, iPad and other eBook formats

at http://TiwakaTiki.com

Other books by the Author

The Parrot Talks in Chocolate

theParrotTalksInChocolate.com

2009

~~~

Death.by.Facebook

deathbyfacebook.info

2010

~~~

A Perfect Analogy

aPerfectAnalogy.com

2011

~~

~ ~ ~

for all the Surfers

and

those on the beach

~ ~ ~

PREFACE

Perfection is best viewed from a distance.

If we look too closely, at anything, we narrow our focus away from its complimentary surroundings. We might see the moles and misplaced hairs on the beautiful fashion model's face. We might very well see the tiny scratches in a paint job that from a short distance looks fantastic on a '64 Mustang.

Paradise is no different. Fill it with too many details, complain about the slow drivers or bad roads and you'll find yourself wondering what you are doing there in the first place. Slow down a bit, skip that second helicopter ride and consider not driving to Hana and back the same day.

The devil may very well be in those details, making us narrow our view and miss the wonderful ways many things have of working together. A coconut tree looks much better on a beach, in the sunshine, moving slightly in the trade winds. By itself it may not project the same feeling. Looking too closely cheats you of the big picture. And, besides, if you look too close at a helicopter you just might find it impossible to enjoy the ride anyhow.

So, step back, take a deep breath, maybe another, and really open your eyes. I suspect that wherever you are you will see your world in a slightly more positive light. If it happens to be cold, rainy and gray outside, it's OK, you *do* have this book in your hands. By the time you get to the last page I predict you will be much better at appreciating all the perfection that already surrounds you.

Everett Peacock

September 11, 2010

Kula, Maui, Hawaii

~~

Dedicated to

the brave men

and women

who ensure my freedom

to sit on a little island

at a Tiki bar

writing stories

of peace and love

big mahalos!

~~

CONTENTS

~~

~~~

Signals. Getting any?

I sure was. It seemed like the whole world was talking, the jungle, the ocean and something deep inside.

It was time to pay attention.

~~~

~ ~ ~

Letters to my Children

It first happened when awakening from a nap in my hammock above the sea cliffs. My eyes popped open suddenly as if someone might be standing next to me, talking. This perch was relatively secret with no road, trail or map to expose it. I looked around just to be sure and felt it again even as I saw no one there. It was a haunting feeling, but not one of dread or fear. It was a presence, strong and definite, happy to meet me and extremely cheerful. I smiled tentatively and said softly "Nice to meet ya."

My mind tickled with a feeling of light laughter and I felt that surging tingling on my skin and inside the back of my neck. My eyes weren't really looking at anything but I saw with my feelings, someone young and vibrant. They were incredibly excited to be here, talking with me as it were. "See you soon," was something I understood after a moment and slowly my interrupted nap reminded me I was once more alone.

I turned back to look at the cobalt Pacific laced with white and thought again about starting a family. This island seemed perfectly suited to sharing with kids. Kids that I could teach to surf, hula and laugh at my jokes.

So, it is to you, my yet unborn children, that I write these letters, these stories. I want you to know how we came to meet and what my world was like before you were born to a super stoked surfer who lived in a treehouse ~ above a Tiki Bar ~ on the little island of Maui, in the middle of the third planet's most wonderful of oceans.

~~~
# Choices

Life seems to usually be running at 135% of its normal speed. Too many options and you soon begin to miss a lot of the good stuff. A perfect example would be having to decide between going surfing and sleeping in late with a beautiful young woman. Either choice would force missing out on the other outstanding option.

Her intoxicating leg, thrown over my hip, would have been so much warmer than the chilly morning wave now sweeping through my hair. I hollered at its abruptness but now, completely transitioned to wetness, I paddled hard through the quiet waters of the deserted bay, once again a sea creature.

The dawning sky finally let me see down into the clearness and to the reef below. My favorite star was just peeking up above the sea promising to take the chill out of the air. Up ahead Sandy turned and lazily stroked into a shoulder high wave, her still dry hair and radiant smile reflecting crisply off the water. Dozens of colorful reef fish raced ahead of her hoping, no doubt, to catch her attention.

I stopped so I could lift up off my board and give her a good surfer-hoot, nice and loud. Sitting there and watching those same intoxicating legs gracefully dance along the wave, I surmised my options: when offered two outstanding choices always go with some of each.

~~~

Jungle Love

Love must surely be the most powerful force around. People that love something usually embrace it to some extreme, even if it can't be any good for them. Some people love to gamble, and unless they are really good at cheating, it eventually does more harm than good. Infatuated strangers get called stalkers when they love beyond their capacity to enjoy reciprocation. Love comes in several flavors, one being the rich and creamy one called Excess. Popular with so many of us we use it to enhance what we eat, or drink, or to feed our need for speed sitting atop fast motorcycles on dark mountain roads.

The world is full of many other such flavors, as evident by the countless books written, movies produced or songs sung. Flavors that make us better are my favorite. Every person alive knows its special tingle.

Here in the jungle we have a flavor few of us recognize until it is far too late to escape. In this beautiful vortex of sweet tradewinds, rich volcanic soils, song birds that can make you cry and waterfalls the flavor is known simply as #9.

I sure didn't recognize it, at first. It kind of sneaks up on you, like a good song that sounds so much better after you hear it a few times. Naturally, it took a parrot to point it out to me.

~~~

It was early in a late morning and I was polishing the bar, preparing my limes and getting things ready for a big Friday. Tiwaka, my ever faithful parrot, was patrolling the perimeter of our fine establishment, ostensibly to alert me to any trash. Occasionally I looked for him, like one might keep a watchful eye on a toddler. There, out at the edge of the lawn, just before the jungle began its magnificent unbroken climb toward the mountain top, he marched. His head held back high, looking like a British Bobby, he stepped high and confident, until he detected something of interest. Immediately then, his demeanor would collapse into that of a foraging dog, sniffing under and rolling away leaves and brush that might be hiding something delicious.

Bugs, no doubt, were specifically designed for the culinary pleasure of birds, evidenced by their extreme joy in finding one. Tiwaka had come up with a large centipede half way around the yard, jumping up and down while the insect tried squirming away from between his beak. For a brief moment I thought I heard old Ococ grunting with fresh hamburger, but it was that bird enjoying his bounty. When the last dozen or so legs finally disappeared he turned into the sunlight and slowly spread his wings. I don't know if he was offering thanks or showing off, but his tail wiggled a little in a silent dance.

After a few moments he recovered from his ecstasy and made a bee line back to the bar. Two quick hops and he was up on the Koa counter, smiling as well as a beak would allow.

"What about the rest of your patrol Tiwaka?" I asked.

He looked back out toward the lawn, apparently having remembered now his original purpose. Before turning his head back to me, his left eye turned to me and blinked twice. I didn't really expect him to finish up, but I couldn't resist to ask.

"No need Boss," he squawked. "Happy parrot now."

I stopped mid polish, setting down the large glass beer stein and looked at him. His vocabulary was increasing daily thanks to Ms. Melita letting him sit in twice a week at her small jungle elementary school, Roots. New words, that I expected. But not his conceptualization of purpose. It took a special gift to understand a way to find happiness. This bird went out in search of something he loved, something good for him, found it and enjoyed it. Humans take note.

"You're happy Tiwaka?" I asked, still incredulous at his statement.

The parrot bobbed his head once, and looked the other direction while scratching his feet along the bar top. I got the impression he was getting emotional. Of course, that could have been my imagination.

"Tiwaka?" I continued softly. "Are you happy here, at the bar?" Quietly I put my towel down, looking around and hoping no one would interrupt this moment. The coast was clear.

The parrot stomped his feet, gathering his courage no doubt and turned to look at me, first one eye and then the other. I knew he often needed time to process his thoughts, so I waited patiently. He flapped his wings a bit, anxious to find the words he wanted to use, perhaps new words he had learned at Roots.

I couldn't help but smile. This bird, my friend of many years, my companion was trying so hard to express himself.

"I love…" he paused, thinking. "…bugs." He flapped his wings a little more, trying to move more words up. "I love…" he bobbed his head twice this time, "…Boss."

That moment, I will always remember, was the only time an animal made me cry without biting me.

"Wow," I whispered, trying to control my voice as well. "Mahalo Tiwaka. I love you too buddy." I picked up the bar towel, found a clean corner and wiped my tear before it fell into the lime bowl.

Just when I was going to hug the feathered beast someone could be heard making their way down our long gravel driveway, on a noisy 2-stroke moped.

"Game faces Tiwaka, customers are early today!" I forced the emotional moment back into some corner of my mind, where I might find it again later. Tiwaka no doubt did the same.

I glanced up at the "Hawaiian Time" clock Shiloh had sent and it was just a moment or so after 12 noon. Well then, it was indeed after 12 somewhere and it had found us. We were open.

A faint blue oily smoke exhaust rose up above the driveway painting where the moped had just been, but it was itself still hidden by the hibiscus hedges. Suddenly the engine stopped, but I could still hear it rolling along the gravel, taking advantage of the downhill.

In a moment, rounding the corner onto the lawn rolled a familiar customer I just couldn't quite place. He propped his now silent transport against the coconut tree conveniently planted there decades ago for just such purpose and walked over to the bar.

He had that semi-permanent smile I had seen before in the little beach hamlet of Paia. Walking directly to the Stool of Truth, he parked it promptly and looked up at the both of us.

"Well, been a while hasn't it?"

Tiwaka walked over to him, pushing napkins and toothpicks out of the way with his feet. Peering closer at the early customer, perhaps to smell his name, he lingered only long enough to avoid being rude.

"Vic?" I asked staring a moment. "You look … good. A little sunburn though."

Vic pushed his hand back through his hair, "Yep, keep losing my hat on that putt-putt of a moped."

"It's your hair! That's it, longer." Now I recognized him as the nuclear sub guy who picked pineapples for a while and then blasted off for Tahiti on a sailboat.

I placed a new Hinano beer coaster in front of him and a napkin. The Tahitian lager was popular here at Tiwaka's Tiki Bar & Grill.

Vic picked up the colorful coaster and looked at the front and back, placing it back down. "Had too many of these I must admit."

"I bet!" I looked quickly into our beer cooler. "Wanna another?"

Tiwaka had retreated a foot or so back down the bar, but was still watching Vic like he was going to magically turn into a big cashew any moment.

"No, no. Thanks." He looked over at Tiwaka. "You still practicing?"

I looked over at Tiwaka, he was nodding.

"He even goes to school twice a week now. Can't believe..."

Tiwaka interrupted me with a loud squawk and then threw his head back, flexed his wings and said, "Treasure Island Keeps Improving."

Vic sat back laughing. "That's right! T.I.K.I." Vic turned toward me pointing at the parrot. "That's gotta be the smartest parrot I have ever heard of, much less met."

Proud as I was of Tiwaka, he still could easily impress me with his recall, and his timing. Vic had taught him that acronym probably a year ago.

"Must be something in the water, I dunno, but he seems to be getting much better at speaking." My partiality was only partly to blame on my bragging.

Vic nodded, not so much in agreement that the bird was smart, but something else.

"Do you have any fresh coconut? Coconut water?" he asked.

Sure we did. A Coco Loco Moco required fresh coconut water, in fact it was served up inside a freshly opened coco, with half the water still inside.

"Of course!" I looked under the bar for my stash of cocos, but remembered, at not seeing any, that I had not fully prepared for tonight. "Uh, wait..." I walked down the bar hoping to find one left over from the night before. Nothing. "Vic, looks like we're out for a moment."

"No worries, I'll wait for .... " he volunteered.

"No, no. I need some anyhow, for tonight. Give me ten minutes." I walked back over to where he and the parrot were. "You want something different instead?"

Vic stood up. "No, but I'll help you gather some cocos bro!"

"Cool." Turning to the parrot, "Tiwaka, you're in charge." I reached under the bar to grab the sixteen inch machete and my ball cap.

"Whoa," Vic exclaimed. "Is that for the rowdies?"

I laughed a little. It was really to open coconuts when making the Coco Loco Mocos, but I always felt better knowing it was there. "Well, usually Tiwaka takes care of the occasional trouble," I looked over at the parrot, now standing tall, his chest thrown out in bravado. "But, it's there to back him up if he needs it."

Vic shot a half smile glance over at the parrot and nodded. He turned and walked with me, out toward the coconut grove. "That bird sure is special, isn't he?"

My emotions were still a little fragile, tough guy that I was and all. I walked a moment with Vic, not answering right away. The warm tropical sun felt real good on my skin and the light breeze pulled my attention up toward the expansive blue ocean ahead of us. Of course Tiwaka was special in new ways I had never realized until this morning.

"Well, it is *his* bar." Deflection was a skill I had learned bartending. "We're almost there."

Vic and I walked along in silence as we finally reached the thousand strong coconut grove. We stood about ten feet above the base of the grove on the high ground, and at least half the trees were still quite a bit above our heads.

Vic whistled in awe, no doubt also wondering how we were going to retrieve any cocos at all. I looked over at him and then handed him the machete.

"You pitch, I'll catch."

"I dunno about…"

"No worries Vic. Just kidding." I took the offered machete back. "I have some shorter Fijian trees over here, in the corner."

Vic was shaking his head, thankful. "I never climbed any that high."

"Me either, not without equipment. I use a deer stand when I do, works great." We pushed through a small banana patch and into another smaller coco grove. All the trees here had large green cocos hanging low enough that we could reach them standing on the ground.

"Yeah, I like this a lot better." Vic breathed relieved.

"These are the better ones for juice." I added. "I pick these on special occasions or when we aren't going to put any alcohol in them."

We cut down a clump of six, weighing about forty pounds.

"Lets drink one right here, shall we?" Vic asked.

"Sure." I cut one loose from the clump, turned it so I could whack off the bottom, opposite from the three eyes most folks saw in the stores. I prided myself in being able to get a nice spout open in four or five swings of the knife. I handed Vic his and prepared my own.

Neither of us talked for a moment as we drank up the cool, sweet water inside. The nutritionist at Mana Foods Grocery said fresh cocos were full of electrolytes, Vitamin C and had various healing properties, some of which I was unfamiliar with. Coconut milk, often sold as a cooking preparation, is made from the pressed white meat inside. The water though, what you found when you opened one, was what we enjoyed.

As I finished my half quart or so I looked out at the big white splashes in the ocean just offshore. Vic was pointing too.

"Whales!" he yelled. "I didn't see many of those in Tahiti."

I watched as several spouts followed the jumping. "Must be a half dozen of them." Sitting my now empty coco down, I looked at Vic. He was still staring out to sea. "So, tell me, how was Tahiti?"

He continued to look ahead, avoiding my gaze as he answered. It took him a moment but he finally did so in a loud whisper, the kind of voice used to keep from displaying more emotion than you wanted to. "Overwhelming." He looked down into his coco, tipped it up one more time and sat it down between us, finished.

I waited for him to explain, as I would for Tiwaka to find the right words himself. Looking back out toward the horizon, the whales, obviously members of the US Olympic Splash Team were getting the most out of their training. Closer, the trees around us were full of birds, no doubt alerting their friends to the imminent availability of some sweet coconut meat. It was a lively morning indeed.

"What I mean," he finally added. "It was intense. In a good way."

"Tahiti? Intense? I would've figured it was relaxing." What did I know, I had never been there.

Vic looked back out to the whales, now slapping their tails and just having a big time of it. "Well, I guess it could be. But, the trip down on the sailboat almost killed us a couple of times. There were only four crew and we had at least ten days of severe weather. The equator was so full of thunderstorms."

"No kidding?" I guess sailing wasn't all sunsets and martinis.

Vic shook his head. "When we finally got into Papeete, we were exhausted. But, we had to leave almost immediately. The guy who owned the boat, our captain, had apparently pissed off the French Constable there on his last trip. If it hadn't been getting dark we would have had to make way before we even docked.

I knew a little French and talked the Officer into letting us stay until morning. The waterfront there was hopping and we ate good at the les Roulottes. I even found the energy to drop into Le Retro for a couple of Hinanos."

"Roulottes?" I asked.

"They're like lunch wagons here, but a little nicer. Tables set out and awnings. Very reasonable food as well. It was ..."

Vic paused a moment. Something had his inner attention and he was fighting to sort it out.

"Tell me more Vic, this sounds like a good story." Encouragement often helped overcome any demons.

He poked at the white coco meat just at the spout of his empty, so I offered to open it up. One swift swing of the knife and it lay bare. I cut mine open as well and threw half out a few feet away for the birds.

"Anyhow, we left at dawn, just at the cops were showing up again. I never found out what this guy had done, but it was enough to keep us moving.

"The captain said we should head over to Mo'orea, but instead of pulling into Vaiare where all the ferries went, he wanted to try the opposite side of the island. I figured he must have also pissed off the harbor master at Vaiare as well.

"It was already afternoon when we pulled silently into Opunohu bay. The two other sailboats we saw turned a hard right into the dock area of Papetoai, but we just continued deeper into the bay. Soon we could see a small thatched building just off to the side. We anchored off about twenty meters.

"We were tired, but glad to be in flat water with no hassles. I wanted to get some distance between myself and this sailor of ill-repute. As luck would have it, two skiffs motored out toward us."

"Good guys or bad?" I asked.

"Yeah, I was looking for guns as they got closer. Pirates or police, I was expecting either." Vic said.

"Geez."

"Fortunately, they were restauranteurs, willing to take us to shore, and to their little eatery. They loaded us up and in minutes we were in that thatched hut drinking and eating. And falling in love."

I looked at Vic, surprised.

"Yeah. One of the ladies there, who drove one of the skiffs, was... incredible. Maybe I was vulnerable or something." Vic picked out another piece of perfect coco meat. "Or, maybe I was ready. She was your classic Polynesian beauty, about forty, funny, easy to be with. She was like a vision in a sailor's dream. The kind that makes you forget the sea forever."

I watched the mynah birds devouring the coco meat out in the sun where I had thrown the halves. Some cardinals were trying to muscle in and get a taste.

"She invited me back to her little home, back up in the hills, as well as the other girl with our boat. The three of us made our way back to this idyllic spot with a view of the bay, surrounded by papaya and breadfruit trees."

Vic pushed his hands through his hair. "I mean, seriously, it was picture perfect. I slept in a hammock she put up in the kitchen and Joanie took the couch. The next morning, Joanie was gone and I found myself alone with Manutea. Breakfast was fresh fruit and some potatoes, with fresh guava juice.

Everything became a blur, like good vacations tend to do to your old mindset. In the late mornings, she took me fishing and diving in her outrigger canoe, in the evenings we drank rum and danced."

I was watching Vic tell this story like he was reciting a dream. I was also wondering why he was sitting here on the opposite side of the equator from Manutea's home.

"Every night we drank fresh coconut water and made love under the stars. She insisted on the coco, opening one from a small patch of trees she had in the back of her place. In the mornings, we made love again before breakfast. And, then repeated the days all over again.

"She taught me how to surf, small waves of course. I speared fish, climbed *short* coconut trees and cooked banana soufflés."

Vic looked over at me, trying to gauge my reaction. I hoped my expression showed quite a bit of fascination, because that's what I felt.

"Well? Go on Vic. I still don't know why you're sitting under a coconut tree here on Maui and not cooking some new banana dish back on Mo'orea." I threw another piece of coconut meat out to the birds bouncing around in the sunlit grass.

Vic stood up. Reluctantly I too pushed myself up as well. I picked up the machete, and kicked the remains of our coconuts out from under the shade and over to the rock concert of birds all squawking and singing and indulging themselves.

"You know," Vic finally said. "It felt like I had been drugged. It was all so perfect, so wonderful. How could that be real?"

He obviously was unsure that his leaving had been the right thing to do, but here he was regardless. We walked back to the still empty bar. Tiwaka was back out in the yard looking for bugs.

Walking around to the back of the bar, I put the machete back in its place and pulled out two clean glasses. As I held them in my hands, turning toward the bar and Vic I had the funniest feeling. I just wasn't thirsty, but beyond that it was a satiated feeling. It was good to feel some power over routine and habit.

Vic waved off a drink as well. Putting the glasses back, I turned to the iPod and and started the playlist going. I had to have some tunes on. Music had always been my clean drug. Clean because it had no side effects and did no harm. There weren't many such things and the ones I could find I surely embraced.

Vic and I both just kind of sat there, looking around at this little jewel of a scene we found ourselves in, letting his story sink in slowly. The light breezes moved through the bar, tickling the bamboo chimes hanging from the ceiling and moving across to the large bamboo patch at the edge of the jungle. The fluffies were racing across the blue sky and the air was so pristinely warm it felt like the breath of God herself. Vic was smiling too, we both were feeling it, we both knew it well. Exquisite existence.

Everyone has had the feeling, a moment of feeling really good. Feeling like you are so happy to be alive, stoked to be right where you are. For some it may have been a long time ago, but you never quite forget it.

Just as I was tumbling down that rabbit hole of thought, a large clump of coconuts fell from one of the taller trees at the edge. This particular tree was so bountiful it could not hold everything it was capable of producing, and as the nuts grew bigger they would simply push themselves away and off the tree.

Several hit the ground with a seismic thump that would have, in the old days, rousted old Ococ from his padded pillow. Two cocos split apart from the impact spraying the grass with juice. Every bird in the area immediately showed up, even Tiwaka made his way through the flocks. They all were quick to drink up the juice still pouring out of the nuts.

As the birds got their taste they retreated a bit, letting the others get a chance. Those that moved away walked slowly instead of flittering about. Tiwaka surely got his fill and began a slow saunter back toward Vic and I at the bar. We both watched him comically enjoy himself as he gracefully hopped, with wing assist, up to his perch. He probably felt as good as we did.

"Hey Tiwaka, are you feeling it too buddy?" Vic asked.

He bobbed his head a little just as the The Platters were finishing up 'Smoke Gets in Your Eyes' on the 1959 portion of our music rotation.

"Tiwaka, what do you like so much about coconut water?" I asked, looking out to the yard. "All your bird friends sure love it."

Vic and I watched the parrot, thinking he would ignore that question after a moment. Suddenly he threw back his head and announced, "Love Potion #9" just before the song of that name began playing.

As we listened to the first few seconds of the song, Vic and I looked at each other and knew immediately. The parrot pointed out one of the obvious things we humans are so good at not seeing.

It was something in the water alright, the coconut water! The birds loved it. Vic and I had drank it and had that old familiar feeling again, of mild euphoria. Love Potion #9 indeed!

Vic spoke up first, like he had finally figured it all out. "Manutea and I drank coconut water...from her patch of trees..." He stood up, excited. "That's the key, like it's an elixir or something"

I was laughing. My wonderment at what to make of that good feeling we had so often, the timing of the song on the playlist, Tiwaka answering our question by simply announcing the next title all seemed too coincidental. I mentioned this to Vic.

"You know as well as I do," he said. "Coincidental and random are just two words we use to deal with things we don't yet understand."

True.

I nodded my head in mild amazement. It was no surprise, the coconut water being something special, but it was new information that made it more spectacular. Perhaps that was what made my Coco Loco Moco so enticing!

Tiwaka was watching the remainder of the birds fly off into the jungle, giggling and singing.

"I love it," I whispered to myself.

Tiwaka turned to look at me and said, "Jungle love." He hopped down off his perch and landed on the bar. "Jungle love Boss."

~ ~ ~

Mongoose
(the other white meat)

In the early days of post-discovery Hawaii, when sugar would soon be the only King left, the plantations discovered yet another problem the world had brought to these virgin shores. Rats.

The sailing ships from North America, Latin America and Europe were infested with rodents, mosquitoes, and roaches. The sailors themselves harbored measles, venereal disease and every scourge any continent could offer. Twenty-five hundred miles of open ocean had been a great buffer for thousands of years against invasive species, but no longer. Today, modern Hawaii is the dubious holder of all endangered species records.

Of course, some invasive species we can live with. Ourselves being one, for the most part. Chickens are another and that brings me to my story.

Rats love sugar cane for the same reason we do. It's sweet, delicious and on this island, readily available. The plantation owners figured if they imported the mongoose it would attack and eat all the rats and that would be that. Plus, the mongoose didn't like sugar cane.

Three problems became immediately evident. One, the rat moved at night. Two, the mongoose moved during the day. And, three, the mongoose loved chicken eggs!

It might seem ironic that one invasive species might eat the eggs of another invasive species, if it weren't for the fact that Bruce loved his chickens. It was more than ironic, it was a big pain in the okole.

Bruce was living one of those storybook lives at the edge of the sea, above a small cove, approached by a one lane jungle road and then a smaller path still through a banana patch. His home was modest, self built and beautifully functional. His wife grew taro and vegetables and the kids caught large fish off the rocks, surfed and sometimes ventured into Paia to see what the rest of the world was up to.

Despite being in his 60s, Bruce was, by far, the healthiest person I had ever met. It could have been a large dose of good genetics but it was certainly reinforced with his diet. Chicken, fish, that which came from the garden and rainwater. No beer, no alcohol, no dairy, no starch.

His free range chickens had two acres of beautiful land to wander, explore and hide their eggs. It was those eggs that the mongoose could not resist. They had already decimated the native bird populations to near extinction by eating their ground nests. All that was left, and plentiful, were the eggs of all the wild Polynesian chickens on the island, and those at Bruce's.

He trapped them for a while, the mongoose, but they were relentless, showing up again and again. One mongoose could wipe out two dozen eggs or more, plus the small chicks it might catch. About a month after they had been discovered by the hoards, he was down to half a dozen large hens and a couple of aloof roosters. Some dogs began to help, but if a cobra wasn't fast enough a canine was never going to catch one, plus the numbers were just too great. Finally he had to begin caging his remaining birds. That was when I showed up one day, to fish.

I had hiked down from the main dirt road, crossed the banana patch and finally found his sunny lawn perched on the forty foot cliffs above the cove. "Yo! Bruce! OK to fish a little?" I announced. There was no other doorbell but my voice.

"Ahoy!" I heard from deep inside the plantation styled home.

Walking over to the kiawi post fence at the cliff edge I watched that funny swirl the ocean gets as a fresh water stream flows into it. It looked like a little kid tickling a big one, then getting overwhelmed when the bigger kid tickled back.

"Hey there! You going to try your luck?" Bruce asked, walking down from the house.

I turned and grinned. Here came the only sixty year old guy I had ever met with six cubes on his stomach, tan and stronger than most guys half his age. It was a testament to clean living. "Yeah, I heard there was an overpopulation of Ulua. Thought I would do my part."

Bruce laughed a little cynically. "Yeah, there's some overpopulation going on around here alright."

I sensed he wasn't talking about fish. "What do you mean?" Glancing back out to the cove quickly, I saw dolphins moving in and immediately thought my target fish population was going to get smaller.

"My chickens," he pointed back up toward his cages. "They're getting wiped out by these mongoose." He shook his head sadly. This was not a hobby for him, he depended on this flock to help feed his crew there at the cove. "You got a moment, I need to figure something out?"

"Sure," I agreed. We both 'had a moment'. In fact we had nothing else to do, but could probably come up with something if we really had to.

I followed Bruce over to his lawn chairs tucked under a hala tree and we both sat and propped our feet up on the fence overlooking the ocean. It was our best thinking position.

Bruce had both hands behind his head, watching the dolphins. "These varmits are wiping out my chickens. I can't trap them fast enough. I must have buried a hundred of them, and they keep coming. It's like an invasion."

I flashed on an old World War II movie I had seen as a kid, well before I should have. It was terribly frightening to see the bad guys so numerous all heading your way. "I don't guess we can call in an air strike eh?"

Bruce laughed. "It would take a lot of them." He continued watching the dolphins.

"You know, I just heard on the radio that the Upcountry farmers are having a hard time with those Axis deer. They are eating everyone's crops. Apparently, no one wants to hunt them anymore."

Bruce looked over at me, thinking about something.

I continued, remembering more of my small kid days. "My uncle showed up a couple of times, I remember, with venison, which he explained was deer meat. I loved it.

"Another invasive species, those deer, with no predators to keep them in check, not even hunters."

Bruce was forming a smile slowly as I talked and he formulated some idea he was increasingly liking. I kept talking.

"You know, if they started carrying venison at Mana Foods, maybe people would rediscover how good it is, and maybe people would start hunting deer again." That seemed like a logical idea to me.

"Have you tried..." I asked but was interrupted.

"Why don't we try...." Bruce jumped up and headed over to the grill pit. "...something new!" He was laughing.

I kept having visions of road kill, which were where I usually saw mongoose. Of course, deer littered many a road on the mainland as well.

"Let me check my traps!" Bruce was running now, excited at the prospect of a new weapon in the Mongoose Wars.

My fishing was going to wait a while, and my lunch was going to be something entirely new. I had made it a life mission to try anything once, if there was a reasonable chance of survival. As Bruce walked back around the corner of the massive breadfruit tree next to his house with two headless mongoose, I knew I could now add something to my own personal Bucket List.

"Well, lets give this a try, shall we?" Bruce laid the two carcasses on his cutting board, next to the grill, where many a fish had moved from this life to the next. After quickly dressing out the animals, he reached under to a cabinet full of oils and salts. "I think some olive oil and some Hawaiian salt should work."

He turned to me for a moment, "Hot sauce now, or later?"

I was still staring at the relatively skinny bodies stretched out on the grill, slowing sizzling. "Hmm, maybe later?"

Bruce turned back to his grill, smoke rising and spinning back toward me. I couldn't help but think it smelled like chicken, but then that was what I was hoping it would smell like.

"This shouldn't take very long," Bruce commented as he turned them both over. He sprinkled them with some more oil and salt and if I closed my eyes, they still smelled like chicken.

"Wow!" Bruce exclaimed, apparently happier about this then he initially thought. "They don't look half bad."

My imagination wavered between the other half that might be bad, and this becoming a successful idea. Bruce and I might become mongoose ranchers by day and bartenders by night.

In a few minutes they were done, and Bruce plopped them on a big plate, poured some hot sauce out on one side of the plate and grabbed the obligatory shoyu bottle. We walked back over to our lawn chairs to enjoy, quite possibly, the first human meal of mongoose ever.

As we sat down and looked longer at the plate than we would have at fish, chicken, steak or even asparagus, we laughed.

"Mongoose, the other white meat!" Bruce pronounced.

I sat back laughing. "That's our angle then, we need to convince everyone on Maui that this stuff rivals chicken." Just like the pork guys did with that slogan.

Bruce was giddy. "Got Mongoose?" and put a small leg up to just below his nose, like a milk mustache.

I waved that one off as a no, falling out of my chair laughing. That leg looked so skinny I had to holler out "Where's the Beef?" I still couldn't stop laughing enough to crawl back up into my chair.

Managing to sit up on the grass I watched as Bruce pulled off a strip of meat and tentatively took a bite. His face was classic, a mix of anticipation and abject fear. Standing up I went back to the plate and grabbed a piece myself. Sitting down slowly I took a bite, eyes closed and trying hard to imagine Kentucky Fried Chicken.

It wasn't as bad as I had thought. It wasn't oily or gamey. It was incredibly salty though, from the seasoning. Bruce was looking at me for my reaction and saw, as I had in him, that I wasn't disgusted.

"Well," I volunteered. "It's better than I expected."

"Yeah," Bruce said, nodding. "But, I think it might be better ground into burger."

I grinned, mongoose meat still in my mouth. "Maybe an extender? Mix it with hamburger, or put it in hotdogs?"

"Sure, they put any kine in hotdogs don't they?" Bruce asked.

I was sure that hot dogs were a mix of whatever meat fragments could be swept up off a production floor before the inspector could get there. But, what would we call it?

"Goosedogs then?"

Bruce shook his head no. "Mondogs?"

That didn't work either. We had to come up with something that would make everyone on this island crave mongoose meat. Other than everyone starving, I was having trouble thinking up a reason.

It would have to be promoted as some kind of delicacy, where only a small portion would be needed. Something one would enjoy on special occasions. It would take some thinking, some inspiration of almost epiphanatic proportions.

"Pass the hot sauce would ya?" I asked, as I closed my eyes and imagined.

~~~

Sweet Sandy

There are some things you could never have planned to have worked out as well as they did. Not in a million years, nor in a million dreams. Such good fortune most likely found you because you made yourself available; available for good things to happen. Simple as that sounds it was usually pretty difficult to actually do. Distractions could sap the potential right out of your life.

These thoughts were coursing through my early morning mind after my afternoon of mongoose fillets the day before. I had mixed up a fruit smoothie so amazing that I had to practically fight Tiwaka off from his insistence on sampling it. Sitting out on the lawn just out from under the thatched dining area I could see the near cliffs and hear the ocean knocking on the doors there. The sky was shaping up to a decision point it had been struggling to figure out. Should it rain, or should it shine? A light mist mixed with some sun showed me how it was still not sure. That was fine, neither was I.

The smoothie had to be one of my best, my recipes were getting tuned up nicely with all the practice. I took another long sip and thought about my extraordinary good luck of late and how it had started.

Right after high school Ma & Pa told me it was time to see the big world. I couldn't believe they wanted to send me off, and they didn't really want to, in their hearts. But, they knew, an island boy must go see the rest of the world or forever be unappreciative of his true home.

So, with an *almost* nicely funded debit card and a new suitcase I joined up with my buddy JB and we set off for San Francisco and the world.

Fortunately, JB dragged me out of there after a week and we headed up to Vancouver, and then to Anchorage. JB had been around a little. He was a great resource at keeping me out of trouble and taught me that every girl I found irresistible was only going to slow down our journey.

We made our way to Tokyo, Singapore and to Bali to surf. Two weeks there and I swore I didn't want to leave, ever. JB worked hard getting me out of there, beads in my hair and incense coming out of my very pores. Bangladesh followed, then Karachi, up to Croatia, Paris and foggy London. We would spend at least four days at every stop, living on the cheap, trying to stay under the tourist radar and getting a taste for the local scene. Both of us were easy going, friendly and willing to learn from the locals. It was a whirlwind tour that continued, taking us to Havana, Caracas, Quito and Buenos Aires.

Finally, we made our way back to Los Angeles, with a side of San Diego and even a taste of Tijuana. After three months, too many spicy meals and way too many infatuations we stumbled tired and exhausted into Waikiki late one night.

It was well past three in the morning when our Quantas flight stopped in Honolulu for fuel and we bade farewell to the rowdy Aussies headed back home from Disneyland. The public buses were already done for the night and so we spent twenty bucks on a taxi to the Park Shore Hotel on the corner of Kalakaua and Kapahulu. Ma & Pa had a condo there, across the street from the unobstructed beach on one side and the Honolulu Zoo and Kapiolani park on the other. Twenty two floors up, corner unit facing in the direction of Diamond Head and we sat out on the lanai and waited for our tropical sun to welcome us back. The lions were roaring at the zoo and JB did his best imitation as one of their free cousins. I could have sworn they answered him in kind.

After a week of hitting all the hotspots and Tiki Bars we met up with Captain Rout taking a longliner fishing boat out of the Sand Island docks back to Ma'alaea harbor on Maui. JB's sweetheart met us in her pickup and drove us back to Haiku.

It was enlightening to say the least. Travel is absolutely the best education anyone can ever hope to enjoy. No one should ever consider themselves truly educated before they've been around our planet at least once.

I had met hundreds of people, seen all kinds of places, eaten and drunk many an exotic flavor. I had seen the exterior of the world and enjoyed it immensely, but I found a most comforting thing back on my little tropical island. It felt so damn good to be back. The early morning waters of Ho'okipa beach wrapped around me like a long lost twin. The heart of my island and my own beat stronger now having proved we shared a soul. Maui was home and I hugged the first coconut tree I came across.

My smoothie was almost complete, I didn't like to think of it as finished, or done, or all gone, but complete. Completely enjoyed. Tiwaka perched on the table and stared at the tall glass hoping to will it over to him with some kind of avian telekinesis. I didn't want to wait that long so I shared it with him, pouring the last bit onto the table for him to enjoy. That certainly made it complete. Perfection had to be shared or it just didn't seem perfect anymore.

Finally, I moved back toward the bar to drop off my glass and there behind the fine koa counter leaned Sandy. She was propping her chin on one hand watching the parrot and I. Her long black hair was flowing around her Tahitian features in that special way only the most beautiful of women have mastered.

Of course, I was partial. I was in love with the most wonderful girl in the world and I could say that with some measure of authority. Her smile, directed at me, was a powerful motivator. If I were Michelangelo I would have painted ceilings for her, if Einstein I would have completed the Unified Field Theory and named it the Sandy Effect, if Lady Gaga I would have invited her to co-star in a video. Being who I was though I asked "Have you been surfing yet?"

She looked down at her hands, lightly playing with a Hinano coaster, then back up to me, eyes all big and lovely. Immediately I saw that subtle hint of playfulness that we had only recently learned with each other.

Without taking my eyes off of her I yelled out to the parrot, "Tiwaka, you're in charge buddy!"

~ ~ ~

Green, White and Blue

We had made it down to my sea cliff hammock right after losing our last pieces of clothing. We kissed like our breath depended on it. The hammock held us, swung us and entangled us like two netted fish. I flashed, for a millisecond, how when I became an old man these times would amaze me. Youth was not being wasted on the young today.

That mischievous look of hers had me laughing afterwards, it couldn't be possible, I thought.

"What's so funny?" she asked, poking me playfully in the side.

I shook my head, smiling. "I don't know," I acted up. "How can you be any more beautiful?" I threw my hands up in mock surrender. "I mean, seriously!"

Sandy laughed the laugh of half agreement and half acknowledgment that I would say that while we sat naked together in my hammock. "You might better get back to the bar. Tiwaka is probably giving away drinks by this time."

She was right. That parrot had the generosity of a Bill and Melinda Gates. "I need a moment, still." We swung lightly in the breeze, the hammock rocking with the guava trees it was anchored to. "I want to soak it all up a little longer honey." She needed a kiss and I obliged her.

This was the same spot where I had that vision of little children waiting their turns to be born, and I wanted to tell Sandy. I wanted to but didn't have the courage to bring it up. Afterall, we were still new at all of this, and I felt it might scare her off. It kinda scared me as well.

Sandy hugged me a little. "It's still early and Coco should be there soon, she can fill in."

I nodded, but said nothing. The view, the warmth and that feeling of all being right with the world was overwhelming my ability to speak. But, I took a deep breath and tried anyhow.

"You know Sandy...this is really, well...awesome." My command of poetic language fell far short of Shakespeare or even Mister Rogers for that matter. But I did fancy myself a philosopher. "Of course, words can't quite put a label can they?"

Sandy looked at me, not sure of where I was going but listening with the patience of a lover. "What do you mean?" she asked lazily, trying to keep a quick nap from stealing her attention.

I gently laid her head down on my chest so she could rest and looked out to sea. It was a musical mix of blue and white textures that I knew ended somewhere, but hinted at infinity. Surrounded by the greens of guava, hibiscus and wild grasses I felt like a bird in his nest. Here, on the cliffs we could both grow a family, launch them into the big wild world and retire back to this place one day, to dream about it all.

Stroking her hair lightly I felt a bond growing beyond my capacity to control it. I was lost in her embrace and I knew I was now lost forever. Surely, I would never want to be found again.

My travels around the world had taught me one of many important lessons. Here, in this land of green, white and blue there was a magic I had found no where else.

This place spoke to me in a way I found irresistible. Words were not the language though. Energy was. The wind moved around me, brushing my long curls away. That was energy. The ocean was the largest battery on Earth, storing immense quantities of energy in the waves and the warmth of its water. The sun itself; its light bathed us in energy. And, the stars at night and the planets all spoke the language of energy. Then, there were us, the humans, and all the animals from the largest whales to the tiniest critters. We were incredible packages of focused energy, self directed and motivated.

Sandy snuggled against my chest, her warmth, her energy radiating toward my own. I hugged her lightly, feeling her sleepiness.

I leaned my head back against the hammock and closed my eyes a moment. I knew I sometimes saw things that some might not agree with, that some might say weren't there. Honestly, I felt I was doing nothing more than denying nothing. For me it was simple observation with an incredibly open mind. One thing I did remember though from Dr. Karimoto's chemistry class in high school was this: today's magic may very well be tomorrow's science.

A few small clouds moved overhead, hiding the sun for a brief moment. I followed their movement toward the great mountains behind us until the sun again beamed down between them. It caught my eye as if to speak. Something was there, something just at the edge of my comprehension. I had met many a person that tried to speak to me, but I didn't understand their language. Some of them tried hand gestures, anything they could to communicate. Here the light was trying and I was desperately trying to move my listening ability a notch higher.

I was feeling frustrated at missing something important, but finally checked it with my normal post-epiphany sanity check. I could be dreaming this all up, I said to myself. Imagination is indeed powerful, perhaps powerful enough to create impossible scenarios. I took a deep breath, feeling Sandy's head rise on my chest and sink again as I exhaled.

Some distance away, I heard my phone ringing in my shorts back on the path we had run down. It was probably Tiwaka or Coco, but I would go with Coco on my first guess.

Reluctantly, I sat up softly, letting Sandy back down gently into the hammock. I went to gather our clothes before waking her. Away from the guava's shade the sun bathed my entirety in a gentle warmth. I felt like a little boy, running along the shore at Baby Beach without a stitch of clothing. That memory, of the sun on my skin, made me turn back toward the bright sky. I squinted up and tried one more time to hear whatever it might be. I had seen the Japanese tourists frown the same way in trying to figure out the menu at Mama's Fish House.

I pulled my cargo shorts back on and tightened my belt around my hips. Out of my pocket the phone confirmed it was Coco who had called. Guess it was time to get back. Despite having had a wonderful time, this mystery weighed on my mind. Picking up Sandy's shorts and tube top, both of our slippers and her hair tie I stood for a moment and looked back out to the horizon.

I tried a little analysis and went back to my foreign tourist analogy. They weren't stupid because they didn't know the language...neither was the local who didn't know the tourist's language. I let that thought wander about a moment and watched some spouting not far off from a pod of whales. The sun was on my back, and warming my neck just as I felt the tingle of recognition, like someone was there. I knew no one but Sandy and I were here, so I let the feeling progress.

Energy was a language? OK. I didn't need to know how to understand it, yet. Then my smile beamed clear across my Sandy perfumed face as it finally came to me. A language indicated an intelligence. In energy then, there must be intelligence!

OK, it was non-human, it was a language I couldn't speak, write or even understand, but it was an intelligence nonetheless. It was there, the same way you could look into someone's eyes and tell.

Walking over to the beauty in the hammock I watched her breath rise and fall for a few moments. She was certainly energy, and so was I. Maybe we could spin off some energy ourselves. I laughed at my almost silly word usage. English surely wasn't the language I needed to master for this one. I gently leaned over and kissed her awake.

"We have to get back to the bar," I whispered into her ear.

She stretched like a tigress, and then demurely took her clothes from me and covered herself. "Turn away why don't you," she giggled.

I turned back to the sea, smiling. It was all working itself out. We were surrounded, enveloped with natural energy and as such an intelligence that was trying to get through. It wasn't insistent though, or intrusive or even obvious. It was going to wait for me to figure it out.

Sandy grabbed my hand as we walked together back toward the bar. The palms up ahead were nodding, they knew all about it. Soon I would as well.

~~~

Tiki Labs

Tiwaka had indeed been giving away free drinks. There were three very happy customers lined up at the bar feeding him cashews and pouring their own rum. Coco was in the kitchen working on some pupus and about to call me again for reinforcements. It was still early in the day, but the air had that feel of impending crowds.

When Sandy and I walked back into the kitchen to check in, Coco stood back a moment from the grill, hands on her hips, and looked at us real good. For a moment I thought she might be mad, but after a second or three, the slightest smile began forming in her cheeks. Her eyes twinkled a little just as her hip moved to the side and she turned fully to us.

"That bird can't keep a secret you know," Coco winked.

I looked at Sandy who was grinning and back to Coco. "What did he say? Besides, drinks are on the house..."

Coco walked up to both Sandy and I and put her arms around the both of us. "He said what we all have already felt. That you two are a couple now." She kissed us each on our foreheads.

"Coco, we are so sorry for showing up late. We got ... distracted for a moment," Sandy admitted, reaching around to pinch my butt as she did.

I threw my hip easily toward Sandy and Coco let us go with a big smile. "You two take good care of each other," she said with all the authority she could muster. "And get out there before that parrot bankrupts us."

I walked out to the bar, leaving Sandy and Coco in the kitchen. Tiwaka was dancing along the bar, head back, tail extended and his wings out to the sides. The iTunes playlist had 'High in the Middle' from the Honk album Five Summer Stories playing.

The three patrons at the bar were all clapping, encouraging the bird to greater heights than he had probably ever achieved. Tiwaka was holding court, the Prince of Pineapple. I moved into position, grabbing a new towel and throwing it over my fresh Aloha shirt.

"How are you gents doing?" I asked. No one paid any attention to the guy behind the bar. The parrot had their attention and their vote.

There was nothing for me to do for a few minutes, so I turned and ran back to the kitchen. Coco was putting on her cocktail waitress outfit and Sandy was at the grill. I looked at Coco for the briefest of seconds, grinned real big and turned to Sandy.

"I need another kiss baby!" I announced, proud that Coco could witness it all.

Sandy puckered up and let me plant a big affirmation upon those exquisite lips. I couldn't look Coco in the eyes for more than a second, so I just gave her a big hug.

"Thank you Coco," I whispered in her ear. She had saved my life while surfing mondo surf at Unknowns and told me then it was for a good reason. Now I knew what that reason was.

Turning to run back to the bar, I found Tiwaka swaying along the bar like a drunk sailor. The three guys had moved over to a table of young honeys from Lahaina and left the entertainer unattended.

"Tiwaka, are you..." I couldn't get the question out before I watched in some horror as the poor bird fell over onto his side, legs straight out like a couple of chop sticks. I ran over to him, putting my hands on him, turning him around but could see nothing wrong. Immediately I turned to the ships bell just above the rum and rang it three times, our emergency signal at the bar.

All eight patrons rushed over to the bar counter, including the three free drinkers probably thinking another special was on.

"Any of you see what happened to Tiwaka?" I demanded.

Plenty of aghast looks and head shakes no. One of the Lahaina honeys said her cousin was a vet and she whipped out her iPhone to call.

Coco and Sandy came running around the corner from the kitchen as I was picking up Tiwaka, now almost as stiff as a board, but still moving his head around.

"Oh no!" screamed Sandy. "What's wrong with him?"

"I can't tell," I shrugged, feeling completely helpless. I felt guilty for not studying parrot physiology when I had that chance at Maui Community College some years back. "Coco? Can you tell?" I turned to her, holding the distraught bird in both hands, like an offering.

"Let me hold him," she said softly, her big eyes already beginning to change to those I had seen only on a few rare occasions.

Sandy noticed those amazing green sea turtle eyes this time and gasped. She looked at me for a brief moment and I could only nod.

"Tell me what is wrong my little bird," Coco whispered to Tiwaka. She put her head gently up to his feathered mane, and waited. She kept her face down, not looking at the small crowd, her expansive black hair hiding her eyes and covering the bird.

Suddenly, she laid Tiwaka on the counter flat and yelled. "Chopsticks, stat!"

Shocked, but always on duty, I reached under the counter and pulled out a pair of bamboos. Her hand was outstretched just like a surgeon's so I slapped them down into her palm, like I had seen on T.V.

"Pull back my hair!" she said with just as much authority, so Sandy and I both reached to sweep back her long black hair so she could better attend to the now prostate bird.

Her fingers manipulated the chopsticks like a Benihana chef spins his knife and with a certainty of purpose, she used her left hand to open the parrots beak, while with her right controlling the chopsticks she inserted them deep into his craw.

Tiwaka thrashed around a little despite his obvious weakness at this point. I noticed that Cocos hair was as smooth as seaweed, silky smooth like seaweed feels underwater. I couldn't see her eyes now, as she bent over Tiwaka, but I knew what they looked like. She was indeed in her special way.

Tiwaka wasn't moving and I took the briefest moment to consider a world without my feathered friend. I shouldn't have done that, as the sadness immediately gripped my chest.

Coco worked the chopsticks around a bit like she was grabbing something and a second later pulled out a massive macadamia nut. She held it up for everyone's inspection, a whole nut the size of a small hybrid car.

She then bent back down to the unmoving bird, covered his entire beak with her mouth and breathed into him loudly. Once, then again. Nothing. She picked him up and brought his head up to hers, touching foreheads gently. I could see Cocos eyes again now, huge, watery and somehow so patient. It was like she knew it was all going to be alright, despite the bird looking damn near death.

Coco was whispering something so faintly I couldn't hear it even standing as close as I was. She then lay him back on the counter, still and unmoving. Placing her left hand on his belly, she moved her right to his feet.

"Tiwaka!" she said as if announcing a spectacular sunrise. "Now!" Her right hand looked to be tickling his feet.

The parrot moved his head slightly left, then rolled it over to his right. Again to his left, as Coco continued tickling his feet.

"Now, Tiwaka, now!" Coco demanded.

Just then I thought I could hear the rumblings of a massive parrot burp moving up through his gut and I stepped back just in time to see a mass of half digested who-knows-what come flying out of his mouth. The crowd moved back in disgust, but as Tiwaka finally squawked and began flapping his wings a bit, they clapped and cheered.

I grabbed a towel, wet it a bit and handed it to Coco. She gently wiped his mouth and lifted him upright. His feet were wobbly but he managed to stand, Coco's hands remaining an inch away in case he teetered.

"Tiwaka!" Sandy said, happy tears rolling down her face. "Are you OK?"

The exhausted parrot made a sound like a small chirp and then followed that with a broken squawk and finally a very quiet "Mahalo."

"Geez buddy, you sure gave us a scare there," I said, trying to sound strong. I moved in closer to the bird, but Coco gently put her hand on my shoulder.

"Give him a moment to find his balance," she said.

I looked up to see her eyes rapidly changing back to those we were all used to. She blinked a couple of times, like she was trying to get some dust out of her eyes, and then with a broad smile growing across her face, looked at me and winked.

"Our little secret, remember?" She said, her right eyebrow went up a little for emphasis.

I nodded, but couldn't help glancing over at Sandy, who had seen it as well. Coco noticed and turned to her.

"Darling Sandy," Coco said, putting her hands gently on her shoulders. "Mea honu kapu."

Sandy nodded, looking down. Instinctively, Sandy then reached around to hug Coco. "Mahalo. Kumu Coco."

The patrons had all retreated back to their little worlds within the bar, back to their own stories, their friends. Coco walked back to the kitchen to finish her preparations and Sandy came up to me softly.

"You think Tiwaka is going to be OK?"

I looked at him as I put my arm around her. He didn't look very energetic, but he was sitting on his perch between the tequila and the vodka. "He looks tired, doesn't he?"

Sandy put her head on my shoulder. "Lets keep a good eye on him tonight. He might be a little embarrassed too." Looking up at me, she smiled in the radiance of compassion I had only seen in mothers. You could see the love she was capable of, if only speaking about my parrot. For a brief instant I could hear those little voices from my cliff side hammock cheering and dancing.

Tiwaka turned to look at us and bobbed his head a little. "Mahalo." He paused a moment and then said it again. "Mahalo." His voice was scratchy and weak.

"You're welcome buddy." I patted his head feathers lightly, remembering my old dog Ococ, Tiwaka's friend as well. "I need you to stick around a while, OK?"

Turning to Sandy, I suggested we pick up the coconut bowls of macadamia nuts and put them away for the remainder of the evening. I had to say something, if only to acknowledge that she now knew Coco's secret.

"Coco is very special isn't she?" I tried, hoping to keep our conversation in line with our promise of secrecy.

Sandy looked up at me for a moment, afraid too to break it. "Yes...my grandmother knew such things. I just never thought I would see anything like it."

We dropped it there and then and went back to replacing mac nuts with peanuts and raisins. I looked up to the parrot perch.

Tiwaka flapped his wings a little, tucked them back under themselves and moved his feet a little.

Somehow the iTunes playlist had paused during all the excitement. I picked up the device to restart it and noticed it had come to the end of the rotation but had not looped back to the beginning.

"Whoa, Tiwaka. You sure dodged a close one there. Even the playlist thought it was the end."

I laughed a little at that and started the playlist at the beginning again, as it should be. "Come Monday" by Mister James Buffett.

~~~

Weekends at Tiwaka's Tiki Bar & Grill were when we got the enthusiasts in. Those were the folks who were fully ingrained into the Tiki culture, recapturing as best they could, those days many decades past when Tiki was hip.

A thoroughly cross cultural invention of the American mind Tiki had evolved from a misinterpretation of early Pacific Islander art and ported over to a mildly irreverent fascination of some fanciful tropical lifestyle. Tiki bars were pure escapism for Vegas weary clubbers looking for the exotic. It was, simply put, a part time adoption of tropical mindset into a mindset not quite willing to go there full time. Everyone loves Hawaii, but few would really want to live there year round. It's just too far away.

Ma and Pa had kept a Tiki Bar in Waikiki back in the late 40s and then moved it to Lahaina in the late 50s and 60s. Tiki was as you might expect then, different. It was more ethnic then, more topless brown skinned girl in a grass skirt serving extravagant drinks flaming away their abundance of sugar and alcohol to the absolute delight of people who had only seen a Milwaukee's Best explode before that.

Yet, it always was a venue for fun, and as fun evolved so did Tiki. Tiki was about fun, and about art. Art changes with the generations and the art of having fun, in a tropical setting, was changing. The old timers might not remember the name of their topless waitress back then but they sure remember the fun they all had, and that was the key. Tiwaka's Tiki Bar and Grill asked our girls to keep their tops on, and for the most part they complied. We were here to have fun.

So, on the weekends, we took a special pride in entertaining the purists, the orthodox Tikiphiles as well as those youngsters who saw it a bit differently. The mix was eclectic and electric, and it worked well because despite your Tiki dialect the base language for everyone was Fun.

I liked to call it Tiki Labs, where we experimented with new mixes, new music and often new people. Throw some Coco Loco Moco at that and you got a sustainable all night party.

Naturally, I invited the local Tiki vendors to come and show their wares. Musicians on Maui were numerous in their blend of rasta, tropical and dance, and Marty Dread did it right on so many occasions they were on a standing invite. Brad Parker was a new painter on the scene making big bucks at the tourist galleries in Lahaina. He could fit a frame containing a 1950s B movie with a carved Tiki quite nicely, adding that Disney surrealism with his mix of light and color.

Of course, there were the zombie Tikis, the African tribal Tikis, the Beaver the Clever meets Tiki crew and even the lustful big eyes, tongues out Tiki that needed a date real bad. Everyone had their interpretation and all were welcomed.

However, there was a line I didn't like to cross, as fine as it was. I didn't want anyone's real culture to feel insulted at the bar. This couldn't be a white man's infatuation with the south seas alone. It had to be a blend, like Hawaii was a blend of races, like Haiku Elementary school was a blend of children, like the 100% Kona coffee at some stores was a blend. I encouraged Tiki interpretations that strayed from their Polynesian roots. Surely the Euros had carved up something similar back in the day. Lets see it! All our carvings had to be smiling, or at least not frowning. Loud colors were promoted, Aloha shirts that came with sunglasses were expected. Tropical drinks that had more than two ingredients were required. Music that made your body want to shed it's woes, clothes and expose its toes were played at max volume.

Tiki Labs was all about trying new things. Don Ho had to wait until Tuesdays.

It was early Saturday afternoon and the bar was already half full. A minibus of Canadians had arrived early and from the looks of it, would be staying in the cabanas tonight. Those folks could really enjoy warm weather! Several of the larger fellows had already shed their aloha shirts, letting it all hang out in the sun. There's nothing like a bare chested fat man in cargo shorts, socks and slippers to tell the world 'I'm having more fun that you!'

I was wiping up the bar from yet another drink that Tiwaka had spilled while trying to walk the counter. His mojo had not yet returned after his near *Death by Macadamia* event. No longer did he prance and dance along the bar to the thrilling screams of the ladies. He wouldn't answer tough questions in exchange for chocolate covered nuts, in fact, nuts terrified him now. People were complaining, a little, about the lack of said nuts, but now enjoyed the California raisins and the Georgia-meets-Tokyo Wasabi peanuts.

Parrots, as a breed, were resourceful critters. They had to be in a jungle where stealth meant survival and you were wearing the most outrageous colors for miles. I felt Tiwaka would get back to normal eventually, but I had to keep him from knocking things over with his unsteady gait until then.

That thought still in my mind, Ms. Melita, the school teacher from Roots showed up to drop off the latest batch of ceramic Tiki mugs. Her school was making them as a fund raiser and we were happy to buy the custom works of elementary art. Amazingly, when the requirement was for smiling Tikis, the kids there did a fabulous job.

"Hey, I heard about Tiwaka," Melita mentioned, looking over at him between the tequila and the vodka. "Is he just going to sit on his perch for a while?"

I looked back at the parrot, easily filling the space between the 1.5 liter bottles. He was starting straight out to the jungle, as if ignoring the action between him and the trees. "I think he got quite a scare." My hands nervously cleaned another oversized beer stein. "I just hope he didn't get any brain damage, that would be a real...."

"Squawk!" Tiwaka interrupted. "T.I.K.I." he spelled, trying to prove my fear invalid.

"Does he spell now too?" Melita asked. "We've been teaching him new words, but not spelling them." She pushed the large box of Tiki Mugs onto a stool and sat down a moment. "Got anything *without* rum?"

"Sure! We've got..."

"Wait a minute," Melita changed her mind. "Better not drink in front of one of my students." She looked over at Tiwaka. "How about some lime in the coconut, on ice?"

I laughed at the idea of Tiwaka being a student, but it was quite true. He attended school to both educate the amazingly fortunate students at Roots as well as soak up more vocabulary himself. Melita got her drink in a shimmering glass Tiki mug I had just found at TikiFarm.com and sipped it lightly. She was watching the parrot with a lot of interest. You could see her blue eyes thinking out loud beneath that mass of curly red hair.

"Why don't you send him over all next week?" She looked over at the stationary bird. "He could use a break from all of this perhaps."

Tiwaka stood there, like a stuffed bag of feathers, listening I knew, but pretending not to.

"You know," I turned to Tiwaka. "That is an extremely good idea." I put my hand out for him to walk onto, and after a short hesitation he obliged. Walking back to where Melita was sitting I put my hand down onto the bar next to her and he stepped lightly onto the koa wood.

"Would you like to hang out with the kids next week?" Melita asked her most colorful student. "We can play memorization games!" She stroked his chest feathers. "Your favorite kind."

Tiwaka moved his head back a bit and opened his feathers full. Both feet stomped up and down and he twirled like a ballerina before coming back around to face his teacher. "Love to!" he announced loud enough for the entire bar to enjoy.

Melita had that talent of making learning fun, in finding the door to any kid's hesitation about school and showing them the open window instead. Roots was the only school I had *ever* been to where absolutely every kid loved going, every day. It was certainly a special place, near us in the tradewind blessed jungles of north Maui. Half the kids walked to school so they could eat the wild sweet guava along the gravel paths. Field trips were to waterfalls and whale watches. Lunch was probably organic, and no candy or caffeinated drinks were allowed. Everyone can remember a special slice of life, of time, when the world was made just for you. These kids would remember Roots like that.

"Well then," Melita said, finishing her lime and coconut. "Bring him by Monday." I handed her a check for the Tiki Mugs and she stood to go. "He can spend the entire week there you know, go home with me. Gabe would love to try out some fresh fish recipes on him."

Tiwaka was certainly more energetic now, going from one foot to the other in his eternal quest to balance himself on the edge.

"That sounds great. See you Monday!" I picked up Tiwaka and sat him back at his perch. "You bird, are one lucky parrot."

Tiwaka turned his head to watch me walk back to my work at the bar, but my back was to him. Coco later told me he bowed so low she thought he would fall. I think he was quite happy to be alive.

~~~

Our Tiki vendors never showed up before the customers. They made a point of showing up while our customers were already here. The particularly clever ones would simply saunter up to the bar, box of goodies in hand, top off of course, and order a drink. Natural curiosity being what it is, someone would inevitably ask them what all those cool nicknacks were in their box.

I didn't mind this tactic at all, it actually gave me a good idea as to whether anyone would be interested in their product. Usually they had called or emailed in advance with a brief description, which I appreciated. Sometimes though, they winged it, showed up unannounced and the results could be unpredictable.

The evening was still early and the crowd thin when one particular purveyor of fine Tiki collectibles showed up, box in hand. He slid up at the end of the bar, placed his box of goodies on the bamboo stool next to his and ordered a Coke.

I pulled one from the bottom of the ice cooler, sat it on a grass coasters and let it shed its icy coat for his enjoyment. He wasn't paying any attention. His eyes were scanning the crowd and naturally he soon picked out Coco with her outrageously beautiful black mane moving above her colorful mumu dress. I glanced once more quickly at him, and caught his age at about middle. I left him alone to attend to other customers and didn't pay any more attention until Coco came up to fill her orders.

She caught Mystery Box Man's gaze and being the good sport she is moved right up next to him, placing her tray on the bar and smiled.

"Order up Tiwaka!"

The bird knew it was his opportunity to play it up a bit and quickly hopped down from his perch between the bottles and started his drunk sailor saunter down the bar toward Coco.

I watched his tail feathers sashay from side to side and Mystery Box Man lean forward from behind Coco to spock out who Tiwaka might be. His eyes got real big when he saw the parrot flexing his wings, throwing his head back and squawking. I was trying not to laugh, but when Mystery Box Man retreated back behind Coco only to pop up again this time behind her I let my belly shake. I think he might actually have been a bit scared.

Remembering that birds were probably all that was left over from the predatory dinosaurs of yore it was no doubt a healthy fear.

Tiwaka got to Coco's drink tray, turned to face her and shuffled one foot, and then the other in his classic display of "Bring it on!"

Coco laughed lovingly and played it up both for the bird, her own entertainment and that of the new guy with the box. "Tiwaka, I need 3 Primos, a Coco Loco Moco light on the rum, but heavier on the vodka and a Lahaina Lassie." She looked over at Mystery Box Man who was staring at the bird. "He always gets it right ya know."

Mystery Box Man found the conscious energy to close his gaping mouth and smiled up at Coco. "Really? How can... how can a bird...you know..."

I had written down her order myself. "Tiwaka," I called. "Bring me your drink order please." The parrot walked over to me as I pretended to get the order from him.

Coco turned to the Mystery Box Man and with a raised eyebrow asked, "So big boy, what ya got in that box there?"

He quickly put his hands over it as if to hide whatever it was. "Well," he muttered nervously. "I don't think it is such a good idea anymore, ya know, what with that big parrot you all got here."

Coco glanced my way to see if Tiwaka had made it back and then turned fully to face the Mystery Box Man. "Well then, why would it not be a good idea?" Her curiosity was famous and she was fully prepared to use all of her considerable skills of persuasion, starting with her radiant smile. Mystery Box Man glanced down the bar once more, saw Tiwaka at my end and went back to talking with Coco.

"You see, I haven't been here before..."

"I know that," Coco interrupted. "Did you call in to let us know?"

This made him even more nervous, but before he could come up with a lame excuse Coco stepped in again. "You don't really have to. But, most people do. They let us know what they might be bringing to show us." Coco moved a little closer toward Mystery Box Man, making sure her hip lightly touched his arm, the one guarding the closed box. She was going to find out what was in that box before the world spun another mile further on its axis.

Mystery Box Man was blushing now, both in the infatuation launched when he first saw Coco and in some embarrassment about his product, which he was still managing to keep a secret.

"Order up!" I announced. Both Coco and Mystery Box Man looked at me. "Three Primos, a Coco Loco Moco light on the rum, but heavier on the vodka and a Lahaina Lassie."

Mystery Box Man looked up from his stool to the exceedingly gorgeous Coco still standing above him. His eyes were incredulous. "How does that parrot do that?" He clutched his box a little tighter.

Coco leaned in close, enough so that Mystery Box Man could smell the light scent of jasmine in her hair and touched his hand atop the box. "Magic, some say. Me? I just think he is clairvoyant and already knew what I was going to order. It's easier that way." She moved her fingers lightly from his wrist to his knuckles. "Some people say the same thing about me you know..."

Mystery Box Man was now officially in over his head and swimming in deep waters. He felt the intoxicating power of Coco's seductive voice moving through parts of his mind that he had not visited in quite some time. Sweat broke out in a sheen over his brows. His pulse quickened and he shifted in his chair a bit. He felt he needed to say something, anything or risk falling into her trance without a hope of ever returning. Gulping, he blurted out, "If, if you're...I mean if you are...clair..voy...can read minds, and all."

"Yes dear?" Coco breathed a little heavily, still moving her finger tips along his wrist and up his forearm.

"Then, you already know what's in this...this box...don't you?" His hands were slowly being guided away from the top of the box even as he willed them to stay put.

"Honey," Coco whispered, going in for the capture, her long black hair falling around her face like a cape. "I know what's in your heart." Her eyes, a very special part of her, remained human but could pierce a man's armor as surely as any sword.

I was returning from table six, having delivered Coco's drinks and saw her left hand already opening the box while the poor guy simply stared up at her. Coco was surely the Queen of the bar and any male patrons were simply squires wishing a moment with her under the guise of a drink. As I watched another moment, making my way back behind the bar, she pulled out something from the box that looked like a toy.

Her eyes never leaving him, Coco felt what was in her hand and with the skill of a magician placed it on the bar between them. "Sir," she continued in her trance inducing voice. "What should I call you? Mystery Box Man? Or..." she stroked his arm while turning her head to look at what she had retrieved from the box.

Tiwaka let out a shriek and hopped back down from his perch, practically flying over to Coco.

Coco stared at the toy parrot on the bar, with a bobbing head no less and almost laughed out loud. "Or should I call you Parrot Head?"

Mystery Box Man blinked a couple of times, coming out of his trance and looked to the bar where Coco was now looking. "Whoa! How did you get that?" He looked back down to his box quickly and saw the box top askew, his hand clutching Coco's arm. Tiwaka immediately crashed into the toy, unable to brake properly on the slick Koa wood and took several coasters with them both a few feet further down the bar.

"Hey! That's why I didn't want to show you guys. After seeing your parrot I knew you would think it silly." He looked duped and embarrassed.

Coco laughed lovingly and quieted down the Mystery Box Man's discomfort. She put a hand on his shoulder this time. "I think it's cute, like you."

I had tried to follow Tiwaka down the bar when he looked like he was in attack mode but by the time I got to where he, the coasters and the toy parrot were it was a blur of flapping feathers and squawks.

"Tiwaka, hey!" I said a bit loudly. Customers at the tables were all looking over at the fracas. I knew better than to just grab the bird, with talons and a beak like he sported. The broom was down at this side of the bar and I picked it up and gently tried to get it between the bar and the bird.

Coco walked around the stools and over to the bar as well. "Tiwaka, it is not a bird silly. It's a toy!" She leaned over and blew air at his head, but kept her hands clear.

Now, Tiwaka knew the word "toy" and after a few moments it must have registered somewhere in that avian brain and he mellowed out a bit.

I looked over at Coco. "Wow, territorial I guess eh?" She nodded.

Mystery Box Man was standing and watching us. Tiwaka finally backed off and watched the toy for any more fight that it might have left in it. I picked it up, but it's head began to bob again and Tiwaka squawked, ready to go at it some more.

"Stop it Tiwaka. It's a TOY," drawing out the syllable a little. Melita had told me that wasn't the best way to reinforce pronunciations, but it seemed dramatic enough. I quickly followed with "Toy" and flicked the head with my fingers. The hard plastic body remained still and the head moved without complaint. Tiwaka stilled a moment watching this. No bird he had ever encountered would let someone flick its head like that. Something clicked and finally Tiwaka mimicked, "Toy. Boss. Toy."

"Yes, it's only a toy!" Mystery Box Man promoted. "With all due respect, uh Tiwaka sir, it is…" he picked up his box and went to leave. "Only a toy."

I held the six inch bobbing parrot head in my hand and decided to see if Tiwaka was on board with it. There was a bit of flat shelf next to Tiwaka's perch so I placed it up there. It was a spitting image of the parrot, even if it was only a macaw.

Tiwaka bounced back up to his perch and acted for a moment like he was going to ignore the interloper.

"Tiwaka?" I asked. "Is it OK dude?" I touched the toy lightly, flicking the head to get it bobbing again.

Tiwaka turned one eye toward the toy and then swung around to face the back of the shelf so that his other eye could confirm. Finally he turned back out to face us and announced, "Made in China!"

"God bless China!" I toasted and Mystery Box Man stopped a moment. He nodded his head.

"Hey, let me buy this from you," I said, motioning him over.

Mystery Box Man turned back toward the bar, glancing for a moment over to where Coco was picking up empty Primos.

"Hey, sorry about the bird going all crazy on your product like that." I sat out a coaster in front of him. "How about some cash for the toy and a drink on the house?" I offered.

Mystery Box Man sat down, again, and nodded. "Sure, that would be great, thanks." He looked behind me at the beer soldiers lined up on two different shelves. "Tsingtao would be great." He smiled like that was a joke but I didn't get it.

I walked over to the refrigerator of uncommon beers and found one, wiped it dry and popped it for him just as it landed on top of a new coaster. "Hey thanks for dropping by too. You must be new on the island?"

He took a long drink of the refreshing ice cold Chinese beer, probably half of it and set it down with a big grin. "Yep, right off the boat, as they say."

His hair was cut distinctly short and well groomed, and as black as Coco's. His eyes looked to be as dark as hers too and he took a moment to turn and look for her again. When he turned back to the bar he grinned up at me and asked, "So, tell me about Coco. If you would."

I smiled at him. Another heart in her quiver of hearts that girl! "Well, she is single, as far as I know." I went to polishing a few glass steins, as I like to do when having to talk carefully, as it gives me time to think. "She is a wonderful lady, as I think you have noticed yes?"

"Oh yes, she is quite stunning. A bit of a magician too I think."

I laughed a little at that, as it was quite the understatement. "Oh yes, she is an amazing creature."

He finished off the beer. I thought I should ask his name so that I could properly introduce him to Coco. "So, if you're going to sell around here I guess I should know your name." I stuck out my hand. "I'm Mister Tiwaka," grinning at my own joke.

He stood, bowed ever so slightly and grasped my hand. "Tsingtao."

I was confused and thought for a moment I had said the wrong thing.

"Do you want another Tsingtao?" I asked, my confusion showing.

"Tsingtao would be great!" and he immediately began laughing.

Coco had walked over and was standing next to the laughing salesman as I turned to get another Chinese beer.

"So, handsome." Coco said, hip bumping her new friend. "What part of China are you from then?"

How did she know he was from China, other than he being Chinese, which in Hawaii didn't mean you were from China by any means? Clairvoyant, I guess.

"I was named after the city I was born in. Creative parents yes?"

Coco looked at me, giving me that smile I had seen a few times when she was real keen on someone. I nodded back my approval, not that she needed it, but it made us both feel good.

"Tsingtao is my name, my home town and my favorite beer." He said, turning to look at Coco.

"Oooh," Coco cooed. "I like that in a man. Consistency."

I laughed and turned to let them have a moment. Tiwaka was quiet and sitting next to his new neighbor, the parrot head. He looked OK with it, but I wanted to reinforce with him that he was with me, and the toy wasn't. I found a small cashew, one he could easily bite into and held it up for him to taste.

Tiwaka watched me for a long moment, which for his parrot mind was a brief second, trying to ascertain my intentions. I knew he was a bit jealous of his smaller look a-like toy so I gently moved my other hand up and pushed toy head to get it bobbing again.

"Mahalo Boss." Tiwaka got the message and accepted my peace offering in one quick bite. I think he was comfortable now with it all.

Coco and Tsingtao were trading phone numbers and acting like teenagers. Well, teenagers from a time before texting. I felt a tug on my heartstring watching them and thought I would go check on Sandy back in the kitchen. I gave Coco the secret hand signal that I was going to be gone several minutes and walked around the bamboo wall and back to the grills.

I stopped at the door and saw Sandy there, iPod headphones on and her eyes closed as her head was back and she was lip syncing something slow. The white wires to the ear buds contrasted perfectly with her tan and the glow of her kitchen heated skin. My God, she was the most beautiful creature I had ever seen, and partial or not, I thought I would simply break in half if I didn't kiss her immediately.

I really wanted to walk up behind her and hold her, but I didn't want to scare her, afterall there were a lot of knives close by. So I thought, with her eyes closed she would still see the lights dim or flash. I walked over to the dimmer and slowly moved it darker, moving slowly, trying to match the movements of her hips and the music I couldn't hear. She suddenly put her arms up in the air and thrust her hips sideways, so I put one arm in the air, threw my hip to the side and brightened the lights. That did it! She popped her eyes open in time to see me with my head back, eyes closed, hip to the side and rocking with both hands up in the air.

She was on me in a second like a tigress, tickling me in the ribs for revenge. Her lips grabbed mine possessively, one of her hands behind my head, twisted into my hair. I never opened my eyes. I felt her put one of her eyebuds in my ear and I moved into her, dancing slowly with 'If I Die Young' by her new favorite The Band Perry. I held her hot skin close to mine and thought I should have given Coco the *other* hand signal giving me more time.

She kissed my open ear and whispered, "What did you tell Coco?"

I moaned a little as Sandy reached up under my shirt as well as admit to the wrong hand signal. "It's too busy out there..."

Sandy squeezed my butt and licked my neck, purring. "Too bad."

I remembered my mantra though; when given a difficult choice, choose a little of both. So, in a few minutes that problem was solved. Quickly.

I had actually come back to the kitchen on other business, and between catching my breath and all I proposed it to her. "Sandy, besides being outstanding and all, I thought you might like to try something different." I volunteered.

She looked at me with a bit of surprise, "You've been gone five or six minutes already honey boy." Slipping on a new blouse she slinked over to me where I was putting on a new Aloha shirt. "What do you have in mind bad boy?"

I smiled and wondered if I should take more vitamins in the morning, but moved on. "I thought you might like to try bartending a little."

Her eyes lit up like I had candy or a good surf report. "Really? I would love to give it a go!" She was jumping up and down. Thank the good lord, I thought, that they didn't sell bras on Maui.

"Would you? I can work the grills for a while." I stood up and acted as managerial as I could fake. "Let's do it for a week and see how you like it."

"Super!" Sandy was smiling as big as I had seen. She really wanted to work out there with all the people, the characters, the action. Her personality was perfect for it. Besides Coco could help her through the rough patches and I was always a couple of steps away. Tiwaka knew half the recipes and could entertain or check IDs. "When can I start?" she asked.

I took one of those instants to look at her. One of those instants where time gets all twisted around and a million moments all work their way into that slice of time. I saw Sandy beaming behind the bar, all the customers cheering as she made the drinks, sang and danced. I saw her kissing me back at the grills, pulling one of my earbuds out and putting into her own ear. I saw her living in a fine treehouse, surrounded by her kids giggling and laughing as she told them surf stories. I saw her glowing in the light of another spectacular sunset, looking at me with the affection of angels.

She poked me a little, laughing. "How about right now?"

"Of course! Yes!" My instant had passed, leaving me a little drunk with happiness, even if it was all my imagination. Imagination, I had long ago learned counted too, as much as reality.

We walked out and around the bamboo wall to the bar. Coco was pouring her own drinks and popping beers with all the bar stools holding up customers. Tiwaka was up on his perch, watching it all, the parrot head silently following his gaze.

"Hey, need any help Coco?" Sandy asked, smiling so big it wrapped around her entire body.

Coco laughed out loud. "You know it baby!" She glanced at me quickly and I gave her two thumbs up. "Grab me a six of Primo."

The bar must have had fifty people and the place was quickly warming up to party mode. Tsingtao held up an empty box from behind the crowd, waving at me and then I noticed the parrot heads everywhere. People had them on their shoulders, on their heads and one guy had one in his beer. Wow! It was time to ring the ship's bell. I gave it one quick pull.

"We got us a new bartender!" I announced. Cheers went up all around. Everyone raised their drinks. Sandy didn't expect that and turned to look at Coco and I as we bowed in her direction. Tiwaka squawked nice and loud, and I turned and rang the bell twice.

Coco, Sandy and I worked the bar together for the next hour. The three of us kept busy as the place filled up. I turned up the iPod to "party mode" and people started dancing out in the grass. The trade winds were hanging in there keeping us all cooled off and the moon, my old friend, insisted on competing with the tiki torches.

I looked around after a while and thought what a great time we were all having. People were singing along with the music, some were just moving their bodies to the beat. Others felt just fine watching it all.

The bar thinned a bit as most folks moved out to the grass. Tsingtao had finally coerced Coco into a dance. Her long black hair danced as gracefully as she did. I recognized many of our regulars and several new faces. All of them were smiling.

Sandy and I stood hip to hip serving up drinks and talking to the customers. She was absolutely radiant. The customers wanted to talk and she engaged them all, while keeping the magic flowing over the ice. She was a natural people person, a happy human.

I got an order for a Coco Loco Moco and went to get a coconut and my machete. Tiwaka always announced right before I would make my first slice, so I looked up to him, waiting for his cue.

He bounced from one foot to the other, getting his mojo up and then with a big flap of his wings, threw back his head and practically screamed "Coco! Loco! Moco!"

My machete came down cleanly, once, twice, done. Out with some of the water, in with the ice, lime, rum, and those other special ingredients. I handed it over to a very happy looking Chinese guy in the arms of an even happier Coco.

I smiled that bartender smile, leaned on the bar with my arms and watched the action. Looking back to Tiwaka I saw him nudging the toy parrot head just enough to get it to move back and forth. He looked over at me, and I could swear he was grinning.

"Aloha!" he squawked.

~~~

The Magic of the Sugar Cane

Later that night, when most of the folks had returned back to wherever it was they came from, I wandered out toward the small kiawe wood campfire on the cliffs. Several people were there, sticking marshmallows into the flames, dropping their chocolate into the grass and giggling at the spilled beers. Sitting in the grass was Coco and Tsingtao, Ma and Pa, Gregorio from up Makawao way, three or four people I didn't know, but suspected were European tourists, and of course, Sandy.

Ma was just finishing up a story about her and Pa's wild times in Waikiki and Lahaina when they first got into the Tiki Bar business decades before. I'm sure there was enough adventure there to fill a book or two.

As I sat down next to Sandy, warming up my bare legs against her silky skin and accepting a fresh and incredibly cold Hinano beer I laughed a little.

"What's so funny big guy?" Sandy teased leaning into me.

I looked over at her in complete amazement. The glow of the fire had her lit up like a goddess, and the twinkle in her big brown eyes had more to it than just a reflection of the fire, or the moon. "Nothing really," I said, tipping my beer up for a moment. "I was just thinking how nice it is out here."

Sandy squeezed in close and snuggled. I kissed her lightly and turned to look out to sea. The ocean was sparkling all the way to the dark line of the horizon, trying to entice the moon lower I suppose. It was a noble effort indeed.

"Your turn," Ma was saying to me as I took another sip of the Hinano. "New guys have to tell the next story."

Everyone around the fire agreed it was indeed the rule and being the last to show up I was it.

"Is that a beer you're drinking?" someone in the dark mentioned. I was somewhat known for not drinking much. Not as a teetotaler necessarily, but as a special occasion kind of drinker.

"Oh yes," I toasted. "Only at fires these days."

A few agreeable sounds mixed in with the fire crackling. I took one more swig of the last of the Hinano and sat the bottle down in the grass. "Actually, I am reminded of a story, if you have a few minutes?"

A few people laughed lightly.

"We've got six hours til dawn, go for it!" Pa said.

I turned and smiled at Sandy, gave her a quick kiss and turned to the circle of friends and family sitting in between the shadows and the fire light. "I see we have some travelers among us," nodding to the Euros, " and so I will tell you a little history as well."

~~~

Most people arrive on Maui by air, from those other islands up in the sky I used to say as a small kid. If the weather is nice, and it's a good bet that it will be, the first thing you notice as you approach the airport is the sugar cane. 40,000 acres is hard to miss, especially when the verdant green contrasts so nicely with the cobalt blue ocean and the white sandy beaches.

Most people know something of the stories about missionaries and sugar barons and wild whalers and figure the sugar cane plant was brought over by some of that crew. History though usually has a more interesting story to tell if you put on your detective hat and listen to the words someone far older than you managed to write down, sing within a song, or etch into rock.

The great Polynesian voyagers moved easily among the giant swells of the Pacific Ocean when only the Vikings were venturing into the Atlantic, some 500 years before Mister Columbus. They brought the sugar cane plant with them from Tahiti and planted it along with their taro. It was a sweet treat best chewed on a hot day tending to your rock walls and water flow.

Refining it into molasses and eventually into those famous white crystals was something that became popular, at least in Hawaii, around 1835 on the island of Kauai. Planting sugar cane within plantations spread to most of the islands and with some extraordinary engineering feats worthy of their own story, water from the windward slopes of the mountains were funneled, tunneled and spread across the sunny, but desert leeward growing areas. Those would be the same areas you flew across when your plane brought you here.

Almost as influential as the coconut palm, this cultivation of sugar cane on Maui, and the other islands as well, shaped human culture and history profoundly. The economy, the political landscape, the towns themselves revolved and evolved around sugar cane. The sweet smell of the smoke during processing, the god awful stench of the fields when the water lay dormant, and the black "Hawaiian snow" of ash that would fall hours after a field was burned are all embedded in island memories.

There is plenty of good and bad associated with something so prevalent, something so good at making money. Depending on who you ask, and in what era you asked, you could get answers ranging from "Sugar put my kids through college" to "Sugar took the water away from our taro patches."

Regardless of any individual human perspective, the island had it's own opinion. It saw it all. It felt the fire of the fields burning in the night, the quenched thirst at its parched deserts. It felt the slow seeping of poisons into its bosom and the sting of fertilizers. It enjoyed the tradewinds massaging the miles of cane on its way to the ocean and it felt useful to those multi-cultured people so enthusiast to work its soil. Maui, as an island, smiled in so many ways as it provided for all those who used its vast resources.

The island also learned, early on, of how such large scale human activity brought it so much adventure and how it eventually reflected so much of that. The massive sugar cane fields became the playgrounds of exploring children, the protector of thousands of small animals (for the 18 month growth cycle), the shield for illegal marijuana growers and all too often the shallow grave of an unfortunate murder victim. Many teenage girls and boys explored each other in their cars parked among the tall grasses. Drinking and partying, even camping by the homeless went unnoticed. Almost every human activity would take place there from the time the cane was head high to when its tops sparked with the tall seed tassels and right up to the point where the great burns took it all away. Everything ugly, everything beautiful had 18 months to explore until the fires reset it all back to zero.

The vast fields, untended for the most part during the growing cycle had always been a favorite place for pakalolo growers. Marijuana, its other name, blended in well with the tall sweet grasses, soaking up the bright tropical light and the clear mountain water irrigation. I suppose it was just another cash crop, like the sugar cane, exploiting the land. Regardless of what opinions were about this particular plant, the problem it created was as old as mankind. Greed was a powerful master. Pakalolo, being illegal and in demand was therefore expensive. Millions of dollars were generated from its production and one important difference it had with commercial crops was that the small guy could make money growing it. You didn't need to be a large corporate sugar plantation. All you had to do is trek out into the nameless sugar fields, at night, carve out a small patch and plant your starter plants. You might check on your garden once in the five or six month growing cycle but you didn't have to. Trek back in before the field was cut off from water, prior to its burn, and you with any luck would have $20,000 or more of Maui Wowee ready to haul back to your Toyota pickup.

The temptation to do this was not frowned on for the most part. Afterall, most of us probably knew dozens of people that smoked it, including many adults older than us. I have been to kiddie parties, with bouncy houses and slippery slides all going and several parents casually smoking pakalolo right out in the open as they discussed the hassles of helping with homework. On more than one occasion I had heard parents saying something like "No Billy, you can't smoke until you're 14. It'll stunt your growth, now go back and throw a water balloon or something (lengthy inhalation sounds followed)." Drug culture is in fact multi-generational. Just like alcohol and prescription meds I suppose.

The sugar cane employees hated it for the most part. The last thing they wanted to do was stumble across someone's patch, trip a booby trap or be tempted themselves. Maui had about a dozen missing persons a year that never showed up, ever, and everyone knew intuitively that they had probably ended up in the cane fields.

We all have our own cane field stories, but nothing compared to that of our high school buddies Ignacio and Enrique. Both of them were pretty good students at Kula High, played a mean game of basketball and could surf circles around most of us, well not me, but most of us. Iggy's dad worked for Maui Sugar and Enrique spent summer vacations as a planter there.

It all started one late afternoon while out surfing an unusually glassy day at Ho'okipa. The wind surfers were grounded and us surfers had perfect conditions in double overhead waves. It had been a spectacular session and after several hours we were all sitting over at Pavilions cooking up hamburgers and some wild pig one of the guys had brought back from Hana. Enrique had a big date that evening and was all excited. His date was probably the most beautiful Japanese girl that existed on all the islands. Her parents had moved to Maui from Honolulu, a little high brow for the likes of most of us, but Enrique, I was told, was pretty handsome himself. He was a born comic and had caught the eye of Jasmine. Some of the guys teased him though, that he didn't have the money to keep such a girl interested for long. That, of course, didn't deter him.

This afternoon, after we had all changed to dry clothes, some guy I didn't know was talking about how 'sugar cane planter Enrique' could never keep a city girl like Jasmine. Enrique jumped up on the picnic table, shirtless and shouted.

"Jasmine knows my pockets are empty," as he pulled the pockets inside out so they hung our like ears on a shaggy poi dog. "But, she knows that's not all I got in these pants boys!" He threatened to pull his zipper down, but we booed him down from that idea pretty quickly.

Near sunset, when the beers were coming out fast and furious Enrique, nice aloha shirt hanging on his muscular frame, went out to start his old Toyota truck. It had been his older brother Esteban's ride and it was old when Esteban had bought it ten years earlier. I heard it cough a few times, turn over then stall. He tried it several more times before getting out to open the hood. This was not a new problem apparently. Pulling out a spray bottle of something high octane he put several shots directly into the carburetor, ran back in the cab to turn the key and with a small explosion it turned over and idled for him. I watched him run back out to close the hood, shoot us a shaka sign and fire off toward Wailea and sweet Jasmine.

"Hope that damn thing doesn't catch fire with that honey of his in it." I said.

"No way dude. He would never pick her up in that thing. He told me he's gonna meet her at Oceans for drinks." Iggy confirmed.

All of us nodded, thinking we would do the same thing, or had already done that once before.

Unfortunately, we heard the next day that the truck had broke down on the run across the island. He had shot more of the magic octane juice in the carb and this time it did catch the truck on fire, burning it to a crisp on the long road through the cane fields that separated the resorts from our side of the island.

Enrique had tried to hitch hike the rest of the way, but after dark it was near impossible to get a ride anywhere. He had been determined enough to walk, but didn't reach a phone for several hours.

The story goes, as I heard it anyway, that Jasmine had thought she had been stood up by yet another surfer boy and had gone off to dinner with some tourist guy with a Porsche rental that ran just fine. Enrique had finally made his way to Oceans around ten that night, dirty and sweaty and overly thirsty. He ended up drinking too much, got in a fight and thrown out. The cops picked him up at dawn sleeping in the kitchen of some saimin shop in Kihei.

Iggy bailed him out that afternoon with the money he had stashed for a new board. Both guys felt tapped out, trapped and with no options short of joining the Army of making anything better of their lives. Maui was not known for its good paying jobs. Maui had, in their lifetimes, become a playground for rich tourists, starry eyed hippies and trust funders. Nothing much had changed for the working folks since World War II. Subsidence jobs were hard to get and rents were not cheap.

Iggy and Enrique knew one thing though. Those tourists, hippies and trust funders all enjoyed a fine stinky marijuana bud, rolled up nice in some organic rolling papers and slowly burning on the beach, the top of the mountain or in their beach front homes.

It was funny though, I had never seen either of them partake. Primo beer yes or an occasional mixed drink, but never marijuana. So, when I heard Enrique bring up the subject at Pavilions I was surprised.

"So guys. I'm sick and tired of being frickin' broke all da time. My cuz he grows only one or two patches. He's got a new truck and next week he's gonna buy a fishing boat. I told 'em I'm in. I'm gonna grow some weed in the cane and make a few bucks."

Iggy wasn't saying no, but was listening real good. His dad had told him stories about growers and most of them were probably not good.

"I only need one guy for help me out. We can split the take. No worries on starters, my cuz said he would set me up." Enrique looked around at the six of us sitting there still dripping wet from surfing that morning. "So what? Whose in?"

No one volunteered. Not that it seemed like it was dangerous or was illegal. We knew the cops never bothered with small growers. It was the cane fields. They were pretty and all, but we didn't want to go tromping around in those endless mazes of sharp grasses, full of the infamous cane spider, stinky soil and the ghosts of a thousand other hapless souls that had never returned. And, at night? No way!

"I'll go with ya bro." Iggy raised his hand and then stood up. "I need a new board." He smiled at his little joke. Everyone knew he could buy a hundred boards with one good crop. "Besides," he continued. "I can ask my Dad where the best spots are. He'll tell me so we can stay out of trouble."

Enrique stood up, walked over to Iggy and gave him a big hug. "Right on dude." He hugged him again. "Mahalo."

That was our second year at Kula High. By Junior year, both Enrique and Iggy had new trucks. The summer between Junior and Senior years they took their girlfriends to Disneyland, flying first class direct from Maui to L.A.

We didn't see them surf much that last year of school. Their grades fell a bit, not much, but no more honor rolls. They were tired a lot during the season, planting and harvesting more than two guys could really pull off. The money had them under its spell. And, it was all cash. No taxes for those guys. I overhead Iggy saying he not only had made more money than his dad, but more than the plantation boss as well.

Things were sure looking good for them. I knew I was a bit jealous at the time, but I made my excuses. I would rather surf than hoof it around in the dark and mud. When I heard Enrique and Iggy talking about their new automatic pistols I figured it was all over my head anyhow. I guess I wasn't as broke as they had been, and my motivation wasn't so much a lot of cash, but a lot of free time. I looked at them like I looked at a guy in a suit on TV, cruising Wall Street. It was cool I guess, but not for me.

Their girlfriends at Kula High were increasingly popular as well. They had nice stuff too, complements of Iggy and Enrique. Even if the boys were gone for a couple of days, which happened about twice a month, no one messed with the girlfriends. There was a level of respect there that no one else got. Not the football guys, or the surf stars and even Hans the new world champion wind surfer. It was local respect. Maui boys, and their girls. No one messed with them, no one even wanted to. They were self made guys and everyone was proud of them, even if they were pot growers. They were cool. Everyone knew them, and both boys were cool with everyone else.

Money though has this problem of letting itself be known to everyone. Word got out that growing on Maui was big business and some rifraf from Honolulu decided to fly over and give it a go. These guys were off-Island trouble and within a couple of weekends, word was out, mostly from the discos and the bars, that some bad asses were around. Off island guys were pretty easy to spot. First, they drove rental cars. Second they threw money around like they were big wigs or gangsters. However, the fact that no one knew them was the dead giveaway. Maui wasn't so big that you couldn't always find someone who knew someone else. It was about two degrees of separation here.

Several months after all that got started, near graduation, Iggy and Enrique came out surfing for the first time in probably a year or more. It was a big time, we caught all the good waves and after one of those old time classic sessions we sat around Pavilions again and talked story. We all finally got a chance to talk with them one on one again. They were still their old selves, just maybe a little more worldly now. Enrique especially fell right back into his jovial ways telling jokes and tall tales.

Right around midnight though, both of them split off for a moment while we just sat there and popped more beers. They looked a bit solemn walking back toward us and then they got our attention.

"Guys, we gotta say something important OK?"

Sure, we all nodded, trying to figure out what the heck it could be.

Iggy spoke first. "You all know what we've been up to these last couple of years." Everyone hooted and laughed. "Yeah, yeah, we know, good times yeah?" More hoots.

Then Enrique spoke, all quiet and serious. "We got some trouble on island, and you might have heard of that too." Everyone quieted. "We got us some Honolulu guys trying to squeeze us out of business. Frickin' townies for god's sake."

No one said a thing. We just stared, not really understanding the depth of their problem. One thing we did well in those days was let stuff settle into our brains without interruption until we did understand. So, we just sat there. Quiet. Settling in slowly...

"We got guys trying to take away from us Maui guys. Taking our local pride, taking our local money." Iggy said all defensively. "You know what that means?"

No one did, but I at least asked. "What Iggy, what the hell is going on?"

"This is what is going on," Enrique said, pulling out his pistol. "We're gonna chase them right the fuck off this island."

Immediately we all sobered up a bit. We knew they had guns and carried, but we thought they were always stashed in their trucks. Now they were brandishing them, all pissed off. It was taking a lot of the fun and fascination out of it for us simple surfer types.

"Whoa dude!" Jackson, one of the younger guys exclaimed. "That's pretty heavy!" We all agreed, and waited for Enrique and Iggy to tell us more.

"What you want us to do?" Iggy challenged. "Just roll over and let some off island gangsters come over here," he spread his arms out toward us, his gun in hand now too. "And take away from our aina?"

"Well?" Enrique now demanded of us. We were all watching their guns more than their words.

Jackson spoke up again. "No way! Of course not." He stood up and leaned casually against the picnic table. The rest of us were keeping our butts seated. "But, it looks like someone is gonna get plugged."

"Damn right, and it ain't gonna be us!" Enrique proclaimed.

Jackson continued. "Look, maybe my uncles can help. Two of them are cops ya know."

Everyone of us turned our attention to Jackson, incredulous that he would suggest the police get involved with anything Iggy and Enrique were doing.

"Say what Jack?" Iggy asked, his eyebrows almost to the top of his hairline. "How are cops gonna help out some local growers chase off some Honolulu rats?" All of us waited for an answer to that one.

Jackson looked at us for a moment, wondering if he was sounding as stupid as it looked. He turned back to Iggy and Enrique. "Because you're local." He sat up on the picnic table now. "They don't want any gun fights going on, or outside crime. You know they look the other way with you guys. Hell, they all have relatives doing the same thing. They're cool with that, but they sure as hell don't want gangsters shootin' up the place." Jackson looked at the rest of us again and asked, "Right?"

Iggy and Enrique seemed to be thinking that one over. They had thankfully put their weapons back into their belts. Iggy leaned over and whispered something to Enrique. He nodded.

"So Jackson, how would something like that work?" Iggy asked, his hands folded across his chest.

Jackson didn't really want to get involved in something he knew was big trouble, but he was like the rest of us. We wanted to help our friends out of a jam that we knew they were not going to be able to manage by themselves. They were just a couple of neighborhood kids like us, not big city bad boys. "Let me know who you think these guys are, or where they hang. I will pass that on to my uncs."

Iggy and Enrique looked at each other and nodded. "Yeah, we can do that. We know where they might be soon." Iggy laughed a little sarcastically.

"Where then?" Jackson asked.

"They've been renting small planes and flying over the cane fields. They spock out our patches and come back at night to rip us off." Enrique looked heartbroken. "They were flying this morning." Enrique gave Iggy a light punch to the arm. "We gotta go, yeah?"

Iggy nodded. He looked back at us. "Guys, it's been good hangin' with ya. Get waves tomorrow or what?"

"Sure, and no wind I heard." I offered.

"So," Jackson spoke up again. "You want me to tell my uncs the scoops?"

Iggy looked at Enrique for a brief second and then back to Jackson. "We gotta think about it." They both grabbed their boards, towels and one more beer. As they were walking back to their trucks Enrique turned and stopped, looked at Jackson. He smiled and nodded his head thanks.

We all had a bad feeling about that entire scene and for good reason. At first light both Iggy and Enrique drove immediately out to their patches, hoping to harvest before the thieves came that night. They had a big patch, worth around $30,000 in a dry field that was scheduled to be burned in a couple of days. Iggy always had the scoop on burn days since his dad was on the burn crew. It was early afternoon and they were cutting and stuffing big Costco garbage bags with the sweet sticky buds. Then they heard it.

"What the..." Iggy stood up from stuffing his thirty gallon black bag. Enrique heard it too.

"Frickin' airplane!" Enrique almost screamed. His frustration was eating at him like a shark feasts on turtles.

They both tried to figure out what to do, but there wasn't much. The sky above them was clear, their patch would be easily seen from a few hundred feet up. The sounds kept getting closer until they could see the little Cessana 150. It was flying a straight line about a hundred yards to the south of them at about three hundred feet. Suddenly, it turned and headed right for them.

"Shit, they see the patch dude!" Iggy cursed.

Enrique was enraged. He could now see some guy poking his head out the window, taking pictures. They were mapping out the patch.

"Screw them Iggy!" Enrique yelled, pulling out his .45 automatic.

Iggy looked at Enrique trying to figure out what he was doing but it came to him pretty quickly. He drew his gun as well.

"Come on boys, come on over here." Enrique coaxed.

"Yeah, we got some for ya." Iggy agreed.

Enrique was still holding his gun down, and advised Iggy to do the same for a moment. "Let them get real close Iggy, then we shoot that damn plane right out of the air!"

Iggy was giddy, he would finally get to shoot his new gun at something other than the range targets in Ukumehame. He and Enrique had been very good students of marksmanship. Like anything they focused on they usually excelled.

Suddenly the Honolulu boys saw both Iggy and Enrique and feeling cocky decided to circle the patch lower and lower, yelling taunts out the window.

"Hey! Thanks for all the weed guys!" Someone from the plane yelled. "You guys are the best!" The plane was in a tight circle now, about two hundred feet straight above Iggy and Enrique. "Yeah, we're gonna hire you to do my mama's garden!" someone yelled from above.

Enrique was shaking with rage, but kept his gun down. "Iggy, you got an eye on the pilot?"

"Yeah dude, I got him."

"Look, lead them about a half inch, that's all, but dude…"

"Yeah Enrique?"

"Unload all you got into the plane, then reload as soon as you can. OK?"

"Got it dude." Iggy confirmed, feeling two more clips in his overalls.

The plane continued into one more circle, the left side leaning toward the boys on the ground, the pilot leering at them as his passengers continued to yell taunts and threats.

"After we take all your weed, we'll be back for your women!" This same guy spit out the window and laughed.

"Iggy?" Enrique asked.

"Ready dude."

"Aim for the pilot's window, I'm aiming for his door." Enrique coached.

Iggy hadn't planned on that, thinking they would shoot at the engine. But things were moving fast suddenly.

Enrique yelled, "Now!"

Both local boys, from good hard working families, from a good school, with great friends and smart minds raised their gun hands high, steadying their wrists with their other hands and in an instant crossed one of those lines in life that you can never retreat back over.

One of the guys in the plane, the spitter, managed to yell "Shit" just as the first four high velocity slugs slammed into the cockpit window and door. Glass shattered all over the three city boys inside as well as the bright red arterial blood of their 19 year old pilot. Not that it mattered in that very next second, but four more rounds found their marks. The pilot dead, and the plane already on the edge of stall as it circled low immediately fell like a stone managing to get upside down just as it slammed into the dry cane thirty yards from Iggy and Enrique.

"Whoa!" Enrique yelled in victory. "Hot damn Iggy, we got 'em."

Just as Iggy was hooting the plane exploded, it's wings almost full of fuel for a day's reconnaissance. Burning fuel and hot metal flew out in all directions, landing on cinder dry cane grass already prepped for a controlled burn.

The concussion knocked both Iggy and Enrique down on their butts, but they scrambled back up and ran toward the plane. They had downed their tormenters and ran instinctively to see what they had done. It wasn't long before they began to absorb the scope of the destruction they had wrought.

"Oh shit..." Iggy hissed. He wasn't looking at the rapidly spreading fire around the plane, but at one of the passengers, broken and half out of one of the windows, his hair and face burning.

Enrique was in shock. His earlier rage was now displaying its dark consequences. He looked down at the .45 still in his hands and flexed his fingers around it a bit, feeling like it perhaps had grown too tight into his hand, his soul.

Suddenly, a scream erupted from the other side of the plane, out of view. It was full of fear and horror, and panic.

Iggy immediately ran over toward that side of the plane, ignoring the mounting flames just a few feet away.

"Iggy! We gotta go dude!" Enrique yelled.

Iggy never heard anything, only the screams and deep inside a growing guilt that was slowly overwhelming him. As he rounded the tail of the plane he saw one of the city boys on his back, outside the plane. His entire body was burning, the clothes almost gone. His arms were flailing uselessly at the flames and at his face, but his screams were piercing. Iggy froze in his tracks, hypnotized by what he had been a part of.

Enrique looked around and saw that the fire was now raging almost completely around them. "Iggy! Iggy! We gotta go! We gotta go now!" He was yelling at the top of his lungs, but he could barely hear himself. The crackling of the dry cane and the increasing roar of the hot air rushing upward was deafening. "Iggy! Iggy! Let's GO dude!" Hot pieces of grass were flying around and landing on Enrique. Frantically he was brushing off the embers as fast as he could. "Iggy, I gotta go, come on!" He turned and ran toward the slim patch of space left between the flames yelling Iggy's name the entire time.

Iggy felt like he had been stabbed in the heart himself. He stood and watched in horror as the poor guy continued to burn, screaming and thrashing. Tears were marring his vision as the scene deteriorated and in a brief instant he asked God to forgive him as he raised his gun hand.

Enrique felt his own clothes catching fire as he ran. He threw his gun as far away as he could, stripping off his burning shirt right after that. He was still yelling Iggy's name when he heard the gunshot.

"Iggy, goddammit, where are you?" Enrique had tripped again, crying out the words in his desperation. He saw one more chance to get ahead of the flames and made his mad dash for freedom and life. In a few more yards he would make the cane road and could run faster there.

Iggy felt a massive relief flood his mind as the burning man stopped thrashing and screaming. He let his arm fall back to his side, the .45 heavy now and done with the task. Just then he felt his scalp get hot, and reached up to flick away what he thought was an ash. His hands felt something quite different though, his hair, his beautiful curly black hair, envied by every girl in his school was on fire.

"Shit!" he screamed himself now, dropping the gun to use both hands to try and put out the flames. It was burning his skin and he pulled up his shirt to try and cover the flames that way. As he did so he felt flames licking at his bare back and turned. There in front of him was the twenty foot tall monster of his childhood dreams. He had had nightmares since he could remember of cane fire monsters sneaking up on him, eating him a little at a time. His father understood, he had had them himself he told young Ignacio.

Iggy tried to yell Enrique's name, but as he drew a breath, the hot air burned his mouth and throat so much he couldn't manage a sound. He dropped to the ground, a few feet from the burning thief outside the plane. The fire was on him. He looked around and could see only the monster weaving in closer, reaching to grab his skin. He looked down at the blackened corpse and screamed as another ember landed on his back.

"Shit, shit!" He stood up and ran but quickly fell, not three feet away, got up and ran again, this time stumbling right back into the airplane and falling on top of the dead guy he had helped leave this world. There was no where to go. "Aye!" he managed to scream, singeing his throat again as he inhaled. His lungs were burning now with the heat, and his scalp was making sounds like bacon frying. The pain was becoming excruciating as he crawled off the corpse and tried to stay close to the ground. In his rapidly growing fear he found an inner comfort from somewhere, even as he vainly attempted to cover himself in dirt. He thought of his mother, her smiles and hugs and of his father showing him how to surf, how to work on his old car. "Please...please," he whispered in prayer. Glancing over at the burned corpse next to him he began to weep that lonely song of pain and unbearable grief.

He couldn't speak anymore, but he did think to himself, as he felt on the ground for what he needed. "I'm so, so sorry..."

Enrique reached the dirt cane road and looked left to see flames crossing the road there, already consuming both of their trucks. To the right it was still clear and he started to run as fast as he could, until he heard another gunshot.

"Iggy! Iggy...." Enrique cried as he felt part of his mind break away from the strong and stubborn man he had become. He stopped and looked in the direction of the shot and saw nothing but hundred foot tall flames roaring in their own victory celebration. His legs began running again. He felt the presence of evil there, and knew, as he ran faster than he had ever managed, that it was a part of him now.

A couple of weeks later, in a little cemetery on the edge of sleepy Wailuku town, at the base of scenic Iao valley, we all saw Enrique again. Iggy's parents were burying him right next to his grandparents. The entire high school class showed up, every single one of the three hundred and twenty-two people that all knew Ignacio so well. For a high school kid, it was by far the saddest thing we had ever experienced. With any luck it would remain so our entire lives. Of course, that was youthful thinking. Enrique looked defeated and about ten years older. His hair was cut short, presumably from the haircut he needed after getting burned. He had bandages on his hands still.

The police and Maui Sugar had never published their findings, but the newspaper carried a story about a small plane crashing into the cane and sparking a fire. Nothing was ever mentioned about the marijuana patches or any of the other drama. Enrique met us at Pavilions that night and told us the whole story, swearing us to secrecy until he could leave town. He said he had told Iggy's dad too, but that no one else was to know. We never saw Enrique again after that, not even at the high school reunions.

The girls from class put flowers on Iggy's grave for several years to come. Everyone talked about him at our graduation a few months later. It was hard on young people to know someone die so young, but it was, in a way I'm sure Iggy would have appreciated, enlightening. We all lived like it counted after that. We quit racing our cars, we quit surfing storm surf, and some of us embraced our little paradise a little closer for it.

When I see the sugar cane fields now, I think about how it absorbs the best and worst of us, of how it cleanses itself and our mistakes with its fire and how it always comes back big and beautiful.

~ ~ ~

Rolling Stone

The moon was not getting any lower toward the sparkling ocean, no matter how hard the sea tried to pull the light closer. It must have been around midnight by now and the fire was feeling especially comforting in the cool late night air.

"Wow, I don't think I ever heard that story before." Sandy remarked. She looked up at me questioningly. "How did you know the parts about Iggy's last moments? It sounds like Enrique couldn't have seen all that."

A couple of people thought about that and murmured agreement with Sandy's question. I was happy they were paying that much attention at this point in the night.

"Good point honey," I squeezed her a bit. "Jackson helped me with that. Before the funeral, which was a couple of weeks after this all happened, and before we saw Enrique again, we managed to get a hold of the coroner's report.

"We weren't sure what had happened to our friends, neither of them were around. When the coroner identified Iggy but not Enrique we knew Enrique must have escaped somehow. It also told us, forensically, about the gunshots.

"The four other guys, in the plane, were all from Honolulu alright. All but the pilot had criminal records." I looked for another Hinano, but couldn't find one. "It was tragic for sure."

Everyone was quiet. I knew one thing for sure about telling stories around a camp fire: don't quit on a scary story or a sad one.

"I do have one more story, one with a happy ending, if you guys are up for it?"

"Only if I can lay down on your leg," Sandy offered. I stretched my leg out for her.

"Yeah, go for it!" The Euro travelers were wide awake still.

"OK, OK. Once upon a time..." I looked around for a Hinano. "Are there any more of those Tahitian beers left?"

It was dark and no one could see anything really that wasn't right next to the fire. None of us wanted to get up, but I was about to. Storytelling had this strange way of making me thirsty.

"Someone looking for Hinanos?" A voice approaching from behind us asked.

Footsteps came up from the dark jungle behind us. I turned as far as I could without shaking Sandy's head off my thigh, but couldn't see until he was right next to us.

"Here ya go dude," he said, handing my a icy bottle.

"Great! Thanks." I looked up at the friendly face glowing in the firelight but didn't recognize him. He was tall, well over six foot, gray and black hair pulled back in a good two foot long pony tail. Beads adorned his tie dyed shirt and even hung off the tops of his cargo pants. Leather sandals and dirty toes finished the look, but he was smiling and that is all that really counted here.

"Got four more with me, if anyone needs?" he offered. Gregorio took him up on one and the Euros took two.

Sandy had seen the beads upside down and decided to sit up and greet him. "Have a seat with us, we're telling stories."

He sat down with most of the grace of an older guy and got comfortable. "Thank you very much. I appreciate the hospitality." He popped his one remaining beer and took a look up and said, "I'm Waterfall."

Sandy immediately livened up. She loved the hippie names that people gave themselves when they moved to Maui. We had talked about that a couple of times and she had explained to any and all that would listen that it was so cool. Some people came here and their lives changed, their minds opened and their eyes became more childlike. It was only natural that they would adopt a new name.

"I'm Sandy," she said, beaming. Introductions were done all around.

"We were about to hear a much happier tale than the one we just did," Sandy prompted.

"Cool, I'm fresh to that." Waterfall said and leaned back on his elbows, a carved ivory pendant sliding across his chest.

Sandy poked me lightly, ready for me to begin again.

"OK," I announced. "Where was I?" I took a long drink of my now half empty Hinano and feeling a little of its long forgotten effects, I began again. "Oh yeah. Once upon a time… there was a young kid I had met back in the day. He wasn't a kid kid, but a twenty something kid all fired up to make his way in the world. The world of Maui as it were.

"A bit younger than me he had found out about a big beach party we were throwing and asked to come. That alone was amazing, most people just crashed our parties. Those were the days of skydivers, live bands, multiple kegs and topless Canadian nurses dancing all night. Oh yeah and big bonfires that could be seen from space. Epic comes to mind and this night was no less than epic with a really big capital E.

"This kid, Stone was his last name, showed up and immediately blended into the party, having a big time, like the rest of us. Apparently he knew quite a few people there having grown up in Haiku somewhere. Not to get off on a party story, but at the end of the night, around two in the morning when most people had either left, hooked up, passed out or wandered away, Stone and some other guy started arguing about a girl.

"Nothing new there, but this one got heated, fueled by alcohol as it was and not really knowing either guy I told them to take it out to the beach. After a few moments Paden, my roommate at the time, said we had better check up on the two drunks, in case they tried to drown each other or do something else stupid.

"These big parties always had an element of chaos somewhere and this was going to be no exception. As we walked across the expansive yard toward the sand we heard muffled yelling. Getting past the last few palms Paden and I saw the two guys locked in a fighter's embrace, down on the sand. I wasn't sure who was who, but one of them had the other's head face down in the sand, lifting it up and then pushing it back down, all the while scolding the guy. Paden and I laughed out loud. Drunks on parade, again.

"Suddenly the guy on the bottom had had enough and pushed up and over, tumbling both of them right into the remnants of the fire and out to the other side. Paden and I figured we better get them separated before they actually hurt each other and ran over, but not before they rolled right back over the fire again and out to the other side.

"Paden grabbed one guy and I the other and we drug both of them kicking and screaming into the water. I had to push mine under twice to get him to shut up, but finally he sobered up enough to get the message. The guy turned out to be the kid Stone. After that we called him Rolling Stone and then later just Mick."

"Mick?" Ma asked.

"Yeah, Mick Jagger from the band called the Rolling Stones." The Stones were not known for any Tiki music, so they had not penetrated every market here on Maui.

"Anyhow," I continued. "Mick apologized later. He was a good guy but had lost it when he spotted his old girlfriend's new squeeze at our party. He wanted to make it up to us and suggested we all rent the state park cabins in Hana at Wainapanapa. He knew the area really well. Needing very little excuse for a campout on any of the islands we invited some friends and some weeks later we had three vans and a couple of pick up trucks caravaning down the infamous curves and valleys of the 'Road to Hana' ".

"Ah yes," Waterfall interrupted. "Hana. The land of dreams eh?"

I turned to look at this guy that I had just met and wondered at his words a moment. It was a little strange to say that, but as it simmered in my head a moment, it did make some sense.

"True. True," I agreed. "Now that I look back at it, those days were dreamlike in a lot of ways." Waterfall smiled and nodded like he knew what I was going to say now.

Sandy squeezed me a bit. "At the time," I continued. "We didn't look at it like a dream. It was more like an adventure train we had simply pointed in one direction, getting off at all the unknown stops to see what was there."

Waterfall added, "There's magic in that rainforest you know. The 'aina, the land, shares with all who move through her."

He was sounding a bit mystical, but I could roll with that. "Well, I'll admit, we returned changed people, that's for sure." I looked around and everyone was still listening so I kept going.

"Our first stop was some distance into the rainforest along the road, but quite a ways from Hana town. Mick said he wanted to show us a beer drinking horse, and since we had quite a bit of beer with us, we thought it a good idea.

"Naturally, we thought it a trick of some kind or a joke, but sure enough after we all gathered along the kiawe wood fence he held up a Coors Lite and looked at us. 'See that horse on the other side of the pasture?' We did. 'Watch this!'

"Mick popped the lid on the Coors can and that distinctive sound known to police, parents and teenagers everywhere echoed through the banana and guava trees across to the ears of the horse.

"Immediately his head reared up, he turned to look at us and galloped full speed over to Mick who was holding the can out. The horse reared up and neighed and finally settled down as Mick began pouring slowly right into the horse's mouth. In less than a minute it was gone and Mick popped another one.

" 'Two's your limit big boy,' Mick said and after that we believed everything he told us.

"It was a week filled with waterfalls on the beach, trucks stuck in the sand, fresh chicken barbeque (and I mean really fresh), bamboo forests, hidden lava tube caves, pristine swimming ponds with no one around and tropical weather. Mick jumped off the bridge at Seven Sacred Pools, sometimes called the Pools of Oheo. It was a good thirty foot drop into a bathtub size pool between rocks. And, he did it three times! We visited the Hana dump where Mick said he used to take his dates to do a little kissy kissy. We couldn't believe he would go there, but it did have an incredible view, up above town, and besides, it had that Hana thing going for it, dump or not.

"We had three cabins nestled in the old lava fields of Wainapanapa hidden by ferns and papaya trees. Since we had some folks that partied more than others we divided the three up. The 'Party Cabin' was where we entertained each other to endless all night laughing and drinking games, including Once I Was A Flying Cockaroach. The 'Sleeping Cabin' of course was where those who really had to went to recuperate. Most of us found we slept best during the day on the black or red sand beaches, or in the shade next to any of the waterfall pools. Finally, there was the 'Stabbin' Cabin' where those couples intent on fulfilling Hana's inherent intoxication could escape to."

"Well!" Sandy sat up. "Did you visit the Stabbin' Cabin?" She playfully accused me by poking her finger in my side.

"No, no. You couldn't go there by yourself." I laughed. "I spent my time at the Party Cabin, for sure."

Waterfall was nodding his head and rocking back and forth slightly. He seemed to be remembering some of his own Hana stories. Ma and Pa were keeping each other warm and the Euros were listening intently so that they might find these places themselves. Gregorio was watching the fire closely and Sandy went back to laying down on my leg.

"Eventually, we had to go back to our jobs, and lives. The trip back toward civilization was almost anticlimactic except for the drama in one of the trucks, the one that had gotten stuck on the beach. Mick had borrowed it and the brakes apparently had some sand, or rocks by the sound of it, stuck inside somewhere. He was only a ramp guy at the local airline and didn't have much money. None of us really did. Surely not enough to fix this. It was going to require some expensive repairs.

"Somehow he worked it out with the owner. Mick worked hard at two jobs and was earning his pilot license along the way on top of that. As for most of the crew that went to Hana that time we ended up all doing about the same old thing we had always done. But, Mick, he worked harder still, studied hard and after some significant bumps in the road became a full fledged airline pilot flying widebody jets all over the mainland.

"After a few years of that though, he transferred back to Hawaii to take a job as a pilot with the same small interisland airline he used to throw bags for. It was an accomplishment that had rarely been achieved. When he pulled into the gate at the Kahului, Maui airport the first time, the big jet's engines winding down, he leaned out the pilot's window and the entire ramp crew gave up a big shout out to the local boy who had done good."

"Sweet," Waterfall said, rocking back and forth.

"Yep, sweet indeed!" I added.

~ ~ ~

Gypsy King

"Well, son, that was a good story. Sounds a lot like some of the adventures in Waimanalo during our Waikiki days. But, I think Pa and I had better head off to bed," Ma admitted.

"Let me walk you back," I offered, but they had their flashlights and made their own way. It looked as if the jungle parted for them as their lights pushed through the darkness.

Gregorio took off as well, having a new load of Angus cattle arriving from Canada the next, well actually this very day. I think I could already see a little light in the eastern sky.

The Euros all took off as well, having a big day in Hana planned and now armed with some stories to follow.

That left Sandy and I, and Waterfall.

"I see a satellite!" Sandy motioned with her arm stretched out toward the sky, still laying down on my leg.

I looked up and searched for a moment before seeing what must have been one of the Iridium crew racing quickly at low altitude toward the rising sun.

"Wonder what it must feel like, to always be falling like that?" Waterfall asked himself, out loud.

Sandy sat up and looked over at Waterfall for a moment, thinking about what he had said, imagining.

"Here, we fall, we hit something pretty quickly." Waterfall added. "Up there," he pointed. "They fall forever." Looking down at his hands for a moment he admitted, "Well for several years anyhow."

Sandy watched the last moments of the satellite as it sped out of view and straight into the incoming star's increasingly bright light. "I had a dream once," she said leaning into my shoulder and looking at the fire. "I was dropping in at Unknowns on a big day. The surf was beyond big actually." She squeezed my arm a bit. "It was one of those dreams where you know it must be a dream but you're still there, having to deal with it."

"I hear that." Sometimes, for me anyhow, it was difficult to discern between memories of dreams and what has actually occurred. When your life is more dream than not it begins to mix together.

Sandy continued. "This really big set of waves started approaching from the horizon, or from space..." she looked up at the stars again. "I don't know, it was like the entire ocean was standing on it's tail."

"Awesome," Waterfall whispered. He was leaning forward, elbows propped on his knees, and holding his head like a trophy. His long gray curls had fallen forward.

"Terrifying," Sandy corrected. "I knew I had to paddle out farther toward them, otherwise I would be caught inside what was going to be a massive whitewater mess.

"You know how it is in dreams, time doesn't seem to behave. Well, I did turn to paddle out, but it had to be miles away. Of course, suddenly I was there, still paddling and trying to make it up the immense face of this giant space wave.

"I looked up at the crest, apparently miles above me, and saw it slap a satellite right out of the sky, out of its orbit! Moments later it was splashing and bouncing down the face of the wave, just missing me. I remember seeing it's shiny metal parts and some bent antennas."

Sandy shivered a little and kept going. This was a pretty good dream I had to admit, even if she seemed a bit disturbed by it. At least she had woken up from it.

"In a moment I found myself near the top of the wave. It looked like it would curl over any second. I was not going to be able to punch through to the other side and I sure didn't want to get pitched backwards trying to swim over the top. I did remember thinking how was it possible that I could breath this far up in space.

"I turned my board around quickly, took two quick paddles back down the face so that I could catch the monster. As I jumped to my feet I noticed another satellite being smacked down by the wave. In the back of my mind I thought I would need to avoid that tumbling ball of metal as I made my way down the face.

"I found my balance and went to turn a little but saw that I was free-falling. My board had not yet connected with the wave, it was so steep."

"Whoa dude! I can see it..." Waterfall exclaimed excitedly then trailed off into some kind of fascinated murmuring.

Sandy looked over at him and smiled. I didn't know until later that she thought he was high on something. We found out later he wasn't, but that his ability to put himself completely into a story often overwhelmed him.

"I've had a few waves where I was airborne for a brief moment before I fell far enough to connect with the water sweeping up the wave. But, this one…" Sandy paused a moment and shook her head. "This one…I never did touch the face. The uprushing wind was buffeting me, and keeping me from actually connecting to the wave. I was doing OK keeping my balance, until I saw one of those crazy satellites come bouncing from the left, splashing and spinning and completely out of control. I tried to swerve right, and somehow did, as the big metal beast swept in front of me and continued down toward the base of the wave, bouncing like a skipping rock.

"I swerved back left and pointed my board straight down, like I would on any steep wave, but still I couldn't stop my free fall. I just kept falling, not going any farther down the wave. I quickly glanced behind me and it looked like I was still up at the crest. Looking back down I saw the wave moving over the coastline and then up the slopes of the mountain, as if it was nothing. Kula passed beneath me and then the summit of Haleakala. In a moment Molokini and Kahoolawe passed beneath the wave, and there were no islands left for it to sweep across.

"That is when I got real scared. I knew there was nothing but thousands of miles of open ocean ahead and I was never going to be able to get back to the beach."

Sandy stopped talking and hugged me real tight. Waterfall stopped rocking back and forth and stared at her. I kissed her black hair and gave her a big hug right back.

"What happened next honey?" I asked. She just hugged me a bit more.

"Yeah, did you see any more satellites?" Waterfall asked. I think he liked that part best.

"No." Sandy stood up. She stretched her legs and twisted her hips a bit. I could tell she didn't want to tell us. "I woke up then." She looked down at me and smiled.

Some things, even for your lovers and friends, are too scary to tell. I looked at her for a moment, to see if I might be able to get the real answer, but she had that look of determination I knew to be resolute.

"You guys need another beer, or," Sandy looked to the eastern sky. "Maybe a coffee?"

"Nature's nectar, or some water would be fantastic." Waterfall asked.

Sandy looked at him for a moment, trying to figure out, like I was, what nature's nectar might be.

"I'll have what he's having!" I said and then leaned over to ask Waterfall about the nectar.

"Oh," he laughed a little at himself. "Any kind of juice, orange, guava. You know."

"Be right back boys." Sandy turned and headed back to the bar for the drinks and I watched her for a moment, thinking about her surf dream.

"She's got a fear built in there somewhere, ya know," Waterfall noted.

I turned to look at him. "Fear? That girl?" I stretched out one of my legs toward the fire, feeling it warm my toes. "I can't imagine that. I've never seen her even flinch."

Waterfall looked at me like he was trying to figure out how much he should tell me of some secret formula. Evidently he came to the conclusion that he could share most of it. "Dreams are a powerful tool. Both those you have when you sleep and those you follow when you're awake." He continued sizing me up to see if I would be receptive to this.

At 5 A.M watching the beginnings of a sunrise at the sea cliffs I am at my most accommodating. "Go ahead Waterfall, that sounds interesting."

He leaned back against his hands and looked up at the lightening sky, took a deep breath and slowly blew it out between pursed lips. I thought he might be going into a yoga trance or something, but pretty soon he straightened up again and leaned over toward me. His eyes were metallic blue, almost reflective and they gave him a veneer of mysticism. It played well with his message.

"Our minds like to experiment. Try new things, discard things that don't work. This is going on all the time, subconsciously. Dreaming when we sleep is one way we see this process."

I nodded. He paused while I absorbed that, which was a good thing. My mind was quite a bit slower at this point. He watched me for some moments and then repeated himself.

"Our minds are constantly trying new ways to sort out all the information that gets presented. Day in and day out we pummel our consciousness with inputs. Eyes, ears, touch, taste and smell. Throw in some heavy duty contemplation and you get an idea of the vast amount of data we are uploading.

"Dreaming, as a lot of people acknowledge, is a way the mind has of sorting out the day's events. Some people though think it is simply the sheen left over from deeper processes that are filing away the stuff that wasn't immediately discarded." He turned to look out toward the east. "The dreams might even *be* the discard."

I glanced back quickly to see if Sandy was returning with our Nature Nectar, but no one was approaching. These kind of thoughtful conversations always made me extremely thirsty, like my brain was running on liquid electrons or something. Turning back to Waterfall I commented "That's cool. I have never heard it put that way before."

Waterfall nodded and didn't say anything, he looked for Sandy as well.

"Have you done a bit of studying on this subject Waterfall?" I asked.

He nodded again. "Yes, got my PhD in psychology right before I dropped out of that whole scene to become the Gypsy King."

That woke me up a bit. Waterfall, the Gypsy King? It wasn't disdain or ridicule that got me alert. I would be a fool to make such judgments immediately. It was the fact that he was so confident in such a proclamation. If he said his name was Waterfall, so be it. Who should say otherwise? Not me, the guy who talked to parrots. If he pronounced himself King of the Gypsies then only a Gypsy could take exception. As far as I knew, I wasn't a Gypsy.

"Gypsy King Waterfall?" I asked politely. "You gotta tell me more about that dude."

"Gypsy King?" Waterfall and I both turned back toward the jungle. Sandy must have overheard us on her way back. "Wait! Wait! Tell me about that." We could hear her moving faster through the grass now.

The pre-dawn light had Sandy glowing as she moved toward us, three tall glasses of color in her hands.

"Here you go Waterfall," she said, handing him one of the glasses. "It's guava and pineapple with a little touch of apple juice."

"Wow, thank you Sandy." Waterfall and I said exactly at the same time.

She handed me the same and sat down again next to me. Oversized straws made it easy to get started.

"So," Sandy said. "I've heard of this Gypsy King. Are you guys talking about that?"

Both Waterfall and I were too busy drinking to answer right away.

"Well," Sandy continued. "I heard he is in town actually. In fact, the rumor is that he is holding a secret retreat somewhere on this side of the island." She looked at us for a response.

I kept drinking but looked at her and shrugged my shoulders. I would let Waterfall tell her about his 'other name'. I glanced at him quickly and he was content to let Sandy tell us more, but his grin was going to give him away soon.

"When I was shopping at Mana the other day I heard some people talking in the deli section. They said this Gypsy King was one of the world's leading experts on dreaming. He had studied at Harvard, Oxford and lived with the American Indians for years."

Sandy was rattling off so much information I wondered how she could be so energetic at this hour.

"In fact," she leaned in a bit toward the remaining embers in the fire. "He is the leading proponent of this idea that all energy has intelligence in it." She shook her head a little at her statement. "I can't quite understand that. Can you guys?"

It got my attention when I heard her say that.

Waterfall finally looked up from his smoothie and caught Sandy's eye. "That is indeed a fascinating idea, if I say so myself."

I laughed a little at that and Sandy looked at me suspiciously, then back to Waterfall. I looked over at him as well and he told me, with his eyes, 'go ahead and tell her'.

"Sandy," I announced. "Let me introduce you to the Gypsy King himself, also known as Waterfall."

Sandy stopped and stared at him.

"Nice to meet you Sandy. You seem to know quite a bit about my teachings." Waterfall leaned over on one hand and extended his other, never getting off his knees. His long curls almost touched the ground.

Sandy grasped his hand politely and shook it once, then retreated back to her seat next to me. She seemed suddenly unexcited.

"Waterfall was just telling me about his Gypsy King thing honey, while you were gone." I sensed she was uneasy.

She looked over at me, with a look of embarrassment. I shrugged my shoulders which in turn moved my eyebrows up. I didn't get what the problem was.

"So," Sandy said a little meekly. "Do you interpret dreams then?"

Now I understood. She had told us that surf dream with the satellites and all. I turned to watch Waterfall.

"Sandy." Waterfall got up and moved a little closer to us. "Dream interpretation is an art I was never practiced in. As I was saying earlier while you were getting us those spectacular smoothies, our minds produce dreams for perhaps two reasons. One, as a way of sorting out the day's activities, questions and fears. And secondly, perhaps less romantic, to discard ideas it doesn't want to hold on to. As any of those processes occur, our minds "see" them as dreams."

Sandy absentmindedly played with the fire, poking it with a stick. "So," turning to look again at Waterfall. "What would you make of my dream then?"

Waterfall looked a bit uneasy, in my opinion. He had already said he didn't interpret dreams, but obviously had some idea about Sandy's. He stood and looked to the horizon, brightening rapidly now. "Why don't we take some chairs over here," gesturing toward the cliff facing the sunrise.

The three of us took up seats in a row, Sandy in the middle, and faced the sea. We sat closely together, armrest to armrest. The air was very still, anticipating as we were, the arrival of the sun. I looked over at Sandy who was still waiting on Waterfall to answer.

"Sandy, I've had a few dreams similar to yours," Waterfall began. "For me I thought they were based in fear." He reached over and gently placed his hand atop hers. "Fear that you have something big to accomplish, but that there may be a danger of some kind that could prevent you for doing so." He looked at her sincerely, then placed both of his hands on his knees and turned to the sunrise. "Here it comes."

Sandy turned to look as well, and we all watched the amazing spectacle of our planet spinning ahead at tens of thousands of miles per hour. The edge of the ocean began to glow ever fiercer, the few clouds above the horizon already bright and happy.

I heard some deep breathing and turned to look at Waterfall. His palms were turned up, resting on his knees, his head tilted forward slightly, but moving back. His lips were pursed slightly and inhaling.

My attention was diverted too long and I missed the pop of light, but saw it immediately enhance both Waterfall and Sandy's faces. He looked as if all the wrinkles and color of age had left him. Sandy was absolutely radiant. I felt pretty good myself.

Sandy grabbed Waterfall's hand and mine and held them all up to the sky. We were all smiling and feeling fantastic and now I know why.

Everyone is beautiful at sunrise.

~~~

Sandy came back from Paia one afternoon, several days after our sunrise with Waterfall, holding two tickets in her hands. She was beaming.

"Wow, still remembering last night I see." I bragged, slapping her lovingly on her butt.

She tilted her head a little and went smug. "No." Disregarding my pout she burst into a little dance, jumping up and down and twirling like maybe she had been taking secret ballet lessons. Waving her hand with the tickets she sang, "I've got us two tickets, two tickets to ride, two tickets to Camp Keanae."

"Where?" I wondered. "What's going on out that way?" Camp Keanae was a great YMCA venue on the way to Hana. It was perched on an outcropping of land that God must have especially designed for large groups of people to gather and celebrate.

I moved in to grasp her dancing hips and steal a kiss. She stopped twirling and kissed me back even while I could feel her feet still tapping. I couldn't help but notice how gorgeous she looked when she was happy. It was like some kind of self fulfilling prophecy.

"The Gypsy King," she exclaimed. "He's going to be speaking at the festival there." She stepped back and continued her happy dance. My quizzical look remained and she finally stopped, put her hands on her hips and said, as if to a small child, "Happy Rainbow Sunshine...you know, the biggest peace and love gathering of the year!"

"Oh yeah!" I did know of that one, and had only been a couple of times, when I was a teenager. It was indeed a cultural experience, a modern scaled down mix of Woodstock, Yoga and New Age Hippies. Great music was a given, as was an array of food and drink that could fill twenty organic restaurants. Speakers and teachers lined up for years to get a spot at this annual celebration of all things hippie.

Of course, these hippies were not the rowdy, spaced out and dirty creatures so poorly portrayed to America back in the day. These people were older, wiser and richer. New Age Hippies were hippies with money. Of course, there were also the truly young free spirits who had to hitchhike to the event and pitch a tent on the vast upper lawns. The majority, though, were comfortable in the local bed and breakfasts, vacation rentals and private homes hidden quite nicely in the pristine jungles. Few, if any, were dropping acid or hallucinating. Most were enjoying wine, marijuana and perhaps some kombucha tea. The organizers, a group of sixty year old San Francisco refugees, were favorites of the local Hana Police who never got a call to come out. Security was private, visible but entirely unobtrusive. If the police were to visit, they did so off the clock, as a guest in their own long robes and beads.

Happy Rainbow Sunshine was indeed a festival of peace and love, to the extent that there had never been a fight, theft or bad trip in as many years as anyone could remember. Everyone seemed to enjoy everyone else's good behavior. There wasn't even much nakedness, if you didn't count topless women. People wandered the environs singing, chanting and making love in the numerous semi-secluded spots. Babies were born by the dozens nine months later and all had names like "Rainbow," "Sunshine" and of course "Kai" (for ocean). If anything it was a fantastic spectacle of people watching.

I looked at Sandy and nodded. "I'm in baby!" I checked the schedule and thought we might be able to peel away for a couple of days soon. "When is it?"

"We leave tonight!" Sandy slinked up to me, putting her arm around my hip. "Coco has us covered." She leaned in to kiss my neck, her hands stroking my back. "All I can remember of last night," she whispered in my ear, "is a blur of pleasure. Can you remind me?"

Happy Rainbow Sunshine indeed!

~~~

Any drive toward Hana is a fantastic treat for your eyes. The only road in the United States that traverses an official rainforest it forces you to stop often and take pictures. Of course, at night it is quite a different experience, more akin to a step back in time to when jungles were places humans never went without a spear, and never in the dark.

Fortunately, my electric pickup truck was quite prepared to protect us with its windows, bright lights and Linkin Park blasting on the stereo. Besides that, Sandy's enthusiasm no doubt created a protective bubble of good fortune around us that no bad luck could ever penetrate.

"I think it is near mile marker 16," Sandy said trying to peer through the darkness out ahead of the headlights.

I had been thinking it was around the next corner, but of course, there would always be a half dozen more corners. This drive toward Hana had to be one of my favorites, but in the daytime it was fraught with other cars, slow moving ones full of tourists and fast moving ones full of locals trying to get to the other side. In the dark though it was all mine. I could take the curves in the middle, avoid hugging the cliff face on blind curves, go as fast or slow as I wanted and only had to look for some other car's headlights.

Finally, near the top of a climb up from yet another valley to yet another scenic outlook we saw the Camp. It was lit up with several campfires and a few dazzling light shows up in the sky.

"Wow! Look at that!" I had to stop and get out. We pulled over to the little bit of dirt off the road and before the thousand foot drop. Across the last valley and bay we would need to traverse was the

Keanae peninsula surrounded in the shimmering sea of tonight's full moon. The water looked like frosted glass that was imperceptibly moving. I climbed up into the truck bed to get a higher view and Sandy leapt up in one shot to stand next to me.

"Thank you so, so much for coming with me." Sandy said, hugging me tightly. "Its going to be so wonderful, look at all the fun they're having already."

The wind must have been a light easterly, a tradewind, as the faint beats of music were moving toward us.

"Come on, lets go!" Sandy jumped down and opened her door. "The organic smores and fireside chants are scheduled for 10."

I laughed a little at her childlike excitement and at my own cynical thoughts, which I would work hard at dismissing. I wasn't so sure an organic smore would taste right, and as for chanting around the fire I was a bit hesitant. My rush out the door to get here had me leaving my cooler full of Hinano beers behind and that might end up being a problem, if I was to be chanting and such.

Fifteen minutes later we were in line to pull up into the parking area. In a moment I was handing the tickets over to a Maori looking guy that had to be seven feet tall. Security was indeed impressive.

"Mahalo and have a good time," he smiled with perfect white teeth. I guess he had never lost a fight. Projecting that much power kept the peace for sure.

Pulling in among the rental cars and local diesels with their Pacific Biodiesel and 'Thank God for Hana' stickers I went around the truck to escort Sandy.

"Wait," she said, pulling something out of her backpack. "Put this on," handing me some kind of cotton pullover. "And, let your hair down." She looked me over like she was dressing an alien. "Lose the hat."

"Wait now…" I protested, but apparently too slow for Sandy.

She walked over and took my ballcap off, threw it in the back of the truck and proceeded to pull off my Kula Cowboy tshirt. I flexed my stomach just out of habit, but she wasn't looking.

"This is a nice hemp shirt that will feel good and help you fit in a bit." It did feel pretty comfortable.

"Look," she continued. "You have awesome hair. Let it flow." She took out my hair tie and let my shoulder length curls fall. Running her hands through it to get it looking the way she wanted she had moved in close. So I, naturally, pulled her closer, her hips to mine.

"Stop it big boy. We got a meeting to attend." She stepped back a moment and surveyed her work on me. "Great," taking my hand and turning to the big meeting hall, lit up with LED lights and candles. "Let's go!"

Holding Sandy's hand was a lot like holding a grocery store helium balloon in a stiff breeze. She was bouncing all over the place, skipping and pulling and telling me all about the cool people she knew who must be here.

I could hear the distinctive haunting rumble of a didgeridoo being played from inside the meeting hall and as we approached the steps I took a deep breath. This was going to be something so different from anything I had done before. That was cool, but I was still nervous. I saw at least a hundred slippers neatly arranged outside the door and leaving mine there as well, I hoped that was all the clothing we would be asked to remove.

"Greetings," a young woman whispered to us as we passed her at the door. Her crystal beads, genuine smile and sparkling eyes portrayed a natural beauty that instantly put me at ease. Immediately relaxing I followed Sandy into the great expanse of the hall.

The entire floor was covered. People of all makes and models were sitting cross legged atop thin cushions facing the speaker who was now putting away his didgeridoo. Everyone seemed to be wearing an off-white organic hemp shirt (which was confirmed later) and quietly waiting for the next event.

Sandy and I followed the wall closely making our way to the back where I could see a few unoccupied spots of highly polished wood flooring.

"That instrument, as many of you know, is a gift from the first Australians." This speaker's voice had the smooth undertones of a professional who understood the power of sound and speech. I glanced back at him as Sandy led the way and caught his eye watching us.

I nodded and hoped he would let us sit without welcoming us in front of the crowd, but alas that was not to be.

"Please open your hearts my brothers and sisters and welcome our two new comers." Everyone turned to look at us, smiling and trying to figure out who we were. "Blessings to Sandy and her friend."

Sandy turned and waved toward the stage as many soft voices repeated her name. It looked like half the crowd knew her. Several people were putting their hands together in prayer fashion and nodding to her, saying her name again and again.

"Thank you, thank you!" Sandy said just as softly. The eyes that met Sandy's soon fell back onto the guy in tow and I tried to smile and look worthy of being with such a famous girl. I felt like her favorite sweater on a chilly evening.

As we took our places on the floor, with borrowed cushions, I laughed to myself and leaned over to kiss Sandy on the ear. Being her sweater wasn't bad duty at all.

The speaker, a well groomed guy in his fifties, began announcing a few events. "We are near the end of our first full day here at the Happy Rainbow Sunshine festival. It has been a spectacular day in the glory of the Universe who loves us beyond any measure."

Everyone picked up on that and repeated chant like, "Beyond any measure."

"Tonight, I know you are looking forward to our famous organic smores out by the several bonfires we have already burning. Please be careful out there. Even with the full moon, or maybe especially because of it, the shadows can be deeper than you might expect. Hold hands with your friends as you move through this wonderful place. And, wear your shoes. At least until you find your resting place in the lushness." He put his hands together and bowed once to the crowd. "Peace and love, my brothers and sisters."

"Peace and love," came the reply from the crowd. Even from Sandy. I didn't say it, but I agreed with it anyhow.

He stood taller for a moment and simply looked at the crowd. Looking around he nodded to those he knew and smiled at those who wanted to know him. After several moments of this he started talking again. "I do have one special piece of information that I think you will all find extraordinary."

It was funny, I could hear the excitement they all suddenly felt even as no one spoke. They must know he didn't speak lightly about such announcements. I would have to ask Sandy who this guy was, later.

"After our blessed star rises in the east several hours from now, and moments after we all enjoy a healthy breakfast in the kitchens we will be treated to an as yet unannounced speaker."

Sandy nudged me gently with her elbow. I turned to her and she was grins from one ear to the other. Her eyebrow went up a couple of bounces. She had the inside scoops I guess.

"Rumors notwithstanding, in this very hall, at 9am, please arrive early to sit and enjoy the discussions of a very close personal friend of mine. All the way from Oregon, by way of Bali, Jaipur, Monterey and Hana we will be blessed beyond any measure..."

"Beyond any measure," they all repeated, but with a lot more bounce in their voices.

"...by a man who has some of the most exciting thoughts on our interconnected universe. Known to many as the founder of the intelligent energy movement..."

People were starting to whisper now. I thought I heard several people mention the name of our sunrise guest from several days ago.

"...a visionary sent from within the heart of all humans, inspired with the radiant love of the stars themselves. The Gypsy King!"

The quiet crowd erupted in applause. Several girls stood up and began dancing in place, twirling and clapping their hands above their heads. The noise was overwhelming. Suddenly a deep base rhythm started and music permeated the entire hall. Everyone was on their feet now, dancing and talking excitedly. The speaker up on stage now had two ladies holding each of his hands as they too danced and celebrated.

"Can I sit up on your shoulders? Pleeeeze?" Sandy begged.

Who would say no? Not I. Bending down a bit, onto one knee I said, "Climb up girl." Sandy pulled my long curls up off my shoulders so she wouldn't pull my hair sitting on it and as I rose up she squealed in delight.

I felt like we should have Tiwaka here, he would have really enjoyed such a large crowd, and the music. He could sit atop Sandy's head and we could have been a living totem pole.

Sandy's feet were curled back around to my back and I held onto her knees, so I could see. And, what a sight it was. The crowd was really tuning into the tribal beat from the drums now. The didgeridoo was going again as were some flutes that had emerged from the robes of those in the crowd. Somehow, they all found the same rhythm and in a magic kind of fusion moved the crowd forward. Sandy didn't weigh that much, and I was strong, but her keeping the beat was going to wear me out soon.

As expected it didn't take too long before some of the younger hippie girls took off their finely stitched and braided tops, to better dance I suppose. It seemed to work. As always, in Maui anyhow, topless women never really seemed overtly sexual. However, they did seem incredibly liberated and proud. It was cool that they could pull it off, so to speak, in such a fashion that fit perfectly into the moment.

I looked up at Sandy to get her reaction and she had already removed her top and was twirling it above her head to the beat. Oh well, I thought, she *is* the most beautiful creature in this room, for that I remained proud myself.

The cushions on the floor had all but disappeared and everyone was milling about, dancing or clapping or simply singing along. I did manage to catch some words being repeated over and over to the drums. Something like "Long live the sun, we are all one..." There was more but I couldn't quite catch it, and then the music began to fade a bit. I looked up at Sandy and she was looking out to the door. Sure enough some of the musicians were headed outside and the crowd flowed behind them.

"Sandy," I said looking up. "You gotta get down girl."

She looked down and pouted a brief second but then nodded. I bent back down slowly and leaned forward so she could easily touch the polished floor. I stood back up and took a deep breath, suddenly feeling covered in sweat.

"Time for smores!" Sandy said, still excited, and shirtless. She looked at my shirt and went to remove it as well. I let her, the cool night air would feel real good right now. "There!" She came up to me hugged me tight and kissed me. "You're mine, surfer boy."

"Yeah baby!" I said and flexed up a bit to show her the goods. Over her shoulder I noticed several older hippie ladies, dressed up in elegant flowing robes and lei. They were watching us and smiling, and for a brief instant I could feel their memories of when they were like us, many years ago.

Sandy grabbed my hand and pulled me outside to the light of that full moon, to the bonfires, the music and the smores. It wasn't crowded but there were people everywhere, all enjoying the moment.

"Hey, wait a moment, I gotta go say hi to someone." She put her shirt back on and skipped, literally, over to talk to some of the people who had greeted us earlier.

I stood there in the moonlight, smelling the night blooming jasmine and feeling the music move the air, the crowd and admittedly, me. Looking around, alone for the moment, I felt like I was soaking it all up from a distance; as an outside observer, even as an invisible traveler from some far away place. All these people, these souls, housed as they were on this island, in their biological forms, were happy with their scene. It was like they had gained favor with God and won a life on Maui as human beings. Tonight, these winners were celebrating that, enjoying the senses a body had and the camaraderie a soul could appreciate.

There were older people everywhere who no doubt were celebrating like this yet again. Of course there were plenty of young adults enjoying it for probably the first time. I felt my moment too now, my slice in time that I would look back at one day, like these older folks were, like the younger ones might, if they were lucky.

Just then I had that feeling again, that one of a presence. It was that tingling under my skin and in my neck that always told me to pay attention.

It was them again, those cheerful and vibrant entities that had visited me at the sea cliff hammock. I let the feeling move through me as I could physically feel my face pull into a very large smile.

Sandy turned and looked at me quizzically. For a moment I could feel her staring at me. "Hey!" she yelled over at me. "Let's go dance baby!"

I raised both arms up in the air and let out a big ol' surfer howl and ran toward her as fast as I could. Yes, I thought to myself and to each of my little visitors, I would name them "Happy", "Rainbow" and "Sunshine."

~~~

A bright light was trying extremely hard to get my attention through tightly shut eyelids. I had ignored the occasional raindrop falling on me from somewhere I couldn't place. The mild sweetness of flutes in the distance, moving on the light breeze, were no match either for my reluctance to exit this dream. Unintelligible voices several feet away were just fine doing what they were doing and required nothing of me. I tried to cozy up tighter to the warm and smooth skin I was holding onto, but that light, growing brighter and brighter was insistent. It wasn't going to go away.

I sat up, thinking I would holler at some guy with a lantern or wave off a flashlight, or even pull a curtain against a glowing television close by. As I did I felt a blanket fall off my bare chest and down to my apparently bare hips. I blinked once to clear what must be my obviously mistaken vision. I blinked twice, turned quickly around in both directions and then looked down to see Sandy, naked as well, half under the same blanket.

"Good morning dude!"

I turned to look behind me, toward the voice to see another guy waking up in the same vast field I was in, just as naked and not nearly as confused.

"Awesome day eh?" He gave me a thumbs up and stood up to stretch, kicking his blanket off the girl next to him. "Sunrise baby, get on up." I felt I shouldn't stare as she sat up, rubbing her eyes, only skin to greet the morning with.

I turned back to the sunrise, laughing at my thoughts that a flashlight was waking me up. Sandy was still out so I gently covered her with the blanket and looked for my pants. They weren't under the blanket on in the grass next to us. Finally I found them, they had been my pillow.

The gently sloping rise I was on had been home to dozens of others as well, all now stirring in the light of a tropical sunrise. It was like a signal from space for all of us to wake up. I guess it literally was. As I stood, in bare feet, and no shirt to be found, I faced that sun, its warmth already sinking into my skin and stretched. It felt real good.

"Wow dude, you and your woman were awesome dancers last night," my neighbor said. "It was fantastic, like you guys are so tuned into each others moves."

"Thanks," I nodded. "I'm starting to remember that now."

He was giving me a big grin, but was still naked. Reaching down to pick up his pants, he put them on a bit slowly and added, "Makes me proud to be a lover too, dude. Mahalo."

"Is that them, Kai?" His girlfriend was asking quietly. She was smiling at me while pulling her hair out of her mouth. She waved groupie fashion and I meekly waved back.

I nodded again and turned toward the cliffs down below us. There was a crowd of folks down there, dancing to some light music, arms up in the air, greeting the sun. It looked something like a chorus line, moving and grooving to those flutes and the wind, and the big ol' bright morning sun.

Sitting back down I looked around a bit more. There were probably fifty campers now I could see, most of them up and stirring. Some music began closer by and I turned to see a much older couple sitting up and facing the sun with their eyes closed. They had an iPhone playing something really familiar, but old. It seemed a little strange, them sleeping out in the field. I had seen them arrive late in a new Mercedes coupe, the type of folks I would have figured for a roof and comfortable bed. Their song which I now recognized as "Good Morning Starshine" by Oliver had their faces bathed in a retro flashback. It was afterall the perfect song for the moment. Old folks rock! Give them enough time and they get it all figured out.

Sandy was moving a bit, but still dreaming from the looks of it. Her eyes were moving quickly left and right under her lids. Those cargo shorts she wore and her hemp shirt were under her head as well. Two bare feet had worked their way out from under the blanket and from the looks of it, were dancing again, moving slightly to some internal song.

The older couple close by had another classic playing now, and several other younger campers had moved closer to join them. The older lady was welcoming the young women with open arms. Her man was showing the iPhone to the guys, the music not missing a beat. "Crystal Blue Persuasion" sang "the sun is arising" like Tommy James and all those Shantells had been here this morning. They had no doubt finished a few all nighters at sunrise as well.

Sandy looked to be waking a little, but turned back over, hiding her face from the light and trying to sneak in a few more winks. My feet were now tucked into the blanket keeping my toes warm. It was a good time to just sit and hang out.

A slow stream of campers were making their way down hill to the showers and bathrooms. Smoke was coming out of the kitchen chimneys.

"Aloha bruddah," my neighbor said. He and the incredibly tan girl he was with had their belongings in arm. "Breakfast should be quite awesome."

"Have a good one," I answered, watching the girl pick her barefoot way through the dew filled grass. Her long braided hair was lightly bouncing on her still bare back as she held on lightly to the guy.

It was funny how I was suddenly relating to this group of people I never thought I would. I had always been more of a Tiki bar guy and not so much a peace and love hippie. Apparently though, there were some shared qualities of both lifestyles. We were all enjoying the same things today.

One important thing I had learned so long ago was that whatever it was you enjoyed, embrace it for the moment, but not for a lifetime.

Every idyllic lifestyle, every beautiful location, every perfect job all eventually became less so. Sometimes it was our own doing, sometimes other peoples. The point was not to invest your life completely in one lifestyle hoping it would remain perfect forever. They never did and besides you would be missing the point anyhow.

Forecasting the future was impossible, so was trying to control how it turned out. All we had, all I had right now, was this moment. If I thought I could perpetuate this for forty more years then this moment wouldn't be as special. I would be cheating myself of its true value. This moment, here on the hill of hippies, with the love of my life stirring gracefully beside me, watching the sun rise powerfully over the ocean was a slice of time the universe had provided for me to enjoy. Maybe I had provided it to myself. Either way, it was something to enjoy and relish, not store in a safe deposit box of hope.

~~~

Breakfast was a simple collection of local fruits and two or three varieties of organic oatmeal. I knew it must be organic because I saw a couple of guys in the back mixing the oats with dried fruit I had seen coming out of solar cookers. The oats themselves had come out of large fifty pound coffee bean type bags. Guava, orange and pineapple juices were plentiful.

Sandy had woken famished. She kept looking at me with a sly smile but wouldn't explain. I assumed it might have been my raucous dancing or the fact that I agreed to sleep on the hill of hippies, naked.

She did look a bit different somehow. Her skin was sun kissed in the morning light, as if the sun was her own personal makeup artist. We had held hands while she hummed on the way to the kitchens.

Walking inside to the long tables was a little like the night before. People looked up to greet Sandy and now smiled a little broader when they look at me. It was a little creepy, so I had to ask.

"Sandy," I whispered. "What kind of performance *did* I put on last night?"

She looked at me like I might be joking. "What do you mean Mr. Swayze?" She giggled like a teenager.

I looked around at the many strangers eating with us and leaned over to whisper again. "You mean, Patrick Swayze? Dirty Dancing Swayze?"

She stabbed a piece of pineapple with her chopsticks, stuck it in her mouth and nodded yes with both cheeks doing the chipmunk.

"Oh my god," I put my head down on my hands. "How dirty?"

Sandy laughed again. "Oh, let me see. Somewhere between debauchery and a tribal mating ritual." She stabbed an orange slice. "Yeah, its a good thing I played along, or you would have looked real silly."

I looked up again, with the guilt of a guy who just discovered his pants were down in the middle of a high school play. "You're kidding, right?" A few older ladies were pointing at me from across the room. At least they were smiling, but it had that Sex in the City feel to it.

She took a long, agonizingly slow drink of guava juice, sat her cup down and dabbed her mouth with a napkin. Then, she turned to me with a serious look on her face. "You were awesome last night! I mean, later, after the dancing. Like an animal, like a possessed animal. A possessed animal madly in love with me." She put her hand on my leg. "It was the best we have ever had. By far."

Well, there is nothing in the world to calm embarrassment like a little bravado. I sat up a little straighter. Let those old ladies look. "Really? I do remember the hammock."

"And, the treehouse?" Sandy added. "And, the bed of your truck?"

I looked at her, much of it coming back to me now. I couldn't help but grin. Yeah, that's how I roll baby!

"Then, in the field, where we woke up." Sandy still had this fascinated look on her face. "Even when you knew people were watching, you rocked on."

"What? People were watching? Us?" I rocketed right back to the height of embarrassment.

"Its like you were possessed alright. You knew they were there, but kept saying this was 'our slice of time', that this was our 'moment of magic'." She leaned over to my shoulder and kissed me there. "Honey." She pulled my chin so I would look at her. "Honey, there isn't anything wrong with it. Last night was a party, a celebration. These people are cool. There were only a few people and they saw it as loving thing, not something exhibitionist."

My mind would just have to deal with it. It took me a few moments, but internally I spun it like the best politico and figured when in Rome...

"Look around you honey," Sandy continued. She would build me back up. "People saw something special in your dancing by the fire, in your wild abandon and," she leaned in and put her head on my shoulder, "in your obvious love for me."

What the hell, I finally thought, surrendering to the moment. I should be proud, not embarrassed. I should teach classes, hold retreats, write a book!

Sandy stood up to go but leaned over to whisper in my ear. "Happy Rainbow Sunshine baby." Kissing my hair, she grabbed my hand to go.

~~~

Outside the kitchens we turned and made for the big meeting hall. A small sign was hastily hung by the entry announcing "The Gypsy King" written in blue felt tip on yellow construction paper. Several hearts were drawn in the corners in red felt tip.

Sandy practically drug me up the stairs where, again, the bead girl was greeting everyone who entered. She gave Sandy a big hug this time and then turned to look at me.

Holding out her hand she took mine and then wrapped it in both of hers. She pulled me a little too close, but I played along to be polite. "I know you are Sandy's man, but I had to touch you for a moment."

She was quite attractive and only held my hand, so I figured what harm could there be. Sandy was standing right there as well, smiling a little, like she knew what all the other young women must be thinking now.

The bead girl closed her eyes and let her head fall back a few inches, taking in a slow deep breath. I looked over at Sandy and she nodded and whispered, "It's OK."

Finally, the bead girl leaned her head forward and opened her eyes. "Your mojo is strong." She looked at me directly as if she might be looking at a magician for his secrets. "Mahalo."

I could feel her release my hand and not knowing quite what to say mumbled something like "Your Welcome" or "I love you too", I can't quite remember.

Sandy had my other hand now and was leading us both out onto the massive polished wooden floor where pillows had already been placed. An aisle way had been left down the middle, so we sat along the aisle a couple of rows back. Few people were here yet.

"Who *is* that girl?" I asked Sandy, looking back toward the door, and then back at Sandy.

"I heard she is Waterfall's daughter." Sandy grinned. "Seems she knows what I already do, about you."

I shook my head. "Well, not everything." I looked back out toward the door and she was looking back at me. Someone approached the door and took her attention away, but she glanced back briefly before speaking to them.

My vision was suddenly filled by an elaborate splash of colors on cotton. Looking up, I fell into the shadow of two middle aged ladies, one of them speaking to Sandy behind me and the other watching me with a sparkling gaze. I nodded politely and turned to Sandy, hoping an introduction would distract the energy beam coming from her libido.

"Oh, excuse me, let me introduce you ladies to..." Sandy said, but was interrupted.

"The most provocative dancer I have ever met!" Sparkling gaze lady exclaimed immediately sitting down on the pillow in front of me holding out her hand.

I felt compelled to take her hand, trying my best to be polite and not get up and run.

"Sapphire and Serenity," Sandy said.

"I'm Sapphire," sparkling gaze lady breathed. "Your hand is so...strong," she complimented. "And, look! Fingers straight out of the myths and legends."

Sandy and Serenity turned to each other to chat, leaving me to fend for myself with what I was beginning to notice was yet another attractive, well kept woman.

Sapphire still held my hand, stroking my fingers like they were something special. "Myths and legends?" I had to ask.

She stopped and let my hand go gently. It took me a moment to realize she had let it go.

"The myths and legends of Buddha." Sapphire explained. "Hands continuously in prayer. You have those kind of hands." She looked down at my lap, where my hands were hiding. Her gaze lingered a little too long for my comfort, but before I could say anything she looked up.

"I would really love to dance with you sometime." Her voice was soft, almost supple and full of promise. She stood gracefully, her dress flowing like a robe. I could have sworn I heard little bells, but I didn't see any. Perhaps they were underneath, hidden away in magical places. "What was your name again?" She asked, as if it was only a word with which to locate me later.

I stood up quickly and offered my hand once again. "Patrick," I said. "Patrick Swayze."

A larger bell rang just then, one tone, and then another, followed by a gentle male voice asking everyone to take their seats. I looked around and the room had somehow filled up in the few moments Sapphire had had my attention.

Sitting back down, Sandy put her hand on my knee. "I might make some good money pimping you out." Her laugh quickly put the thought out of mind; the thought that she could indeed.

"No worries honey," I assured her. "Disappointment is something all of them will have to learn to live with." Sandy liked that and kissed me deeply in front of everyone and the world. "Yeah baby!" I thought. Nothing makes you feel as special as making your lover proud to have you.

Suddenly a white orchid blossom fell in front of me and then several more all around me, and in my hair. A young girl, maybe a teenager, was walking down the aisle throwing them gently up into the air above the pillows. I looked behind me and there were three other girls all doing the same thing. Beyond them I could see that the crowd had grown even more, with dozens of people standing along the walls in the back.

The entry door had a dozen people blocking it as well. I looked for the bead girl but she wasn't there. Just as I thought that she appeared on the slightly elevated stage. She was holding a small incense container that swung lightly from a braided rainbow colored rope.

Immediately clapping greeted her entrance from all around me. The sun joined in by breaking through the morning clouds and spun through the crystals hung in the eastern windows. The rainbow refractions decorated the entire hall in a hippie version of the disco ball, and I had to admit, it looked fascinating. The light was literally twinkling, unobtrusive but everywhere all at once.

"Light fairies!" someone exclaimed, their voice full of genuine wonder.

Sandy was giggling, holding up an orchid to see if she could touch one. I turned to look around and almost everyone was doing the same thing. Up on stage, bead girl was simply holding her upturned hands forward, full of flowers, and watching the light come to her.

"Good morning!" Bead girl finally said, looking out to the crowd. "Good morning to all of you who have made the journey to be here," she spread her arms out to embrace the hall. "The magic I feel in this room, right now...the beauty our star is sharing through the morning sky, through our crystals...is beyond any measure."

I knew that one, and joined the crowd in repeating "beyond any measure." Sandy squeezed my hand when she heard me say it too.

"Today," bead girl continued. "Is our second day of celebration. Yesterday and last night especially..."

I caught her looking right at me now!

"...was a magical time for all of us." She left me and returned to scanning the crowd. "Today we will start out with inspiration and music that I am sure will lead us into another spectacular evening." She glanced down at me briefly again. I was going to have to stay very close to Sandy.

Music began, from the back of us. Light drums, bongos I guess, and a flute. Some bells filled in as I could feel the vibrations slowly approach. Fighting the urge to again turn and look, I lost, and turned to look. Four musicians were moving up the aisle, moving to their beat just as easily as they played. They kept the volume low.

"In a moment we will have a speaker join us that many of you may have never met before. He is a fortunate traveler among us, one that has seen so many incredible miracles. Miracles, he tells us, that we can all see, if only we make the effort not just to see, but to listen, to touch, to taste, yes even to smell. Our bodies, as they are made, are perfect for experiencing this wonder all around us. We too, as he says, are also fortunate travelers."

The musicians had moved up to the stage now and spread out, two to the left and the other two to the right, sitting down on the leading edge, playing softly as bead girl continued.

"I know him as Waterfall..." clapping interrupted her so she waited until the last few finished. "I also know him as Dad, and feel especially fortunate to have been able to live close to him for all these, what twenty two years now?"

A few people laughed at her joke of such longevity in youth. Sandy leaned on me a bit. I put my arm around her shoulders and leaned back a little on my other arm.

"Many people know him by another name, and I wanted to explain that briefly. It is not so much a name he invoked but one that was bestowed upon him by some of the leading thinkers and philosophers in the intelligent energy movement.

"The Gypsy King is a bit of a play on words. As the leading originator in the theory that all energy harbors intelligence he is jokingly called the King. However, the Gypsy title goes to his expanded ideas that are quite outside the circle of what has been developing among his peers. For that they call him the Gypsy, almost an outcast among the already fringe thinking of I.E." She paused a moment. "Sorry, I hate acronyms, but I sometimes fall into one!" I laughed at that. I had fallen into a few myself. "I.E. or intelligent energy."

Bead girl picked up her rainbow braided rope until the incense container, still burning, rose up slightly off the floor of the stage. "His ideas force us to give up quite a bit. We are self centered as humans. Not selfish per se, but self centered. We are individuals and it is natural for us to relate to the world, to the universe as a 'self', as an entity of one. However, as you will hear, perhaps we are more than that." She stopped and looked down a bit. "I feel it now. I feel that my 'self', my individuality is," she looked up at the crowd again. "intrinsically part of a force that moves throughout the universe." She sat the incense down and went to sit down at the front of the stage, as the musicians were, her legs dangling over.

"It's like life exists by default, everywhere. Energy fields bathe the universe and it is these little eddys of energy that spin up, or whirlpool and become humans, or trees or animals of innumerable count. We then live and think and have consciousness via these same fields of energy. It's like a cell phone, it doesn't work unless it's in a field of cellular energy being broadcast from a tower.

"That said, the idea continues that we are all part of these same fields of energy, we are all connected that way. We are all connected with those that have already passed, with those that are yet to be born."

She was looking at me again and I felt that tingling in the back of my neck again, that presence. She nodded almost imperceptibly and continued.

"Waterfall...wait," she put a hand up. "I will now call him the Gypsy King...he will speak to this a little more logically. He likes to put a more scientific bent on the explanation." She paused and looked around to the musicians, still playing softly. "I think he would try and describe God to the point where we could all build one," she laughed a little at herself. "Except of course, we don't need to, do we?" She stood and raised her hands high in the air. "Please, welcome to Maui, to the Happy Rainbow Festival, to your own hearts, the one and only Gypsy King!"

As uproarious clapping ensured I leaned over to Sandy's ear. "Wow!" I was more impressed than I thought I would be. This would be far more interesting than most sermons I had heard before.

Sandy's eyes were lit up like Christmas morning and she whispered back. "I'm so excited!"

The musicians took their cue from bead girl and started playing a little faster and a little louder. She walked down the aisle dancing a bit and moving to the back of the room. The entire room was so full of excitement and continued clapping that I wondered at the enthusiasm. Could this guy we had met at the campfire at Tiwaka's be that big of a deal? I had never heard of him, but then I didn't get out that much actually. It reminded me of how I discovered the band Linkin Park, they had been big for years before I ever heard their first song.

He was no where in sight yet, but I felt the anticipation as much as any of the other fans in the room. Maybe this would be something new in my world. If anything, Sandy was totally into it and that alone deserved my undivided attention.

Finally, the crowd at the entrance parted slightly. Those in front turned and began clapping again as I saw his long gray curls move into view. Several people whistled and I think there were a few girlie screams but the sounds were playing tricks on my ears. He moved over in front of the stage, nodding to the crowd, raising his hands and grinning like a kid. Several girls ran up and put flower lei around his neck, kissed his cheek and retreated.

I noticed he didn't have any notebooks with him, or apparently any notes at all. He was dressed in long white, loose fitting pants, an oversized woven shirt of various colors and was sporting a bandage over most of his left hand. I studied his face closely for reluctance, or annoyance or impatience, having seen that in so many speakers waiting on a crowd to settle. It spoke, to me anyhow, volumes about their intentions and confidence.

Sandy and I were close enough to hear him laugh lightly and grin like ice cream was on its way. He looked around the stage, found a pillow and promptly pushed himself up to sit there at the edge of the stage. Limber enough still to fold his legs he turned to the musicians and signaled them to play a little louder. The clapping began to die down and we all seemed to focus on the rhythm of the music for several moments. He was moving and grooving to the beat like the rest of us and I found that instead of waiting on him to get started I let that go. I wasn't in any hurry, and neither was he.

Bead girl walked past me up the aisle back toward her dad. She had a tall glass of water in one hand and a bowl of fruit in the other. Sitting the water on one side of him and the bowl on the other she leaned in to kiss him on the forehead. She seemed to signal the musicians who brought down the volume gently and in a few moments stopped altogether. The crowd soon became quite full of silence.

His grin was a bit disarming, but it seemed genuine and sober. He looked around at everyone, and I think he really did make eye contact with all there.

"Yes, I feel that good." He remarked, taking a small sip of his water. "How do you all feel?"

I wasn't going to answer that, didn't feel like I wanted to but Sandy spoke up quickly, as did many others. "Awesome", "Fantastic", "Full of love", "Wonderful" echoed throughout the room.

"We are here to have fun aren't we?" He seemed intent on engaging the crowd. I just hoped he didn't start calling people up on stage.

"Yes," I whispered quietly to myself. I turned to look at Sandy. She was all over this, fascination moving through her features like water.

"Me too." He held up his bandaged hand. "I had a little too much fun last night I guess, burned my hand out by one of those wonderful bonfires." Murmurs of consolation moved through the room and he nodded. "I was so anxious to get that marshmallow off the stick and onto my graham cracker that I forgot it could be that hot."

We all laughed, we had all done that before, maybe not as bad as him, but we knew that mistake intimately.

"Energy is quite powerful, in so many ways." He turned his hand in front of him, inspecting it as it were. "I would like to speak on that, but later."

"Does it hurt sir?" a very young voice asked from behind me. I hadn't seen any kids in here but there must be at least one.

"It does son, a little bit." He held up his hand again to look at it. "But it'll grow back." He took another sip of water, watching us over the rim of his glass. After a long moment he sat it back down and folded his hands in his lap.

I could hear a tabla and flutes outside playing, at some distance, but carrying in on the breeze. The sun had moved high enough up in the sky to quit our windows, allowing the shade to color the room. Smells of plumeria moved in instead, from just outside, plunging me back to my Haiku Elementary days where I remembered them so plentiful. I could hear Sandy's breathing, and my own, light and steady. I took a deep breath and watched the Gypsy King.

"I would like to tell a story first, about dreams." He paused a long moment and then continued. "Not the dreams of sleep, but those we pursue." He let that sink in a moment. "We all strive to make our dreams work out. A few of them do, and a lot of them haven't yet."

I heard bells in the distance now, musical enhancements to the tablas and flutes. Mynah birds were squawking just outside and far in the distance I know I heard waves breaking.

"Some dreams we learn to live without," he nodded his head as if he were thinking of a few of his own. "And, a few tug at our souls from a hook set so deep we are caught forever." He looked up at us. "For those it is best to go along for the ride."

Looking over at the bowl of fruit he picked up an apple, absentmindedly moving it from one hand to the next. Letting his words settle in our minds he continued with the apple for several more moments.

"Personally, I have found the most satisfaction in the simple *process of* dreaming. Imagining new things. The hope, the excitement alone are enough to keep me alive." He sat the apple back into the bowl and turned to drink his water again. I could see his speaking was purposely measured to give us time to understand the weight of his words.

"Besides, I have seen many a dream of others, and a few of my own, cross over that line from floating my happiness to becoming an anchor against it." He looked down at bead girl and smiled one of those fatherly smiles you know tells a story of mistakes and a redemption.

"Invest most of what you have, or what you are, into such a dream and it gets all Goldman Sachs on you: too big to fail."

Those of us who read the news laughed a little at that.

"You can't move on, you can't improve. You're trapped in a dream that was a sugar-coated nightmare all along."

He stopped to drink again. Always just a sip. Always watching us over the rim of his glass. I found that interesting, strange but interesting.

"I would just say that it is best to understand life is full of change. Every time you fight that you will find frustration. Every time you plan for that you will find options and opportunity. Some dreams will fail, that's OK. When one of yours does fail, let it, move on and pursue another."

At that he came up off his pillow and took the small leap to the floor. He took a few steps down the aisle, looking at those he knew and waving a little. "I'm a little energetic right now."

"Me too honey!" It was Sapphire, standing up and twirling herself around like a top.

Several others stood up to stretch and move around, and I guess that was the signal for a break. "You wanna go outside?" I asked Sandy.

She looked indecisive. "Sometimes," she whispered. "He gets into some real interesting discussions on these breaks." She put her hand on my shoulder. "Go without me, I'm going to hang out and see what happens."

Sapphire and the bead girl were crowding around Waterfall as he mingled so I made a clean break for the door. Out in the lush field a game of Frisbee was getting started. They were using the big heavy versions that moved on the air currents like dirigibles. It looked like the idea was to move the several they had going in crossing patterns, watching the gentle updrafts put a little action in the game.

I caught an errant one on its way over the cliff and got invited by default. There's nothing like a little field Frisbee to clear the mind of all that intellectual stuff.

~~~

"Back for more?" Bead Girl asked as I approached the door about an hour later. Her smile was friendly enough. Maybe it was my imagination but she looked hungry.

I looked at her with my best 'I know you like me' smile and said, "Yes ma'am, I am." I peered inside and Waterfall was talking. Sandy was still where I left her. "Did I miss much, uh, what is your name? I'm sorry."

Bead Girl smiled big at that. "Well, you have actually. Waterfall is discussing the idea that the contradictions between science and religion are unnecessary." She looked at me to see if that was going to throw me for a loop. It almost did. "My given name is Hehunakai," she continued. "Translates to ocean mist you know, keeping to the H2O theme in the family and all."

I laughed a little too loud at that, and had to step away from the door when I saw a few heads turn my way. "Nice to meet you Hehunakai," I said, shaking her hand.

Still holding my hand, she asked, "And what, pray tell, shall I call you?"

Her eyes were peering at me along some invisible pathway that conducted sexual energy like water. "Overwhelmed," I replied, retrieving my hand gently.

"Ha!" she laughed quiet enough to keep our conversation private. "Overwhelming might be a better name."

I had to steer this somewhere else, then I remembered an angle. She had looked right at me earlier when she had spoken during Waterfall's introduction. "Tell me, Hehunakai, what of this being connected to those not yet born, like you were talking about. You looked at me when you said that...and I thought that a little, well. I thought that a little unusual."

She was watching me like she knew what I was going to say and enjoyed seeing she was correct as I continued to talk.

"I've had these, I don't know, feelings? Like I was sensing..." I honestly had to catch myself. I hadn't even told Sandy about this and here I was opening up to this woman I barely knew.

"Children?" she finished for me. Her eyebrow raised to complement her confident smile.

My guard was completely down now, she did look at me on purpose when she said that. "Wow, how?"

"Look, its OK Overwhelmed. I believe a lot of people have those feelings, especially when they are thinking of starting a family." She leaned back against the railing, glancing inside the door. "You might go in now, looks like they are taking another break."

"Thanks!" I said, touching her shoulder. "Thanks Hehuna..."

She interrupted me there and said, "Just call me Bead Girl."

~~~

It is entirely possible that I had said 'Bead Girl' a little too loudly earlier, but I didn't think so. It is also entirely within the realm of possibilities that I was getting high on all the pakalolo smoke wafting throughout the festival, however slim that chance was, and imagining all of this. Or, I guess it was not impossible that I had been hit on twice by a gorgeous, bead bedecked mind reader. Whatever the case, my name was going to remain Overwhelmed at least for the rest of the day.

Waterfall was signing some books as the break continued and I was able to sneak back to my cushion next to Sandy. She was talking to Serenity, I think it was, sitting on the other side. I tried to remain focused straight ahead and not engage anyone in conversation. Things were moving beyond my simple *Tiki Bar mixologist who surfed a little and lived in a treehouse* world.

I didn't realize my hands were shaking until Sandy grasped mine and asked how I was doing. "OK I guess."

She knew better. "Your hands are quivering. What happened?"

I didn't really want to answer. Glancing over at Hehunakai, aka Bead Girl, now purposely ignoring me I guess, I nodded toward the door. "Ask her. She reads minds."

Sandy patted my hand reassuringly. "Who, Waterfall's daughter? Yeah, she's kinda of famous for that, you know."

"What?" I exclaimed quietly. "How do you know that?"

Sandy looked me in the eyes and sparkled her answer with kindness, knowing I was in over my head, "I keep up on things you know." She pressed my hand tighter. "She is considered a facilitator more than a parlor trick magician. Her kind help people better understand what they are already thinking, things they are having trouble understanding."

I looked at Sandy for clarification, "Her kind?"

The bell toned again, like before, to get everyone back to their seats. A second tone followed right after that. I glanced over at Bead Girl and she was moving toward the stage again, as Waterfall took a seat.

"I'll tell you later," Sandy whispered. She squeezed my hand once more and then let go.

The musicians began a light rhythm as Bead Girl (I should really call her Hehunakai now that I knew her name) began a slight dance to the tune, her eyes closed and her hands moving to a silent hula.

I watched her intently now, liberated from my feelings of being her sexual conquest and now looking for her alien antenna. 'Her kind' was reverberating in my mind. What 'kind' would that be? Waterfall seemed pretty normal, if not a little eccentric in his views. The key must be her mother. I wonder what she was like? Maybe she was the alien and Hehunakai was the love child of an alien and Waterfall? My mind was racing with silly what-ifs.

As she moved gracefully through the song she suddenly began to sing, softly at first, almost chant like. I couldn't quite pick out any words, but the syllables were harmonizing with the music perfectly. After a moment, almost as a refrain, voices echoed her from the back of the room. I turned to see both Serenity and Sapphire in the aisle moving toward the stage, their hands moving the same way as Hehunakai's. It was beautiful and classically hippie. It was entirely mesmerizing.

As Sapphire passed me, moving slowly and spinning occasionally, she glanced down at me with that look of 'see what you're missing big boy'. I wondered if she were a mind reader as well.

Eventually, they joined Hehunakai at the front of the stage. Their voices were in a pitch tuned so fine they must have been practicing for weeks, back on their home planet no doubt.

I kept entertaining myself like this, I knew, as a protection mechanism. There were so many things here that I didn't understand, that I was afraid of to some degree. My feelings of a happy childlike presence on the hammock and again last night before the bonfire. My uncharacteristic primal dancing and lovemaking, in front of strangers no less. My first encounter with a mind reader. Not to mention being saved by a turtle on that huge day surfing last year, and Coco's connection to that. Mystical (if that was the right word) things were happening all around me. Now, at this festival I found myself in an environment that didn't discount such things but rather embraced them. And I thought Los Angeles *was* strange. It was going to take some getting used to.

Serenity, Sapphire and Hehunakai lowered their voices just as the music quieted and bowed as one as they finished. Everyone was impressed, not just me.

Waterfall stood and opened his outstretched hands to the girls. "Are they not amazing creatures?" Everyone clapped more, especially me. "Serenity and Sapphire were so gracious to join us on tour and now they are back home on Maui, loving it with all their hearts." More clapping, as they both moved back down the aisle to their seats behind me. Sapphire winked as she passed, of course.

"My beautiful daughter Hehunakai." Waterfall had his arm around her. "She reminds me so much of her mother, whom we both miss so very much."

Hehunakai looked up at her dad, some tears in her eyes.

"We both share in her appreciation of what it is to be graced with an existence here on this planet. She always spoke of that gift, and that we should never take it for granted." He leaned over to kiss Hehunakai on her head. "We look forward to seeing her again."

Hehunakai moved back to her seat up near the front. Waterfall took a moment to regain his composure, evidently falling victim to the same moment of sadness his daughter had.

"As I was saying earlier..." He took another deep breath, still fighting it. "Earlier," he now continued. "Earlier I spoke a bit about how science and religion are really two different schools of thought trying to describe the same wonder of God.

"Religion typically relies on the believer's faith and considers analogies a viable story telling tool. Hell and heaven, good and evil are purposely reduced to purely human terms so that, I imagine, we can relate better.

"Science disregards that attempt, typically, and often misses the big picture with its focus on the minutia of details and the burden of proof..

"However, there is a movement now toward a consolidation. In my opinion science does a better and better job of describing those wonders of the universe that religion has attempted to describe all along.

"Disregarding the extreme views of both disciplines, of course, we find that, for example, evolution is no simple matter. Intelligent design is an answer to this, that there is obviously some intelligence in the amazing design of life. That would be evidence of God would it not?"

Waterfall laughed a little to himself as he considered his next thoughts. "Many scientists, having no proof of an intelligence behind natural selection, scoff at this idea. That is because they haven't looked closely enough. They admit they don't understand why many of the processes work the way they do, how our genome manages to produce humans and not something entirely different. Science has a long way to go to be able to prove what the religious faithful already know.

"I offer no proof today, but I do offer this consideration before we move on. Science must admit to the fact that human intelligence is not unique in the universe. And religion must admit that there is no less beauty in God's work if you understand its mechanisms."

Waterfall moved down the aisle, his hands behind his back, in contemplation I guess, walking silently. At the back of the room he turned and headed back toward the stage. I watched him measure his pace gently and precisely until he reached mid room.

"We can discuss any and all of these ideas outside of this room later. It is best, I think, to germinate these seeds, these ideas, and then to leave with them in our minds, to percolate and grow."

He moved back up to the stage and leaned against it. "I'll be available to talk about anything, at the bonfires, the waterfalls, of course, and anywhere you happen to find me."

I looked at Sandy for a moment and she turned to smile at me. This was pretty heavy mental gymnastics and she was into it. Maybe she could explain more of it to me later.

"Lastly, let me talk just for a moment on energy, on I. E. or intelligent energy. I promise I won't get too deep into this. Let's touch on the highlights and if you're interested in more, we can sit and chat during the festival.

"I'll also be holding a retreat at the Wainapanapa cabins next week as well."

Waterfall sat back up on his cushion on the stage, folded his legs under him and looked to be taking a yoga pose for a moment. I looked at Sandy and she was grinning and rocking back and forth a little.

"This is gonna be good!" she whispered.

Waterfall looked around the crowd and then to the windows facing out toward the ocean. I followed his gaze. White puffies were floating in on the tradewinds against a blue that was only a few shades lighter than the sea below. I turned and looked out toward the mountain framed windows on the other side and could see the deep green of the peaks and valleys there. One thing I could understand about all this was that inspiration was easily available here. Open your eyes, take a moment to soak it all up and your mind would show you things you would never have found otherwise.

"We are indeed in a most beautiful place," Waterfall began. "You are all so fortunate." He looked at the crowd closely for a moment and then closed his eyes.

"Nature..." he spoke with his eyes still closed. "Nature insures the success of its various projects with overwhelming numbers. The coral reefs reproduce by spawning countless seed into the vast oceans. Pollen, fruit and the insect world all produce copious amounts of material in order to insure success."

He finally opened his eyes, but remained looking down, speaking clearly and loud enough for those in the back to easily hear.

"Space is easily the most prolific of them all. Innumerable stars challenge the concept of infinity, pushing the known numbers quite beyond our comprehension.

"Nature, and I speak of Nature as the all inclusive natural universe, is very adept at promoting itself."

He looked up now and smiled briefly then kept going with his thoughts.

"Energy is one of the most common things in the universe. In fact, I would challenge anyone to describe a place devoid of it. I propose that it is Nature that provides this boundless supply of energy, similar to how it does pollen, insects and life itself here on Earth."

He stood up now and walked down the aisle a few steps, looking at us all for signs he might be losing us. I think he found it in my face.

"Now, that's not too deep eh? Nature is bountiful and energy is everywhere. Simple for the most part, yes?"

I saw a few heads nodding tentatively in front of me and I had to admit when he reduced it down it was easier to hold onto.

"OK, good." He turned and walked back to the stage, leaning against it. "This next point is even easier to grasp, since we are all beneficiaries of it." He folded his arms loosely and glanced down at his daughter and winked.

"Consciousness is something we all enjoy. It's what makes intelligence possible. It is something special that comes in almost as many varieties as life itself, perhaps even more. Humans have it, of course. Dolphins, whales, your pet dog or cat." He looked over at me. "Your parrots even!" He smiled as Sandy poked me in the ribs.

"Consciousness includes the definition of awareness at its most basic level. Plants have it don't they? They know where the light is and grow toward it. They know enough to launch their seeds into the air or stick them onto a passing animal so that they can succeed on wider ranges. That is an awareness of their surroundings and thus a form of consciousness.

"How do we come to have consciousness? It is certainly not unique to humans, and I repeat that because it is important to understand this discussion is non-human centric. We are the beneficiaries of consciousness, not the originators or the owners or the creators of it.

"I don't want to go off point too far, so I'll ask again, how do we come to have consciousness? I propose that it is yet another product of a prodigious Nature. A distributed product. Distributed through out the universe by energy. Thus the statement that 'within energy there is intelligence'.

"Not that energy itself is intelligence but simply that energy is the carrier. We have evolved, our brains have, to take advantage of this, more so than any other creatures on this planet."

He stopped again to let all that soak in. It was pretty far out for sure, but I guess you could twist your mind around it to a degree where it *could* make sense.

"My point then evolves to this: If our consciousness is derived from a common source, then we all are connected that way. We are also connected then by that same source to all other things with consciousness, big and small.

"Look at it scientifically. Everything in nature is influenced, or connected, to other things in nature. Nothing stands alone. It's easy to see all life here is dependent on the sun, or the earth. The earth of course has a very cozy relationship with the moon, and the sun. Our sun is in orbit around the center of our galaxy, and our galaxy is moving as well, to some rhythm of a far away drummer. Molecularly or gravitationally, all things are indeed connected."

I looked at Sandy to see if she was getting all of this. It was hard to tell.

"Therefore, as everything in nature is dependent, or connected to other things in nature, then so are we. And, so is our intelligence. We are connected intellectually to each other and to the entire universe."

Waterfall laughed a little at this, perhaps at himself. "Of course, that's why walls were invented. Walls break this connection to some degree and encircle us in individuality."

He walked over to Hehunakai and held out his arm for her. She stood up next to him, seemingly comfortable with everything he had been saying.

"Walls are OK, just make sure you have a door or window you can open."

He bowed low with his hands together. I wasn't sure he was done until I heard the clapping. My head was spinning and I was going to have to buy the book in order to re-read this several times. It was indeed interesting, but I wasn't sure how I could make use of it. The general idea didn't seem to conflict with what we already knew at the Tiki Bar: Life is good.

~~~

Halle Haleakala

I was missing Tiwaka. I really felt like I needed to tone down my cosmic conceptualization and just talk to a parrot. Simple stuff, like should I use lime or lemon, serve brazil or cashew. However, that was going to be a few hours away. As Sandy and I were pulling out of Camp Kaenae there were two young hippies thumbing their way back north.

"Hey, they look OK, let's pick 'em up," Sandy said. She turned to check out the back seat, and moved one of the sleeping bags back into the flat bed, through the open window.

I agreed, they met my secret requirements for getting a ride: the guy had a shirt on, they didn't have a mangy dog with them and there was no visible mud on their faces. Amazingly enough I passed up hitchhikers on a daily basis that failed this.

"Howzit," Sandy greeted them as they ran up to the window all smiles. "Where you going?"

"Oh thank you so much!" The girl looked young, maybe twenty tops. The guy looked younger. "We're trying to get to Little Beach before dark."

"Hop in, we can take you to Twin Falls," Sandy offered.

Both of them jumped in the back seat, small backpacks on their laps and sunburned faces full of hope.

"Little Beach," I announced like some kind of tour guide. "Is about four hours away." It was already noon, and their goal of getting there by dark, hitchhiking, might be tight. I looked back in the mirror at them. "You might see some naked people there," I laughed. Everyone, well almost everyone, knew that Little Beach, on the opposite side of island, was a famous nudist hangout. Literally.

"Yeah, that's OK with us," the girl said. "We're sunscreen salesmen!" She laughed out loud. Really loud and shrill.

I looked over at Sandy and we both cracked up at each other's expression. These guys would be a fun distraction for the next hour.

Sandy turned around in her chair to talk with our guests. I couldn't help but notice those intoxicating legs again. It was immediately easy to forget about those lonely ladies at the festival, especially if I got analytic about it. I had seen a lot of athletic and healthy female bodies dancing in the firelight, the moonlight and the flashlight and none could hold a candlelight to Sandy. OK, one could read minds, but beyond that, she had them all beat.

"So," Sandy asked. "I think I saw you two climbing the banyan trees."

"Yeah mon, that would be us!" The guy had a Jamaican accent that followed perfectly with his long dreadlocks and the rasta colors in his red, green and black shirt.

"Those trees were so perfect, weren't they Jaz?"

"Fantastic my babe."

Sandy was nodding, but rested her head on her arms as she talked. "I loved those trees."

"I love the shade," the red headed girl said with an honest appreciation. "The sunshine always looks great from under a good tree."

Some hitchhikers were talkers and others kept it to a minimum. My senses were telling me we wouldn't need the radio today.

"Hey, I recognize you now!" The girl exclaimed, talking to Sandy. "You were dancing with that totally rockin' sex machine hunk of a God's gift to women!" She turned to Jaz. "You remember those guys?"

"Ya baby, you said I should take lessons," Jaz wasn't too enthused with her enthusiasm.

Sandy was laughing. "You mean *this* totally rockin' sex machine hunk of a God's gift to women?" She was tapping me on the shoulder.

I was whistling lightly, trying hard to sound like anything but a whatever it was she called me. I turned quickly to look in the back. Jaz was watching me like she must have been talking about someone else. The girl was awestruck, probably from having said what she did in front of the sex machine hunk.

"No way!" she whispered at maximum volume. "Cool beans baby!" I looked over at Sandy just as she was giving the red head a high five.

Sandy gave me a little punch in the arm. "Yeah, he's all mine, found him on Craigslist under Lost and Found."

"No way!" the red head cried. "I found Jaz in the ice cream aisle at Mana Foods!" I could hear her plant a big kiss on him. "What a coincidence!" She was giggling like a kid.

Sandy was punching me in the arm again. "So, nice to meet you Jaz," Sandy was saying. "I'm Sandy, and this is…"

"Overwhelmed," I interjected. I was still liking that name.

"Awesome name, Sandy," the red head said. "But, Overwhelmed sounds like something you made up." She reached up and tapped my shoulder.

Now, I have met a lot of people who went by names their parents would never have given them in a million years, but I never heard anyone say they were 'made up'. I was going to ask her hers but she beat me to it.

"My mom gave me that year's most popular name but I recently made up my own name. I love made up names."

Jaz was being quiet but finally jumped in. "Go on my honey, tell them this week's new name." The inflection in his voice told me he found it entertaining and cute.

"Oh yeah!" she was obviously stoked to be talking about her new 'made up'. "Halle. Halle Haleakala. But not Holly like Christmas holly. Halle, like Halle Berry Halle."

I looked over at Sandy, again and caught her eye. My eyebrow went up as my smile curled up big on both sides of my grin. This was good stuff!

"It all started," Halle began. "With a trip up the mountaintop for sunrise. Jaz and I were drinking our organic bean and groovin' on the colors and the cold. It was the most amazing place I have ever been. Except maybe in Jaz's arms that is."

"Ya mon, beautiful it was. Just like you Halle."

"Isn't he just wonderful?" She asked us.

Sandy agreed and waited for Halle to keep going. It took only a few microseconds.

"So, there we were sipping the Joe and tuning in to the cosmic and all, and I suddenly found myself, like, I dunno, but like awestruck!"

"Ya mon," Jaz agreed. He kept it short though, knowing Halle would fill in all the details.

"I got this vibe, like from God or something, that I was on this mountaintop for a reason. We were on the top too weren't we Jaz? Right up on the roof of the building that sits on the tippy top. Rangers chased us off once, but when they drove back down to the visitor center we climbed right back up.

"You know, I'm not the tallest person around, so I wanted to make sure I was higher than the tourist masses."

"We were baby, we were eh?" Jaz was laughing a little.

"Ya mon!" Halle mimicked with perfect pitch.

I knew that double entrendre. Altitude wasn't the only measure of high they were talking about.

"We finally caught a ride back down to Makawao and had some lunch, and then we met those crazy Canadians. Jaz was all stoked, since they all had dreads."

"Ya mon, they were Irie fo' sure Halle."

"Unreal they were, and they were going back up to the summit for sunset, so we caught a ride right back up. What is it with Canadians? They party like it's 1999 all the time."

"Irie baby. Irie." Jaz added, laughing at the memories himself.

"We got back up to the top about an hour before sunset. It was so cold I thought I would freeze, but they had plenty of blankets. We were just walking around, blankets around our shoulders and getting in the pictures of the tourists."

"Ya, we were part of the attraction baby." Jaz added.

"After the sun went down, the Canadians said we should go look for the aliens in the crater," Halle said matter of factly.

Sandy perked up at that. "Aliens? Like space aliens?"

"Yeah, like from deep space or something. They said aliens had been living secretly in the crater of Haleakala for decades, since the '60s. One of them said that because it was a full moon that we might more easily see them moving around."

I didn't want to discount any ideas people might have about such things, but I did wonder why aliens would pick one of the most popular tourist spots as a hiding place. I had to ask.

"Halle," I asked, looking in the rear view mirror. "I've heard that alien in the crater thing before, but I never saw any on the like thirty camping trips I've had up there."

She was quiet for a moment, but it was only a short moment. "No way! That might explain how you got to be such a good dancer then. I understand that aliens are really into dance."

"But, if I didn't..." I protested, but she wanted to keep talking.

"I know you didn't see them. Of course not. They are not something you could see, or touch, or chase off. Can you imagine what would happen to aliens from somewhere outside of Earth? Geez, look what happens to Asian or Haitian boat people trying to escape bad places, or East Germans fleeing over the old wall. Study human history a little, and I mean only a little, and you too would keep yourself invisible as well."

Jaz was being quiet and Sandy was just listening, wondering I think, how we got on the subject. I loved debating this kind of stuff and as long as she didn't cop an aggro attitude I was willing to keep asking questions.

"Halle," I asked, sincerely. "I would have thought that aliens, being able to make the trip all the way here, would have superior technology. That they wouldn't be afraid of us."

I think I heard Jaz murmur something, then Halle answered.

"That's assuming they were humanoid creatures that needed space ships to propel their butts around the cosmos. From what I heard they found themselves here, on Maui by accident. They are not biological, but some kind of, I dunno, spirit or energy. Travel for them is simply shifting some kind of quantum entanglement from one phase to another."

Now it was my turn to interrupt. "What? Halle, you gotta tell me something. Who is telling you aliens found themselves here by accident?"

They were both quiet in the back seat now. Jaz whispered something to Halle.

"It was the Canadians that gave us the ride that afternoon. They said they heard it from the nene geese." She kept it short, and waited for me to respond. I didn't. The story was getting a bit crazy so I figured I would drop it.

Sandy spoke up, feeling Halle's anxiousness. "Halle, what the heck is quantum entanglement?"

Jaz again whispered something to Halle, and I got the funny feeling that he was telling her to tone it down a bit, like we might let them out of the car if she continued too much crazy talk.

"Well," Halle answered. "Quantum entanglement was the thesis for my Ph.D."

I looked up in the rear view mirror and almost ran off the road.

Halle giggled a little at that as I pulled back onto the thin strip of road. "It is the property that has been observed between two quantum particles that can be separated by any distance, but that reflect each others state, instantaneously. In 2008, at an experiment I attended in Geneva, a minimum speed was measured at 10,000 times the speed of light."

I glanced over at Sandy who caught my eye. Did she believe this story or not?

"That's funny," Sandy said. "And, I thought you were just two sunscreen salesmen."

"Ya mon, that's our cover," Jaz said. "Keeps us out of the crazy house ya know."

We all laughed at that, taking some of the edge off the conversation. I had to jump right back in though.

"OK, so these aliens. Are they shipwrecked here or something?" I asked.

"Exactly. Whatever their technology was it broke. I know one thing, quantum teleportation or entanglement is one finicky process.

These guys were probably experimenting and missed one of those infinite variables that keeps our own guys guessing. Poor bastards."

OK, I thought to myself. Shipwrecked aliens hiding from the nasty ol' humans made a little more sense than most of the theories I had heard. But, why hadn't I ever felt their presence during my numerous trips to the top of the mountain and all those campouts inside the crater? I was open minded afterall, in fact I had just met a mind reader! Why wouldn't I be approachable...wait. What if these aliens were mind readers? STOP! I told myself, this train of thought was getting spooky.

"So, Halle, where did you get your Ph.D?" I asked, trying to clear my mind of that last thought.

"Jaz and I were both at Oxford. Two months ago for me, and just last week for Jaz here."

"Wow! Congratulations to both of you!" Sandy exclaimed. She turned further in her seat to talk to Jaz, directly behind her. "Jaz, what was your thesis?"

"Biogenetic Pharmacology. I've just landed a job in Ft. Lauderdale, so we thought a trip to Maui would be a good idea. Before the games begin." He had lost his Jamaican accent suddenly.

I slowed down a bit to make an especially tight turn leading onto a one lane bridge. Another car was already approaching so I stopped. It was a good chance to quickly turn around and ask a question face to face. I looked at them and saw incredible youthfulness.

"You guys sure seem to have done a lot being so young and all. How..."

Halle knew it was coming I guess. "19. Jaz is 20."

"Really?" I admitted to being amazed, yet again on this trip.

"That's why we're hitching. No one will rent us a car unless we're 25, credit card or not."

The oncoming car was clear and I pulled out on onto the bridge. It was another of those ancient concrete structures that made me wonder how much longer it could possibly support several thousand cars per day. Not to mention the 3,000 gallon fuel trucks that made the run every other day.

A light rain was picking up as I climbed out of the valley, creeping up the middle of a thousand foot cliff face carved out of the reluctant jungle rock. Glancing down at the battery meter and seeing 22% I figured we had just enough to get home. I had forgotten to plug in back at the festival.

"Would you mind if we stop up at that look out? For a picture?" Halle asked, sounding more like a teenager this time than a scientist.

"Sure, but it's raining a bit." I pulled over onto the graveled area overlooking the jungles leading to the sea below. There was only room for one car here.

"Perfect," Halle breathed as her and Jaz quickly scrambled out the doors.

It was raining good now, enough for constant wipers, but they looked undeterred, almost relishing it. Halle ran up to Sandy's half open window and handed her a small digital camera.

"Will you please take our picture. While it's still raining?"

Sandy laughed, turned to me to blow a kiss and stepped out into the rain. Halle and Jaz were holding each other tight and getting soaked. I could see big rain drops pelting Sandy's back, her light blue t-shirt catching them like a thirsty animal.

Sandy was trying to keep the camera dry with one hand and hold it with the other. But when Halle and Jaz suddenly turned and dropped their pants to moon the camera, she almost dropped it.

"Quick! Take this too!" Halle was yelling. "This rain is cold!"

Opening the door quickly, dripping wet, Sandy was laughing hard. "I can't believe those guys. Wild ones!"

Rushing in the back door like a couple of school kids, which I guess they no longer were, the two hitchhikers were having a big time.

"That will make the best Christmas card Jaz!" Halle's red hair had turned two shades darker when it got wet. And she looked a couple of years younger still now.

I pulled back onto the road, ahead of a tour van and fought the rain for directions. My wipers were going full blast and I glanced down at my battery meter again. 19%. Damn electric cars. Well, it wasn't the car, it was the batteries. When would someone come up with a battery that could keep me from worrying? Or a method to keep me from forgetting to plug it in?

Distraction would keep me from worrying so I remembered we had got on the alien thread when asking Halle about her 'made up' name.

"So, Halle tell us the rest about why you are Halle Haleakala."

"Oh sure! Well, after all that alien talk with the Canadians I had to try it. You know, try and talk to these birds that they call nene geese."

Jaz was laughing now, unafraid of hurting anyone's feelings. "Ya girl, that was hilarious!" I thought I could pick up his Jamaican accent returning.

"Yes, I must admit. I did look silly down on the ground trying to coax that bird closer with grass seed. And, honestly I never did hear anything from those geese. The Canadians said that the birds were on to the aliens, that they could sense them there. I dunno."

Jaz spoke a little more seriously, again without the accent. "Both of us are excited by our work in science. But, I think I can speak for both of us when I say we understand that our science, modern as it may appear, is still quite undeveloped. You've heard it said before, today's magic is tomorrow's science. Well, today's science is then tomorrow's primitive precursors."

"Yep," Halle chimed in. "Our science is so primitive that we might be missing more than we can even imagine."

We were almost at Twin Falls, our turn off back to Tiwaka's Tiki Bar & Grill, I couldn't wait! The rain was letting up a bit. Sandy turned to them, all motherly and all, and asked if they would be OK.

"Sure! We're good. If it rains again, we'll go hide under the bridge." Jaz seemed confident with that.

Halle hadn't quite finished her story. "About my name, I never finished. Later that night, as I sat up at the summit, you know, I felt something there. I don't know what it was. Aliens, Nene, God or my imagination. But, I fell in love with it, and so I took that name. For now."

I pulled over just at the bridge and they opened their doors. I looked across the road at the farm stand and the converted school bus they used to sell from. It had a roof extending out from the front.

"You could hide under their roof," I said pointing out the bamboo and palm thatching. As I pointed, the clouds above the summit of Haleakala in the distance parted enough for us to see the observatories against blue sky beyond.

Halle turned and looked back at me, pointing to the sight and grinned. As she ran across the road with Jaz to the farm stand, her hand was up, index finger pointed up. Number one I guessed.

I pulled back out slowly onto Hana highway and glanced over one last time. Halle was standing up straight, saluting us, Haleakala shining in the clouds beyond. Jaz was looking over at her, smiling.

~ ~ ~

Got Poi?

As I pulled onto the unimproved road leading down to our long dirt driveway I saw a new poster on the last utility pole. Right under the "Eat More Rooster" bumper sticker was a picture of a young mixed breed dog sitting in the lap of an elderly lady. It was titled in big bold letters "GOT POI?" Under the picture was a phone number and then a handwritten appeal. "I've already lost my husband and most of my mind. Please help me find my poi dog."

Poi was a term we all used for mixed breeds, especially in dogs. Generally, they were more healthy with their mixed genes to protect them against all the pure breed problems. No hip dysplasia in this group. Another big advantage was that you could always go to the animal shelter and find a new poi puppy for free.

"Hey I know her," Sandy said as we drove slowly past. "Back up, I gotta call her."

"Really? Who is it?"

Dialing and looking back as I reversed, she said "It's Auntie Kealoha, oh my god!" Sandy was rereading the poster. "Arthur died?" She had the phone up to her ear. Looking at me with a small tear in her eye she whispered "lost most of her mind?" She wiped the tear as she looked down waiting for the call to answer.

"Auntie, its Sandy. I just saw your poster on Ulalena road," she was leaving a message. "I am so sorry about Arthur, I hadn't heard.

Listen, we're gonna look for Poi and let everyone know he is missing. Call you tomorrow OK? Love you."

I drove on for a minute before asking. "How old is she, Auntie Kealoha?"

Sandy was bummed, but sparked up a little. "She's near 90. Her and Arthur used to run a swim camp when we were little. They were old even then. So nice, they would hang all of our towels up in the milo trees when we left them on the ground and ran out to the field to play."

Her appeal, admitting she had lost most of her mind was something I never expected to see on a lost dog poster, but, there it was. Bold, a cry for help, or a joke. I wasn't sure. I was only sure about one thing. I had 12% left on the fuel and I was already coasting down the driveway.

~~~

The next morning I had made two hundred copies at the downtown Kinkos of the Got Poi? poster and spent about half of them on the way home, hitting every utility pole in Paia, Makawao and along the Hana highway. That afternoon, I started a Facebook page for Poi and sent an invite to everyone we knew there. I had some friends at the Maui News who found it cute. Got Poi? (a play on the Got Milk theme) was catchy and they ran a short front page article on it. Sussman over at the local radio station (one of the few that hadn't automated to a mainland satellite feed) put on a public service announcement. I even offered a reward at the bar: two free Coco Loco Mocos and a picture with Tiwaka to anyone offering a credible lead.

After a week though nothing happened. No calls, no sightings and I figured it wasn't going to happen. Sandy had been visiting Auntie Kealoha daily and came back every time sad. It was the only companion that old lady had at this point. We both felt a little helpless.

One early afternoon while getting the bar ready and entertaining Tiwaka with all my hard work Vic rolled in. After parking it on one of the stools and chit chatting a moment he asked about the Got Poi? poster just below Tiwaka's perch.

"Sad story that one," I said. "Poor old lady just lost her husband of something like sixty years and now the dog."

"Geez, that sucks alright." Vic was looking at the poster closely. "What color would you say Poi was?"

"Was?" I asked.

"Well, yeah." Vic shrugged. "What color?"

I turned to look at the poster, prompting Tiwaka to flutter his wings like I was paying attention to him or something. "Brown, I guess. Why?"

"Short hair brown poi dog, about two years old I would guess. And, the old lady is like 90 you say?"

"Yeah, losing a little you know," I pointed at my head. "She needs her pet."

"I would guess her eyesight ain't too good either, right?" Vic asked, leading somewhere, but I wasn't sure.

"Look, yeah, OK? She's a sad old lady losing her mind and her eyesight. What's your point Vic?"

"Don't get your panties in a bunch. I've got an idea."

I pulled out the waist of my shorts out to see if I had mistakenly pulled on a pair of Sandy's panties and somehow got them in a bunch as well. Whew. No, I had not.

Just then the Kihei Ice truck pulled up. Usually he got to work hustling out the ice so he could make his next stop. Nothing keeps you busy like selling ice in the tropics. This time though, he walked right up to the bar, something in his hand.

"Hey guys," he said.

"What's up?" I looked at him, something was indeed on his mind.

"I've seen your Got Poi? posters all over the northshore. Got some bad news." He put a dog collar on the bar. The tag said "POI".

We didn't say much for a moment.

"I, well," he looked around for anyone else. "There wasn't much left of him. I had pulled over to check my tires and saw something in the ditch. It was the right color, so I checked the collar." He stepped back and said "Sorry guys."

Vic picked up the collar and looked at me. "Perfect!"

~~~

The next morning I found myself walking next to Vic down a concrete path surrounded by cages. The noise was deafening as they all tried to get our attention. Big and small, young and old, three legged and uninjured, they were all well represented at the Maui Humane Society.

"This one, what do you think?" Vic had spotted one that sort of matched the poster we carried.

"Well, maybe, but his tail looks different doesn't it?" I noted.

Vic studied the poster again. "Yeah maybe a little, we could ask them to cut it shorter?"

No. "Let's keep looking." There must have been over a hundred dogs in here, the vast majority of them mixed breeds. This was Poi Central. Vic was walking up ahead of me, like a kid, intent of discovering the prize first.

Twenty minutes later the puppy dog eyes were getting to me. All of these poor critters needed a home, soon. It reminded me of the poverty I had seen on my one world trip. So much of it, what could you do? Deal with it, I guess. That's what I did then, and that's what I was doing now.

"Voila!" Vic pronounced. "This is our guy! Right here."

I ran up the few steps to catch Vic and look into the eight foot by eight by eight cage and there stood, wagging his tail, the spitting image of the dog in our Got Poi? poster.

"Good job Vic!" We noted the number on the cage, made our payment for shots and some flea medicine and a few minutes later we were rolling down the road with an incredibly grateful dog.

Pulling into Tiwaka's an hour later, Vic and I were still singing. "Got Poi dude? Yeah bruddah we get poi!" Our song didn't rhyme or even sound like a song, but we were singing anyhow. Poi, the reincarnated one, was still wagging his tail, his new collar fitting just right.

Aunty Kealoha never knew the difference but did mention that Poi had gotten a lot nicer since his absence and had a real healthy appetite.

Sandy was stoked too, cooking us a celebratory dinner that had to be one of the best meals I had ever had. Vic and I shared the two Coco Loco Mocos prize and stood proudly on either side of Tiwaka as Sandy took our honorary picture.

I heard, from a reliable source, that the picture of Vic, Tiwaka and I still hung on the wall of the bar long after we were all dead and gone.

~~~
# If, Then, Or

It felt good to be back behind the bar, back near the ocean cliffs nestled in our protective jungle. Protected from the Crater aliens, conscious energy and whatever quantum entanglement was. Here, surrounded by my polished wood, sparkling glasses, refrigerators and Tiwaka I felt safe. Home. Happy.

It was an illusion I was quite content to perpetuate. Tiwaka felt it too. Both of us were quiet in thought, comfortable again in our daily rituals. Our little tiny world had rhythm here, a song that we knew very well, and could tap our fingers to forever.

I reached down to fish out a couple more mugs to polish and looked up at my feathered companion. He had just returned from a week at the Roots school, with a glowing report card from Melita. Apparently, to almost everyone's surprise, he had been quiet and cooperative. The kids all learned a lot about parrots, birds in general and that all important human-animal relationship. Tiwaka was so loved that he was voted by the kids to be something between a pet and a little brother to them. It was good to have him back though, and I could see he was comfortable up on his perch, surveying his domain.

Routine and quiet had a magical way of getting you to think, about other things than what your were robotically doing. Fifty glass mugs could bore you to tears. But in my case I let my mind wander to other more entertaining ideas.

I had always found fascinating the causality of everyday events. *If-Thens* I called them. IF this happened, *THEN* this would follow. It was a fun mind game to occupy my time.

For instance, a night at Tiwaka's could provide hundreds of *If-Thens*. IF Coco wore her black mumu, *THEN* all the middle aged guys would puppy dog her all night long. IF the Lahaina honeys would sit at the bar, *THEN* Tiwaka would try to sit on top of one of their beautiful heads and peck at the young men competing for their attention. IF I snuck back and gave Sandy a kiss, *THEN* I might get one back, or two.

OR! Wait, that was even better! IF – THEN – OR! That added a whole new dimension to my game, one that really did a better job of describing events. IF Coco did wear that black mumu, *THEN* all the middle aged guys would vie for her, *OR* she would just dance with them all.

I turned to look at Tiwaka a moment, thinking of some IF THEN OR with him. His left eye immediately fixated on me, like a tiger might stare at a gazelle. Of course, when he turned his head to gaze at me with his other eye you felt more like he was a near sighted tiger. I continued to look at him. My hand gently cradled my chin, so that my brain could think better, without having to support that obnoxiously heavy skull it found itself trapped in.

"Tiwaka, you ready for a little game?" I asked.

He nodded his head suspiciously, threw his chest out a little like the big bad shield he must imagine it to be.

"OK, here we go. I'm going to ask you a question, an IF question and your answer will be the THEN. You know, IF, THEN?" I wasn't so sure that was even a clear question.

Suddenly he leaped down onto the bar and flapped his wings enough to move the napkins right out into the air.

"Darn, that was my first one. *IF* I offer you a chocolate covered nut...." I opened the drawer for the treats. "*THEN* you'll fly down to the bar." I watched him closely as I pulled the chocolate nut from the ziplock bag. "*OR* maybe you'll sing a little song?"

Tiwaka was watching the nut, and nothing else. I could have grabbed his tail and he would still be watching the nut as I twirled him around over my head. *IF* he were a dog, *THEN* he would be drooling, *OR* having bitten my hand, already eating the nut....

"Come on Tiwaka. You must have learned a cute little song at Roots this week." I paused, trying to speak keywords he already knew to prompt his memory. "Song? Sing Song Tiwaka?"

He didn't move, but kept looking at me. I watched his feet for the first clue of a thought moving up to his head. Sure enough he started pawing at the bar with his left talon. I could almost see the words work their way higher. Up to his tail feathers next as he shook his butt a little. Next his wings fluttered a little and finally his head bobbed and twisted a few times. His eyes looked a little scared. Perhaps his brain was working at maximum capacity and it was spooking him.

"Come on Tiwaka, I know you got it in ya," I coaxed him. The chocolate covered nut was safely ensconced in my hand, but clearly visible, for a song.

He looked at me just as the words began pouring from deep inside his throat.

"My life is like a whale,

too long for pants,

too big to fail,

so just laugh and love,

and always dance."


I guess we all have moments like this, where you suddenly realize your previous idea of someone was so far off to be simply ridiculous. Like Halle Haleakala, I thought she was just a ditsy teenage hippie girl smoking her way to the edge. Boy was I wrong. She was a brilliant scientist living at the edge of the edge.

Now, Tiwaka had always impressed me, and I loved him dearly. But his vocal talents were for the most part memorization, parlor tricks for the bar and the patrons.

Of course, this little song was another memorization as well, but in my current state of mind lately, it seemed spot on. Funny how your emotional state can color reality any shade you need it to.

"Wow, Tiwaka," I said like a proud daddy. "That is so good dude! Did you learn that at school?"

"Mahalo," he said back, bobbing his head.

I wasn't sure why he was saying 'thank you' in answer to my question, but he followed it with one of those words that often got stuck behind the first one.

"Melita." He then repeated what he wanted to say. "Mahalo Melita."

"You betcha dude. Thank you Melita," I said holding up an empty but clean beer mug, polishing one last spot away. Tiwaka had picked up that joy of learning that all the kids had at her little jungle school. If only they could duplicate that a million times over around the world. Things would be a whole lot better.

"Well, well!" Coco was walking around the corner, beaming from here to way over there, those perfect white teeth gleaming with something more to say.

"Howzit Coco girl, thanks for covering for Sandy and I. The festival was..."

"Overwhelming I hear." She moved up to the stool in front of my station, still smiling the grin of yet unspoken knowledge.

"OK," I said a little resigned. "What did you hear?" I was a bit curious at her use of the word 'overwhelming'.

Coco looked around to see if we were alone first, then folded her hands and whispered loudly. "I'll never look at you the same way!"

I put my head down in my hands. "Oh Coco, I don't know what it was..."

"No, don't. I won't tease you about what you're thinking." She paused a moment. "You're thinking about the dancing right?"

Another mind reader in training! "Yes, well, yes."

"No honey. It's your love for Sandy. It's," she leaned back a bit trying to work the word up, like Tiwaka scratching his foot on the bar. "It's just wonderful."

"Thanks Coco. I think she is really special, you know that."

"Oh yes, I do know that. You two, together, are one of those special things the universe gives us. To show us what is really possible."

"Now, Coco, you are getting all cosmic on me girl." I protested. Right or wrong, she was moving me in a direction that I had been too far down lately.

She laughed a little at that. "Well, we are sort of, like, in the cosmos, are we not?"

I hunched my left shoulder a little, polishing a new mug.

"This little ol' planet of ours is a nice place to hang out, but it is plop smack in the middle of the cosmos ain't it?"

"The middle?" I teased, looking up at her with a smile.

"As far as I know," she said. "Perfectly in the middle." She shrugged and lifted her head. "Why not?"

Tiwaka squawked from his perch where he had just finished that large nut.

Coco looked up at him. "Glad to see him back. I missed him. Tips are way better when he's around." She turned and went into the back to get dressed. I noticed her black mumu draped over her arm.

"Tips are going to be real good tonight honey girl," I said to an empty bar.

~~~

Sandy came skipping in like a little jungle fairy, singing and waving her arms. When I first saw her in the corner of my eye I thought it was a little girl escaped from happyland or Twin Falls. On second glance I watched her cross the bar lawn before seeing me and catching herself.

Self consciously she looked down for a moment before looking up and waving.

"Hi honey!" she said loudly, walking over to the bar.

"I was digging those moves Sandy. Looks like you were having fun." Leaning over to kiss her I put down my bar towel. "What's got you all tuned up this afternoon?"

She looked at me, those big brown pools of love blinking a couple of times. "I dunno. But I am feeling really good lately. Really good."

When guys stumble across this kind of stuff, they just wag their heads and try to keep it all masculine between themselves. "Cool dude, good on ya, you must be working out." We keep it short. We never go through *that door*.

However, I had learned there was a whole other world out there, on the other side of *that door*. Especially with Sandy. If I gave her a short answer she would think I was dismissing her or not acknowledging her real message. So, I tried hard to walk through *that door* every time I bumped into it. Often though, I had to hold her hand to keep from getting completely lost.

"Well, Sandy, you look good. I mean better than usual." I walked around outside the bar and we both sat on stools. I kissed her on the lips lightly. "You do seem different, since we left the festival."

She had been looking down a moment. "I am." Looking up again, letting a long beautiful curl grace her cheek she added, "Something changed inside me there. Something good. I just can't place it." She picked up my hand and held it. "It's feels like a piano being played inside of me. I can feel each note harmonizing with the previous one, as they kinda march their way up the scale. Weird yeah?"

I had heard of marching to a different drummer and I guess Sandy's was a Steinway. I knew mine had always been a 1959 Gibson Les Paul slide with the B string tuned to a second G and named "Berneice".

"A piano? Have you ever played one, maybe as a kid?" I asked.

"A little, on weekends when my mother would drive me into Papeete for lessons. This sweet old French lady was so patient with me, and," Sandy grinned. "She had the best beignets I ever tasted."

"Are those donuts or something?"

"Fried donut globes, covered in confectionery sugar." Leaning in close she added, "Almost as sweet as you darling."

I must have blushed, as Sandy pulled back a little and laughed sweetly. "You really are something aren't you?" She was looking at me like she was going to out bid everyone at the ladies luncheon Buy a Date fundraiser.

"Well, yes I am!" I threw my shoulders back, pumped out my chest and patted myself on the head, all at the same time amazingly. "I can surf the big waves, mix a mean Coco Loco Moco, talk to parrots, and throw a party people talk about in retirement." I walked around like I was giving an interview to Geraldo on the set of my next movie. "Yes ma'am, I don't dance with the stars, but I sure as hell dance under them." I playfully slapped her butt as I moved past her, in my slow motion acceptance speech. "I can free dive to a hundred feet, skydive *with* my eyes open, fly the space shuttle on autopilot, and kiss you until the cows come home...which sounds like a real good idea..."

I swung her into my arms, wrapped her up real tight belly to belly and slowly swung my head down to hers and those full lips. It wasn't my first kiss, but this was one I would remember in whatever rocking chair they parked me in at the Hale Kokua home for old folks.

She moaned a little and squeezed me right back. Her fingers were exploring the back of my head, as if she could pull me any closer. I heard another sound somewhere far away, in my head. It must have been me slapping myself silly for being so damn lucky.

Time has a particularly interesting way of slowing down when it wants to. But, it's not like in the movies where everything looks like it is trying to push through air that is way too thick. This was different. This was a flood of thoughts and feelings that are crammed inside of a brief moment. A richness that normal Time just didn't have the bandwidth to handle. Time was being real friendly right now.

Sandy moved her hands under my aloha shirt, rubbing my back and exposing it to the warm sun. My toes, and hers no doubt, were wiggling in the cool green grass of the lawn. I could smell the jasmine in her hair and the warmth of her breath, the breath from down deep.

"We've got to..." she tried to mumble, but I covered her mouth again with mine, trying to keep the moment going. She squeezed me once, and then pulled away an inch. "We're in the middle of the yard..."

I didn't care, but I guess I kind of did. Part of me didn't care, probably that same part of me that had let loose on the hill of hippies.

Time went right back to its normal speed and I sighed a bit. She was right. Parts of me had gotten closer to her than should in a public place.

"I've got an idea Sandy," pulling her hand toward the bar. I had had this idea percolating for some time. It was time, I knew it and I think she did. At least I hoped she would.

"What are you looking for?" She giggled as I ran behind the bar, looking in the storage area.

I found it and brought it up to show her.

"Your machete?" she exclaimed, but with not as much surprise as you would think.

"My special machete dear. The one reserved for opening only the finest coconuts." I ran back around the bar, hearing my mother's voice automatically tell me not to run with scissors. So I was careful.

With the machete in my left hand and Sandy's in my right we ran off into the coconut patch at the edge of the lawn. I looked around quickly and found one of the shorter trees with a perfect bunch of cocos hanging low and full.

"Here, sit right here, I'm gonna open a coco."

Sandy sat crossed legged in her yellow sundress and bare feet. Her hair was untied and falling all around her shoulders, keeping her smile from spreading out to her arms.

I reached up and with one sure swing had two cocos in my hand. One of them gave me that "I'm your man" vibe and I let the other fall to the ground.

"Here, I'm just going to open it a bit..." I was talking to myself more than anything. I had a focus issue going on right now that was taking every free electron my brain could issue. In a moment, with all my fingers intact I was done.

I have always been a bit of a history buff and I knew I was going to make some in a second, so before I fell into Sandy's mesmerizing gaze I took a quick look around. The sun was out, and the sky was a blue bird playing with cotton. The summit of the mountain was shimmering up above, somehow matching the vibration of the cobalt sea in the other direction. Yes, I thought to myself. This is perfect.

Sitting down opposite of Sandy, holding the opened coconut so it wouldn't spill out, I took a deep breath. This is not something I had ever practiced. I looked at her, my mind telling me I had something to do. Her youthfulness was one I suddenly saw decades into the future where she was still beautiful. Right now, she was absolutely breathtaking, so much so that I had to take a few deep breathes.

"Yes!" she said and giggled.

"Sandy," I began, and then heard her. "What?" I looked up.

"Go ahead big boy," she teased.

I think she had said yes, but I wasn't sure. My mind might be playing tricks on me, maybe she had said 'dress', maybe her dress was getting stained in the grass? Or, maybe I had sneezed and she was saying 'bless' you? Oh my god, I was just going to have to keep my composure and do this.

"Sandy, you know that we are, you know, like really into each other. Right?"

"I love you," she said sweetly, her head tilted slightly.

"Oh, I love you too baby!" I blew her a kiss and laughed a little, mostly at my own nervousness. I was getting distracted. Yikes, this was harder than I thought.

"Sandy," I kept saying her name, even when there was no one else around. "Sandy," Yikes! I said it again.

"Yes?" she reached out to help me hold the coconut. That was cool, and a good idea before I spilled it.

"You are the best thing that has ever happened to me. Ever. Really, I mean ever."

She was nodding and smiling.

"I have been drawn to something kind of powerful lately. I'm not sure what to make of it, but when I sat down last night and thought it through, it always came back to you. You and me."

I held the coconut out toward her, so it was between us better. Now, now was the time! I had to blurt it out.

"Can we have children together?" There! I said it.

Sandy laughed out loud and almost spilled the coconut. I quickly took a short drink of it and handed it to her. She took it and watching me the entire time took a long slow drink.

"Of course, but don't you think we should get married first?" She asked, with some considerable amount of twinkle in her eyes.

I sat up straight. Hadn't I just asked her that? "Sure! Didn't I just say that?" I searched my databanks for a replay but nothing had been written to disk. My mind was way too fluid for that.

"Yes, yes! Will you marry me Sandy?" It was worth repeating.

"Yes, I will marry you!" Sandy said. She threw the coconut to the ground and jumped on me.

~~~

Coco was walking around the tables, picking up the coasters and putting them in a woven basket. Her black mumu was stunning, especially with her in it. I swear it was amazing. She had to be sixty, but here on Maui, sixty was the new forty, with privileges.

I don't know how long Sandy and I had been distracted in the coconut patch, but the clock told me it was still early afternoon.

"The road's closed. At Twin Falls. I don't think anyone will be here for some time," Coco announced. Then she looked at us briefly, back to her basket and then abruptly turned toward us again. Her face was a mix of questions.

Sandy blurted it out. "We're engaged!" She held up her left hand where I had put a woven palm frond ring. I had seen it done at the tourist stands around the island and liked it. We would pick out a gold ring together in Kahului later I guess.

Coco stood up straight, both hands on her hips and nodded slightly. "Well, I must say! It's about time! Congratulations to both of you young'uns." She walked out from under the thatched roof of her tables and held her arms out wide.

I thought she wanted to hug Sandy first but she insisted on hugging us both at the same time. It was a long hug full of deep sounds and laughter. I think she was blessing us in her own way.

"Go on you two. It'll be hours before, or if, anyone shows up. I'll hang out here just in case." Coco kissed us both on the forehead and pushed us out into the world, as it were.

Sandy looked at me, with some excitement in her face. "Hey, let's go surfing!"

"Sure! That's the second best idea I've heard today!" I turned and ran for my board sitting atop the naupaka bushes. "Wait, how big is it?"

"I dunno baby," Sandy looked up at the clouds. "The winds are offshore though."

"Let me climb up and spock it out real quick. Just in case we need bigger boards." In two minutes I was forty feet above the ground and well above the jungle canopy. The bay at Unknowns looked so good I had to blink a couple of times, pinch myself only once and look a third time. The surf was lining up as sweet as one of those biegnets in Papeete and small, maybe shoulder high. "Hey, it's small, I'm gonna take my mini-tanker!" I called down to Sandy below.

"OK," she looked around for hers as well, finding it underneath the deck.

It seemed we lived in our surf trunks and never had to change into something to swim in. I had stashed wax at the beach for years. It made such spontaneity easier to pull off. Minutes later we were at the water's edge.

Reaching down to scoop up a small amount of sand, right where the last wave had retreated and left a line I then threw it into the ocean. Shark repellent that was. Sandy was already in the water, pulling herself forward with strong powerful strokes. She was beautiful, but she was most beautiful in the water. It was like she was some kind of ocean princess, or maybe I was just in love and making that all up.

She looked back at me, obviously racing me now to the lineup. Her right foot came up and wiggled in tease, just as I poured on the energy to catch up. Putting my head down and reaching deep and fast into the clear water I sped up. The wind was pushing a little as well, blowing out from the valley behind me and into the faces of the waves as they took their last chance to impress and stood tall.

A set was pouring in across the reef on the left side of the bay. We had missed most of it, but Sandy looked to be in position for the last one. I was still far enough back to watch her move into the heart of it, turn, paddle and leap to her feet just as the six footer flung itself up and forward. The offshore breeze was light, but enough to brush the vertical wave face with a glittering smoothness. The bright colors on her board reflected all the way down the wave. It was as if the wave was amplifying it all for us. Sandy and her board were playing in the mirror.

I watched those same intoxicating legs flex and bend as she made the drop and pushed up into her first turn. Her hair, still dry for the moment, was flying back behind her like a million little kites. I had to stop and watch, I just had to. Besides I was a little out of breath.

The wave was peeling nice and evenly, holding up longer than usual with the wind there to help. Sandy let the board rise up the face about half way and then pointed it along the line leading to the deeper water of the bay where I was. She had the inside edge of her board set in the wave and walked up quickly to the nose of her mini-tanker. First, a few toes and then her entire foot was hanging over the front. A second later, her back arched and her arms back slightly, she inched her other foot up there.

Suddenly I heard a whooping howl from up on the cliffs. Turning quickly, I saw a woman in a black dress waving her arms and jumping up and down. It had to be Coco. She must be hooting for Sandy's hang ten! Cool!

Sandy had her arms up in the air, holding that balance for another moment before the wave started to slow down. Immediately she stepped back a few and turned the board down toward the front of the wave to get some speed. Making another graceful bottom turn she turned back to the top of the wave just as she got close to me. I knew what she was up to now.

Just as the wave passed beneath me she carved a hard turn right back at the top of the wave, spraying me with a shower of water. OK, she was boss, but now it was my turn!

Another set was already moving in and I paddled hard for it, wanting to make the first one, so I could show off to Sandy. The horizon had a sudden funny look to it, like those days when the swell was too big or stormy. I pushed that thought away though, it was sunny, springtime and the entire ocean looked calm elsewhere. No whitewater anywhere but on the reef, as it was supposed to be on a nice mellow day.

Something made me glance back up at the cliff and Coco, I guess it was Coco, was still there waving her arms and pointing. Geez, that wasn't good. Now, I was a bit anxious. Turning back to the horizon as I paddled harder, I could see what all the excitement was about. It was a sneaker set! A big close out set! Just like the ones that finally made me give up surfing Waimea Bay on Oahu. I hated those. During winter at Waimea every tenth set, or sometimes only once a day a much larger set would push its way into the lineup. I guess it was the ocean's way of reminding you of something, but I didn't like it at all. It always involved getting hammered because you were too close to shore to get out and over the big waves. Or you had to choose, often within only a few milliseconds, whether it would be better to race out and try and get over the crest of the biggest wave, avoiding all the certain chaos back inside. That choice had gone wrong many a time with me. Rushing out to get over the waves, I had found myself in the wrong place at the wrong time as an even bigger wave picked that spot to hammer the Earth with everything it had. The white water chaos inside such a situation might hold you down and tumble you but the guillotine of a monster wave could break bones, easily. Not to mention your board, your leash and certainly whatever good mood you might have been in.

This time my choice was easy. I was too far out to turn and run. I had to make my luck outside. I had to try and paddle out and over the big ones. Looking back quickly for Sandy I couldn't see her. She had to be on to this already, and sure enough, I saw her even with me, paddling her heart out. Her face looked a bit worried, as I'm sure mine must have.

We were both heading toward the middle of the bay as best we could. There the waves would be in the deepest water and less likely to break on top of us. It was a tricky proposition with a close out set. It was definitely going to break across the entire bay, unlike the nice set before it where they had begun peeling on the side reef and then slowly lost their power in the deep middle bay. So, the trick was to make it far enough outside while also aiming for the middle of the bay. You couldn't just paddle straight out, you would not hit the advantage of the deepest water, and you couldn't just aim for the middle of the bay as you wouldn't get far enough out.

Sandy looked to have a good angle, maybe twenty degrees or so and I followed her. My arms were full of adrenaline and I caught up with her in half a minute.

"Whadaya think babe?" I asked, almost out of breath.

She glanced at me quickly forcing a smile. "Close," she paddled deeply now with me. "Gonna be close."

It was. We were about twenty feet apart now, not daring to get any closer in case the wave did crash in front of us. We didn't want our boards to hit each other. We figured we were close enough to the middle of the bay now and were powering out straight to the horizon and the first wave.

It was enticingly beautiful, moving its incredible mass up from the ocean depths, all blue and green and infinitely powerful. The wind was rushing up its face and I knew we could make this if we both turned and paddled quickly.

"Lets go!" I screamed at the top of my lungs.

"Go for it!" Sandy yelled back still paddling.

The last thing I saw as I was aiming my board down the cliff of this huge wave was Sandy's feet and the back of her board punching through the top of the crest. She had made it over! Good. Now all I had to do is make the drop.

It was a little too late though. The top of the wave was already foaming and instead of pitching over into one of those picture perfect tubes was simply collapsing on itself from the top. Slowly collapsing, starting with the top hundred tons of seawater first.

I could feel the water all around me. I expected to get tumbled or launched at any second, but I held my balance on my board somehow. I was encased in whitewater, but as I fell I came out of it. Came out of it just in time to hit the clean face below. Instincts gave me a free pass as I caught the wave just right from free fall and compressed my legs in compensation. My bottom turn was not to be though, I didn't have a chance if I rode it that far down. The wave was already going to break across the entire bay, with me or without me. I chose the later.

I had one chance of rocketing up the face of the wave and up and over the top. It was one step short of a suicide maneuver. If I mistimed this, the top of the wave would simply grab me and take me over with it. However, my speed was good and I made it maddeningly quick to the top of the wall. It had decided to wait that one instant I needed.

As my feet left my board and we both cleared the top Time again did that funny little thing it likes to do. The moment was rich with the texture of adventure. I was airborne, some thirty feet in the air, the massive neck of the wave under me and moving away. I was spinning slowly, my board now far away from me at the end of my leash. The cliffs behind me were easier to see now and I could swear I saw something in black diving into the sea. As I spun further around I saw Sandy again. She was just paddling into the next wave, a huge monster. It had to be twenty something feet! Where did this set come from? Geez.

This huge wall was barreling down on me and I was preparing for hammer time. No way around it. Falling into the water I quickly took off my leash and set my board free. Damn, it was gonna be a long hard swim. Immediately I began hyperventilating, trying to pump my blood full of life giving oxygen. As I was bobbing there, getting ready to dive as deep as I could to escape I saw Sandy free falling from the top of this mondo beast. It was just like in her dream, the one with the satellites. As I dove down I had my eyes locked on her. She was still free falling.

~~~

Diving deep under a big wave is probably the best maneuver for success when trying to get away from it's crashing, other than staying on the beach that is. The water was deep enough for me to easily clear its invisible grip and the peppering of the white water on the surface. The scary part is not this diving under but surfacing and seeing what is next. That was going to be worse. The next wave had already broken, it was fifteen feet of rolling whitewater thunder. Underneath it would be a swirling butt chomping roller coaster. Taking another couple of deep breathes and then one really big holder I dove again.

Relaxing, amazingly enough, is the best way to conserve oxygen. I pulled my arms and legs together, tried to tuck my face into my body to protect those boyish good looks. I got hit hard by the first of it and then lifted and spun. Feeling myself move in toward shore was reassuring, that is where I might find my board and if not, at least shallow water where I could rest. The trick was always not to panic. As long as I didn't slam into a coral head I would be fine.

Sandy would probably be sitting on her board, having lost her top again and laughing. I could just see her there, having just had a great ride and wondering when I would be done goofing off underwater.

I surfaced after a moment just in time to see one last wave to dive under. Another deep breath and I was under, but I could feel the cumulative weakness creeping up on me. It could be quite insidious, masking its danger under the umbrella of adrenaline and excitement. But, I knew better, having learned about that the way I usually learn best: by mistake.

Finally, the set was over and I began making my way toward the beach. It was still a hundred meters away. I had to float a bit, doing a lazy back crawl and avoiding the last of the outflowing currents from inside the bay. I hadn't seen Sandy yet, maybe she was already on the warm sand, soaking up some rays. Must be nice!

Just then I swam into something below, at first I thought I had run into the reef. Turning over to look out for the next coral head, I saw I was still in deep water and instantly panicked. Damn! I had thrown in my magic sand as shark repellent! WTF!

I tried scanning all around me, but didn't see a thing, until the big green shape approached from the surface. It was, thankfully, a big Hawaiian Green Sea Turtle. I should have known.

"Hey! How about another ride?" This would really impress Sandy, wherever she was. It quickly got underneath me and gently rose up so that it was basically floating me on top of its shell. Both of our heads were up and clear of the water and it accelerated toward the beach.

Someone was already there, but the water was splashing in my face so much I couldn't clear my eyes fast enough to focus. This turtle was fast!

I shook my head, throwing my hair out of the way and most of the water the turtle had been throwing up. There on the edge of the beach, still partially in the water, laying in the sand was Sandy, surrounded, I think, by two more big turtles.

"Come on! Hurry up dude!" I yelled at the big turtle still rocketing in toward the sand. The spray was pelting me so much I was blinded yet again. I couldn't use my hands to shield them or wipe them clear or I would fall off.

"Sandy!" I yelled. "Sandy, shake it off girl! Shake it off!" I was screaming about as loud as I could, and getting mouthfuls of water. I started to choke a bit and the turtle slowed down. "No, no! Keep going!"

Finally, about twenty meters out I got another clear look and hovering over Sandy was Coco, in her black mumu! She was pounding on Sandy's chest and then before I was blinded once again by sea spray I saw her lean over to do what must have been mouth to mouth.

"Oh my god!" I cried. "Sandy, cowgirl up! Come on!" We were almost there and I could hear Coco yelling too.

"Live! Sandy! Come on, live!"

Finally, I was 'feet on sand' and ran up to them both. Sandy was covered in sand, her eyes closed, water drooling out of the corner of her mouth. Right then she coughed and threw up water, and sand, as Coco turned her head to the side.

"Good girl Sandy!" Coco said, with incredible tiredness in her voice.

"Sandy, oh Sandy girl!" I leaned over and kissed her forehead quickly, trying to clear her mouth of debris. There was sand compacted into her ears and all through her hair. "On my god Sandy, are you OK?"

She coughed again and opened her eyes, looking scared and confused. She tried to talk but only made the hoarse sounds of the nearly drowned.

"I think she'll be good now, I think..." Coco murmured as I looked up.

"Coco! What's wrong..." I asked as she fell over herself, exhausted.

Quickly, I got between both Coco and Sandy now, trying to help both of them. Two giant sea turtles were hovering very close by. One was up on the beach right next to Coco now and the other was only a few feet into the water, looking at us and snorting.

Sandy looked to be recovering so I turned to Coco. My hands went to her head, she felt cold and clammy! Her mumu was torn in several places, but clung to her religiously. I pushed her long black hair away from her face and leaned over to listen for her breathing. It was weak, but steady.

"Coco! Coco, you saved her! You and your friends," I turned to the turtles and nodded to both of them. "What's wrong with you..." I was asking when I suddenly figured it out. She had brought Sandy in, from out on the reef. Coco was soaking wet, her own hair full of sand and looking exhausted. She must have carried Sandy in somehow, wearing herself out in the process.

Sandy had rolled over to her side and was throwing up again. I turned quickly back to her, patting her back out of habit and making sure she was clear of anything that might block her breathing. Her chest was moving quickly as she seemed to be catching up on her oxygen.

Turning back to Coco, who now was lying very still, I saw she still had her eyes closed. Her chest was moving slightly.

"Coco," I whispered into her ear. "Mahalo, mahalo my dear Coco. You saved her life."

Coco coughed a little but didn't move any more. I think she was trying to speak, so I put my ear to her mouth. I could see her chest was still rising and falling, so she was OK.

"I, I didn't..." she coughed again. "I didn't save Sandy..." she coughed a little more.

"What? Coco, you saved her, I saw it."

Coco opened her eyes slightly and then her mouth, trying to speak again. I leaned over closer.

"I saved...two."

I sat back up dumbstruck. Two? What did that mean?

Sandy was groaning, and I guess that was a good sign. I turned back to her and she was trying to get up on her hands and knees.

"Easy girl. You gotta move slowly..."

"I gotta...throw up..."

On her back were several lacerations, apparently from the reef. I went to hold her head, but she yelped as I touched her right side, near her ear. Pulling back my hand, it was covered in a good deal of blood.

"Sandy, you've hit your head pretty good, and you've got some good sized cuts on your back." I tried to comfort her as best I could. At least she seemed to be coming back from it, hurt but certainly repairable.

I turned to back to Coco. And, she was gone! Quickly, I turned back to the water. There, three giant sea turtles were moving back out toward the bay. The black mumu was half submerged in the shallows.

"Coco?" I yelled, my voice getting raspy finally. "Coco!"

The three turtles moved slowly out to the deeper waters. The surf had subsided, now a gentle waist high tumbler ever now and then on the reef. My hands went up to my head, had Coco washed away when I wasn't watching? No way. She sure couldn't have got up and walked away, not from what I saw of her exhaustion. My mind was reeling.

"Did you find my board?" Sandy was saying behind me. Turning I found her standing now, her hand up to her head, blood dripping down her face.

"No, but we gotta go, you're bleeding." I walked up to her, put her arm over my shoulder and began the trek back up to the bar, and the phone. I didn't know if she would need stitches, but she needed a concussion check at the least.

"Wait a sec," I asked as I gently turned around to look back for Coco. Nothing, even the three turtles were gone now. Her mumu was still on the beach. I guess it was OK, knowing Coco. She had this way of showing up and disappearing when you weren't looking. Back at the bar I would ask her what happened and it would be solved.

Sandy moaned a little. Turning back to her and the trek uphill I figured Coco was alright. But, the thought still nagged me. Later, I would come back and looked for our surfboards.

"Did you see my wave?" Sandy asked.

I struggled a bit as we walked uphill. "Yeah baby, it was huge!"

She spit out some more seawater, but in a nice Sandy kind of way, the way a wine taster does. "I think it kicked my ass."

I laughed a little at that. "Yeah, but at least you didn't lose your top this time."

~~~

I ended up taking Sandy into Maui Memorial for a checkup. She did need stitches in her head and they gave the lacerations on her back a good washing. On the way home, the pain started to kick in, and the questions.

"Are you sure it was Coco giving me mouth to mouth?" Sandy asked, trying to remember how she got to the beach.

"Yeah, I talked to her myself. She was exhausted. I guess she pulled you in from the impact zone somehow." I had sworn to Coco I would never mention how it was her that had pulled me out of trouble as well, the year before.

Sandy was holding her head like one might balance an egg, one with a small crack in it already. "All I remember is hitting my board on the wipeout, before I got pummeled on the reef." She tried to sit up, off the seat back. "I hit the reef at least once that I remember, and then somehow I was in the channel, holding on to those turtles."

We passed the sign announcing Paia town with the sticker plastered underneath "Don't Feed the Hippies". I always laughed at that irony. It was that hippie culture, the commercialization of that free-love culture that made this town something more than a place for cane workers to buy milk and beer.

I looked over at her quickly as I navigated the jaywalker rich street. It was probably the first time I had ever seen her look less than lovely. Her hair was a rat nest of tangles, her eyes were both quickly turning black and blue and she was swollen. Slowing down for another immortal jaywalker, the kind that think cars can do them no harm, I put my right hand down on her thigh. It was a benign gesture but I was immediately reminded that her legs were going to always be intoxicating. Since I was driving I put both hands back up on the wheel.

"You think Coco was on the beach and saw it all happen?" Sandy was still trying to figure it out.

I knew what I thought, but it would have to remain just that, a thought. I wasn't positive I had actually seen Coco on the cliffs waving at us, warning us of the outside set of waves. But, I was pretty damn sure. I wasn't positive either that I had seen her dive into the water from that height, some thirty feet, and into the water. But, again, I was pretty damn sure. Knowing what I had known for a year now, I had a really good idea what had gone down.

Coco and her turtle friends had pulled off another rescue at Unknowns. I was going to have to buy her a Lifeguard shirt as soon as I could get to the County store in town.

"I don't know Sandy." I felt like I was lying, but I really didn't know for sure. "Coco does have a way of showing up just when you need her? Remember how she covered us when we went to the festival? That was her day off and she just showed up." I looked over at Sandy with my eyebrows all raised. "Weird huh?"

Sandy just moaned, answering and complaining at the same time. "I'm just glad she was there, or you know..." We both knew.

We drove past Ho'okipa, the windsurfers on one side and the canefields on the other. It was quiet for a few miles.

"I guess our boards are toast."

"Probably half way to Molokai by now," I guessed. "I'll go down in the morning and see what I can find."

I was thinking about what Coco had said, about two. I was thinking about that a lot, imaging what it meant, and I was kind of excited.

"Wasn't is just this morning that we, you know, got engaged?" I asked. I was laughing a little, what a day!

"I know!" Sandy managed. "I was hoping we could go out to dinner and celebrate. Polli's or maybe StopWatch, drinks and some steak." She laughed but quickly cut it off when her head complained.

"I know baby. We could at least get handicap parking."

She hit my leg. "Hey, I'm not that bad."

Scooting over toward my door a little I said, "Yes, yes you are!"

We both laughed as much as the pain would allow all the way back to Tiwaka's. It would be the last time we did that for a while.

~~~

"Where's Coco?"

I looked around as I helped Sandy out of the truck. Someone answered that they didn't know. "What do you mean? She's not here?" I asked, trying to keep the frantic inflections out of my voice.

Pa was looking engrossed behind the bar, the recipe book was open and several bottles of rum were surrounding it. Ma was busy trying to bus a couple of tables and Tiwaka was marching up and down the bar. Suddenly I felt a big ball of fear move up into my chest from way down in the ground where they wait like lightning.

"What's wrong?" Sandy asked, trying her best to walk with swollen eyes and a sore body. "Did they say something about Coco?"

"Yeah," I whispered, afraid to make it real by repeating what I had hoped was a bad dream. "Coco isn't here."

"Sandy darling!" Ma came over quickly. "Oh my goodness! You look..." She caught herself. "Here, let me help you. Come sit down."

I tried not to run over to the bar where Pa was looking up recipes, but I did anyhow. The afternoon and evening crowds were probably already on their way and it might get real busy soon.

"How ya doing?" I asked, bringing up the coasters from under the bar.

"Not bad really." Pa confided. "Tiwaka showed me where the olives and limes were."

I thought that bird was probably looking for the chocolate and happened across the olives and limes by mistake.

"So, no Coco?" This was beginning to worry me. Should I have stuck around the bay to see where she had gone?

"No, son." He looked at me for that instant required to let me know he felt concerned as well. "I heard she helped Sandy out of the water. But, she never came back to the bar after running down to the cliffs."

"The cliffs?" I said, mostly to myself, but loud enough for Pa to think I was asking him about it.

"Yep, she was up here, tending to a few customers and suddenly I heard someone ring the ship's bell. I came out of the shed just as she rounded the corner and took off.

"She was running! Fast. Never knew she could move like that." He was still cutting limes and putting them in the bowl. "We couldn't figure out what was going on, so I just took over the bar and Ma got to the tables.

We were both silent for a moment. Pa was moving steadily, keeping his thoughts to himself. He had known Coco for as long as I could remember. He knew she was a special lady, a part of our family at Tiwaka's.

"Look son, that was three hours ago. Something must be wrong. She would have been back by now."

"I know," my voice cracking a bit. "She was exhausted up on the beach with Sandy, and then, she…" I paused thinking about my promise to her. "She, well, she…"

"Disappeared?" Pa added. His eyes were looking at me with the depth of understanding you only see when both people understand a secret.

My surprise poured all over my face. Pa nodded and went back to cutting limes. "Maui is a very special place, as you well know. Coco came to us some years ago, when we lived closer to the bay. You were just a little keiki then. Before Tiwaka even."

I leaned heavily against the bar, wondering how much he was going to say. Glancing over at Sandy and Ma, and then back at Pa and his focus on the limes as he talked, I knew then that they both knew far more than I did.

"She needed some help. Back then, I had a small boat that I used to explore the coastline. Back in the day, before you ever saw anyone out here in these parts. It had a good motor, which I was quite proud of actually. Anyhow, she had some friends, she called them friends. Friends that had been swimming and got caught up in a net."

Pa finished his lime cutting and put the bowl aside. Turning to look at me he continued. "We both hopped in my boat and sped out the bay and went north up the coastline. It wasn't far, maybe two valleys up. The surf was small, summertime and all, and fortunately the winds were light as well. Not much swell. She pointed me over to the rocks leading into this little valley. The bay there was small and you could see a little stream feeding into it from above.

"Anyhow, up against the rocks I could soon see a big nylon net partly up on the rocks, and sure enough around something in the water. Something that was struggling.

"Coco started screaming and splashing the water with her hands as I got as close as I could. Suddenly, she just jumped out of the boat and started swimming over to what appeared to be sea turtles.

"Turtles caught up in the net. There had to be a half dozen of them, all flopping around and making sounds."

Pa shook his shoulders a little at the memory. "The sounds were pitiful. Frightful. You could tell those animals were terrified and were drowning.

"I threw my little anchor out, not worrying if it grabbed or not. I found my fish knife and jumped in after Coco and those turtles. I had the knife in my mouth as I swam over toward them. Coco looked frantic. But, she had something else going on to. Something about her was different. Her eyes. They were big, or something. Big, and watery, but I figured she was crying.

"Anyhow, I started getting that net cut away. It took me quite some time too. Those turtles were thrashing around and screaming. I'm just glad none of them bit me. You've seen those beaks!

"Finally, Coco and I got to working together, me cutting the net and her getting them peeled outta there and away. First one, then two and three. Two more made the break right after that. Then we got to the last one..."

Pa paused there, and turned back to the bar. He picked up another lime, squeezing it slightly in his hand. "The last one. Well...it wasn't moving at all. I got it free, but it wouldn't swim away. Coco was really crying now, and I gotta admit, it was pretty darn sad. Both of us tried to keep it up above the water and we moved together, swimming into the little beach there.

"It was then that I got the distinct impression that these turtles were not just friends. She acted like they were family. It was really quite amazing, to me anyhow. All the turtles were up on the wet sand, waiting as we brought that last one up with us. Coco was crying uncontrollably. I tried to console her a bit, but her sobs were rocking her body. The others moved in close to the dead turtle then, and touched it with their heads and some used their flippers. They were making different sounds this time, light hissing sounds. Sounded a lot like, well...I dunno, maybe it was turtle crying sounds.

"There wasn't much we could do I guess. Sure wasn't much I could do, so I just sat with Coco and the other turtles for over an hour. Finally, Coco got up off the sand and walked back into the ocean. I watched her in case she was out of her mind with sadness or something and might do something, well, you know, hurtful. To herself.

"She rinsed herself off, going completely under water. Turning to walk back up to me I watched her wipe her eyes over and over. Then, she sat down, right next to me, putting her hand on my shoulder. She spoke very softly. I was afraid to look at her, thinking I would cry too."

"You," she said. "You have helped save my friends. My family," she said so softly I wasn't sure she had said it. "My brother here has moved on to wait on us."

"She had called the dead turtle her brother and that got me to thinking. Before I could mull that over much, she started talking again, this time a little louder. She was speaking to all of us, well the turtles and me I guess."

"Today," Coco said. "We will honor our dead, and we will celebrate our own lives and thank this man who has saved so many of us."

"That's when she took me by the shoulders so that she could look at me, and there...that is when I saw her eyes again. This time, there was no hiding it, no me mistaking what I was seeing."

Pa put the lime down, spun it with his fingers and picked it back up. "Her eyes were huge, and brown and watery, like...well, like one of those turtles. I was beyond words. She continued to speak to me, holding my shoulders firm."

"You, and your family will forever be in our gratitude. Please have us, all of us, our kind, as your 'amuakua. We will be your protectors, as you were our rescuer."

"Wow!" I exclaimed, genuinely surprised. "Really? How long ago was this then?"

Pa put the lime down. "Decades. I haven't really spoken of it since. There were times when I thought I had imagined her eyes, her change. I dunno." He shook his head a little.

"Look, Coco..." I had to say it. "Coco saved me last year you know. I never told anyone. She helped me out of the bay when I was in trouble. Saved my life for sure."

Pa nodded and smiled. "Our family 'amuakua I guess."

I smiled. We had an 'amuakua! It was something very few people acknowledged or even spoke of. Especially, those not of Hawaiian ancestry. But, the way I looked at those things was that the Hawaiians were simply aware of a force that had already existed in the world for all people. Just like the North American Indians and their animal spirits. Anyone, of any culture or background, could tap into the same energy, the same magic, if they were honestly open to it.

"Where was this bay? Maybe I can go back there and find her?" I had my arm on Pa, needing an answer.

Pa looked at me a little sadly. He was thinking about something he was hesitant to say.

"Come on, maybe she needs help? I could drive her to the hospital!" My pleas were sounding childish now, even to my own ears.

"You cannot take her to a hospital son. You know that."

"Tell me anyhow Pa! I can go see her, I can do something!"

He took my hand and looked at me, tears fighting to escape. "Look, that bay, that valley, was developed years ago. They launch jet skis there now, right where that little beach is. They were chased out of there a long time ago."

"Where would they go?" I asked the universe as much as I asked Pa.

He shook his head. "I don't have any idea. Soon after I helped her that time, she came to work at the bar with us. She kept saying she owed us. I told Coco that wasn't true. Anyhow, it was a ways back that she mentioned they had been forced to leave that bay.

"She never said where they went, and we let her have her privacy. I don't have a phone number for her, or an address."

Pa looked around a little. "I don't even have a social security number for her. Her checks never are cashed, and she refuses to talk about that. We have kept all her funds in a separate account, for that day when she might need them."

I looked at Pa for a moment. He had really had an interesting life, far more than I thought. It's funny, but when you look at old people you always have a hard time seeing them as young. Seeing them as strong and vibrant and full of their own adventures and secrets. It was something I needed to work on, understanding people had so much more going on than you usually expected.

"Look, Pa. I'm going to go back to the bay for a moment."

"Sure, go ahead. I'm good here. Tiwaka is full of hints, as long as I keep the chocolate nuts coming."

I ran around the bar and over to Sandy and Ma. They both quit talking and looked up at me. Sandy, poor Sandy, had two good shiners now and her lips was swollen. She was putting some kind of salve on her face as well.

"I'm going back to the bay for a moment. Maybe Coco is there...maybe our boards have washed up by now."

Ma touched my hand a moment. "Its almost dark, take a light with you."

I looked at Sandy. "Go ahead," she said warmly. "I'm good. I can feel myself healing already!" Ever the optimist that girl.

~~~

The last light of the sun was just sliding up the opposite cliffs of the bay as I finally got to the water. The sky was holding all the remaining light but the purples and dark blues were already pouring in as shadows. I had about thirty minutes before I would need my flashlight. In the tropics twilight was short and sweet.

"Coco," I said none too loudly. "Are you here?"

I stood silent and still hoping that my short question might get an answer. The water answered lightly, lapping at the shore. Several birds answered far off into the jungle. The coconut trees atop the cliffs answered in song as the trade winds swept through. A lone airliner, still climbing up toward the mainland blinked its wing lights in a silent answer as well.

But, no Coco.

I started around to the left side of the bay, where I could manage climbing over the large boulders that stood in the water there. Maybe our boards were lodged in there. I was afraid though. Afraid I might find something other than a discarded surfboard.

The black crabs scurried about the boulders, hiding from me but still raising their eye stalks high enough to see around the corner. A couple of good sized eels slid away as I continued my bounce from one rock to the next. Soon I was at the corner of the bay, able to see a little around to the north. I felt a compelling need to go further. It was getting dark though.

Just then I thought I saw something, maybe one of the surfboards. A few more jumps and I could get a better view. Stuck relatively high up in between two good sized boulders was Sandy's board. Even from several feet away I could see the nose was broken off. Making my way closer and closer until I could grab it, and working my way lower toward the water, I finally had it.

Amazingly it looked to be in pretty good shape except for he missing four inches of the nose. One of the fins was gone but all of that was repairable. My light was quickly fading and the rocks had been tricky. I looked at the ocean with a keen eye. It appeared to be pretty calm. It would certainly be easier to paddle back rather than tackle those rocks with a surfboard under one arm. Of course, there was no easy way to get into the water, without just jumping in from atop the boulders. Looking one more time for waves, and seeing none, I tossed Sandy's board out a few feet from the rocks and followed it myself. The water felt really good, mostly because I had feared hitting a rock on the way in. It felt really, really good. In a moment I was up on her board, and paddling it as best I could along the edge of the boulders.

The rocks were evidently home tonight to a crowd of yellow tangs, their black stripes disappearing against their almost fluorescent yellow bodies. There must have just been a big hatching of eggs a few days ago. Several adults were swimming around with tiny babies in very close proximity. I saw one particularly beautiful adult tang with only one baby tagging along, swimming out ahead of the others. I felt kind of sorry for her, all the others had plenty of babies.

It was interesting to see her there, out in front. Just two fish by themselves....two.

Back on the beach of the bay I turned and watched the water again, for a sign, any sign of Coco. Nothing. No turtles, nothing. Turning to go something caught my eye up in the sand at the high tide mark.

I had to use my flashlight at this point, the shadows were hiding a little too much for me to be putting my hand down into something unknown. Reaching down and pulling it half out of the sand where it was buried, I found Coco's black mumu. My heart sank right then and there. She had not retrieved it.

"Coco," I whispered now. "I've got it. Your mumu, girl." I turned to watch the horizon again, already merged into the sea with the cover of late twilight. "Coco. Where are you?"

With the surfboard under one arm and the black mumu in my other hand I watched for a long time. The sky was empty now. No clouds, no sunlight, no stars. The bay was quiet and the jungle behind me silent and dark.

"Coco," I cried. Holding the black mumu up to my face I took a deep breath. Her scent was mixed with the salt of the sea, her coconut oil and the plumeria that she loved.

Sitting down heavily into the dark evening sand of the bay I let my tears fall into the black fabric freely. Nothing could be heard except for my voice repeating over and over.

"Two."

~ ~ ~

Olowalu Sunrise

It had been two weeks after Sandy's big wipeout and the trip to the hospital. The moon had gone from new to full. We had six days of rain and eight of none. The ice truck had visited five times.

And still no Coco.

I had been to the bay twice a day, every day since, morning and evening. Nothing. There had been no turtles, no dolphins and no fish. I had even hung her black mumu up high in the trees where she might see it. Every evening though I took it back down, folded it as best I could and carried it back up to my room in the treehouse.

We had needed help in the bar and Ma and Pa had called up one of their old Lahaina crew to come fill in temporarily. Marciana was a lot of fun, probably as old as Ma and Pa combined, and she knew every aspect of the gig. She could make any and all drinks, work tables, chat it up with the customers and make Tiwaka behave.

I told myself I would be sad to see her go when Coco returned, and then fought the inevitable thought that Marciana might be with us a long time.

Sandy was almost completely healed by now. Her face was back to its gorgeous glow, but her back kept a few token scars. I told her they looked a lot like reef tattoos and that made it sound a little nicer.

We were all getting a little used to Coco being gone, but I still held out hope. All of our fishermen friends had scoured the coastline, looking for Coco or any injured turtles. I made up a story about her being in a boat that may have run into a bunch of turtles and crashed. It got a few eyebrows but no one questioned beyond that. And, no one had found anything.

~~~

Distractions were being offered to me constantly. Eventually I bit and agreed to go to Lahaina and check out some refrigerators one of the resorts was getting rid of. Since every other bar on the island was hip to this I was going to have to get there early. I packed up the truck with a cooler, swim fins, mask and a towel the night before and set the alarm for 4 A.M. Whenever I went to the west side of the island I made it a point to go swimming. No real reason other than it was a good rule as far as rules went.

The drive across Maui from the tropical side to the desert beaches with no street lights or traffic was disquieting. I thought of poor ol' Iggy in the cane field fire. That got me to remember a couple of surfers over the years that I had known before they drowned. I hadn't thought of any of those guys in a real long time. After a while your dead friends seemed to transition from people you hung out with to historical figures. People you knew back in the day. Those memories seemed to get enough time wrapped around them to soften the edges and only let the good stuff out. The weird part was that I was part of that history too, having surfed with them and eventually would do that same transition.

As I rounded the pali and dropped down to the beach road it was still pretty dark. I still had a couple of hours before the resort was going to let anyone in to bid. Perfect time for a little morning swim at my favorite west side reef.

Pulling into the left turn lane across from Olowalu Store and dropping into the dark one lane drive I parked in the circular turnaround at the end. My timing was looking real good. Softly and quietly I got out and closed the door. It was just a few meters to the water from here. There was light in the sky now.

I could hear a soft rolling of a still sleepy sea moving across the pebbles and driftwood. The whales had long since made it all the way back to Alaska so their playground was unblemished with spout or splash. The tradewinds had not yet strengthened enough to spill across the peak of Pu'u Kukui and sweep west out to Lahaina Roads, the waters between the islands. The few clouds still hanging onto the island of Lanai, eleven miles to the west, were just catching the first rays of the morning sun. You could almost hear those clouds bragging about how they are first to brilliance at daybreak and last to sleep amongst all the other parts of paradise.

I almost tiptoed across the expansive old plantation home lawn, approaching the water as if in a tractor beam, drawn steadily toward the sand. Several large banyan trees covered the distance in that motherly embrace of a toddler, leaving just enough room to feel a little freedom. All the mynah birds were still quiet, but several were watching me closely, unwilling to find me enough of a threat to wake the others.

My path through the thick and humid air fragrant with plumerias and still open jasmine suddenly changed to a thinner salt fragrance. My subconscious attitude instantly changed from an independent land dwelling person to a part of the sea about to rejoin itself. On land I was a unique human, but in the sea I became a part of a neighborhood. A lonely morning was about to become a dance with friends.

Dropping my towel and keys on the edge of the grass I moved into the dry sand, then farther to the firm sand, and finally to the mushy border between island and ocean. My mask got a quick rinse and something to keep it from fogging up. Body surfing fins went on firmly and with just my surf shorts on I let my weight pull me into the deepening lagoon. I immediately ducked under completely, then went up for a big breath and dove again for the reef opening.

Several Humuhumunukunukuapua'a chatted up the day's activities around a large brain coral. Shrimp moved nervously ahead of me, and soon enough I spotted a dozen green sea turtles in less than a minute. I gazed at them for a long moment. They paid me no attention. The water literally crackled with the sounds of crustaceans and in the distance the great dolphins.

Just before making the reef pass I surfaced for another breath and checked the shadow on the water. I still had another couple of minutes before the sun, high in the sky but still behind the massive Kahalewai or West Maui mountains rose here.

Diving down a little shallower this time I moved just under snorkel depth enjoying the flight. There must have been a thousand fish in view.

Looking forward before surfacing again, I could see the sun shining down about a hundred meters away on the surface and moving my direction. I quickly went up to grab some air and then tucked and dove to the sandy bottom twenty feet below.

Grabbing onto some hard coral I pulled my feet to the bottom and looked up to the sky on the other side. It was time to release a little air, both to extend my down time and to decorate my room here. The surface above was lightening quickly and just as my first little bubbles moved about half way up, the sun broke over the top of the mountain and raced down to my little place on the reef.

A bird-like parrot fish swam between me and the sun, then another giving chase. After a full minute I felt it time to leave. Slowly ascending into the light felt slightly spiritual and despite the analogies it always felt like the right direction to go anyhow. Releasing more bubbles tickled the light into bending over in laughter, falling all over itself. It was so cool when someone as hyped up as Light could slow down a little and let their true colors show. I kicked just slightly, rising in time with my artwork.

As I drew in a big breath at the surface, I could feel that nice early morning sun warmth on my face. The wind had shifted a bit offshore and I could pick out plumeria from the sea smells. I moved onto my back and floated for a short while enjoying one of the few things in this world I knew for sure: it's always a good day that starts with sunrise under the ocean.

~ ~ ~

Dancing Fleas

The refrigerators were too old and energy inefficient for my taste so I let the guys who owned Maui Electric stock buy them. By the time I got out of there though it was noon and time for another swim.

Baby Beach was close so I left the truck parked in hotel parking and walked over to the relatively secluded cove just over the dunes and through the naupaka bushes. I was peeling off my shirt and putting my keys in my hat just as I came around the corner.

This particular little beach was a favorite for young moms and their little keiki since the surf never reached into cove around the half moon lava outcropping. It was sandy, secluded for the most part and today, full of topless mamas. I always cracked up a little at Maui and its generous population of bare breasted women. What I found funny was that I found it unusual at all. I sure couldn't imagine having to strap something to my chest in this heat and pretend to be comfortable.

Some of these ladies had a tan line but most of them didn't. Some were breast feeding the littler tykes. There were even a few nannies there. All the toddlers were naked.

If was a little refreshing on some level. They were doing what they wanted to do, despite the occasional gawks of mainland tourists. They were playing with their kids, and they were enjoying the ocean. We could all do that a little more.

I guess I was the only guy there, over two anyhow. Oh well. I jumped in for a few moments and then with a tip of the old hat, I left them to their sun and baby lotion.

My watch said 1 P.M. but the sun was saying hot, so I drove over to the giant banyan tree in Lahaina for some lunch and people watching. Both could be had inexpensively.

There must have been fifty different vendors set up under the acre canopy of the 150 year old tree. Several large wooden posts had been placed under various limbs to support them up off the ground. All of these posts were wrapped in different colored ribbons. Painters, potters, lotions and potions were all for sale. Hats, pareos, towels and other art you could actually wear were displayed. Plenty of fake ivory carved into any number of whale, heart and hook shapes were out under glass for sale. I overheard one vendor admit it was bone and not ivory.

Over in the corner of all this action, set apart by their lack of anything for sale were the ukulele players. Six musicians surrounded by dozens of tourists taking their picture. After picking out a fresh spam musubi and a guava juice I wandered over closer. The music was frantic but organized, moving so quickly I could barely follow the melody. Little kids were jumping up and down and flashbulbs were blinking almost as fast as the chord changes.

Uku, or flea, and lele or dancing described this instrument perfectly. Those fast moving fingers were like the little flea, fleas that were dancing and these musicians were making it happen.

Finishing my guava I walked back to the docks, just behind all this action. The charter fishing and whale watching businesses were all well positioned here to take your dollars and dreams out to sea.

A little girl was crying as her Mom tried to explain that the whales were not here this time of year. All this despite the big permanent sign announcing "Whales Watched Here!" Her dad was running back from around the Lahaina Inn with ice cream, no doubt as a consolation.

Several bus loads of older tourists were piling out and making their way to one of the double decker observation boats for a leisurely cruise around the area. Whales or not, it was still an outstanding way to spend fifty bucks and an afternoon.

I sat down to finish my musubi next to a row of bicycles all locked up along the railings. Every crew member on every boat here probably rode their bike to work. Most folks here that could ride did. It was a small harbor town, so bikes worked well. I gazed down the lineup. All of them were old beach cruisers enjoying their last days by the sea, just like those people still climbing up on the double decker cruiser.

After a few more minutes of casually watching the movement of people, boats and ice cream cones I got up and found my truck. It was unscathed in the tiny parking spot just under the furthest reach of the giant banyan.

The ukulele guys were still going strong as I pulled out into the steady flow of small, clean rental cars parading down Front Street. A little perspective was refreshing and Lahaina, rich in history as well as people always gave me pause.

In a little over an hour I would be back home. This time, I wouldn't run back down to the bay. Coco was gone.

~~~

Long Lost Brother

Tiwaka was being especially frisky lately, and it made me wonder if it might be springtime for the old bird. Of course it was already summer, but I couldn't explain that to him. Birds all over the jungle were hooking up and flying around like young fools in love. Tiwaka couldn't help but notice this. Later I would learn that Tiwaka didn't miss much.

"Hey Tiwaka," I suggested. "Go on out there and play with the other birds dude." Trying to break his shy moment I picked up the old Led Zeppelin drum stick and held it out for him to climb onto. He looked at me for a moment longer than my patience, so I put the drum stick back onto the bar.

"Well, are you just gonna sit there all day?"

He flapped his wings with enough force to move some napkins around and squawked loud enough to ring my ears. Mynah birds out in the grass immediately took off for the safety of the upper coconut trees.

I looked at the now empty grass and shook my head. "Well, you scared them all off. Are you just gonna..."

"No!" Tiwaka announced. He looked down at me, presumably for my reaction to that. "No worries!" he said this time. That big old colorful crooner took a short leap down to the bar, turned to glance at me quickly and continued down to the ground. From there he waddled out into the sunshine and the green grass.

In my mind, he had played it all wrong. Scaring off everyone in advance was no way to get playmates. But, alas, I was wrong again. When it comes to bird psychology human logic does not live anywhere close.

Tiwaka strolled right out into the middle of the green grass. There he simply stood for a moment, then began opening and displaying his wingspan. When they were fulling opened, he began a slow turn, a spin. His head was bobbing back a bit and then he began to whistle. It wasn't the normal shrill he was capable of but one resembling a C note. A few seconds of that and then he changed it to a G note. Almost immediately after that he went to F. Then back to C for a long moment.

I could hear birds up in the trees getting louder and louder and Tiwaka continued his slow spin and whistling. Soon, little finches began gliding down to within inches of him, chirping and bouncing about. Right after that some big lumbering doves, fat with worms and rotten mango, came bombing in, standing about a foot away from the outer edges of the great wingspan. Finally, the mynah birds arrived. Dozens and dozens of them, all trying to mimic Tiwaka's C note.

This went on for several minutes as the mynahs got better at getting the C note down. Soon they were singing it perfectly along with Tiwaka. Of course then the doves added some base with their cooing and the finches were left with the refrain, mostly a complimentary treble.

The entire yard was now full of birds! Incredible as it was, I forgot to take a picture. No one would ever believe this one.

Suddenly, the cacophony stopped and Tiwaka brought his wings back in. The flock was silent. Tiwaka turned back toward me, and the bar, bobbed his head once, and then began to chirp. Some kind of multi note chirping, like he was talking. Not English, but avian. It was rapid and detailed. Low notes and high notes and everything in between. It had to have been a full minute before he stopped and the flock was silent again.

Tiwaka stood there looking at his jungle friends and then slowly spread his wings out again. His signature obnoxiously loud squawk followed and then the feathered masses took off, chirping, cooing and chattering excitedly.

As the hundred or so birds finally left, Tiwaka waddled back slowly, his head down a bit. Maybe he was looking for bugs, but my impression was that he was a bit sad. As he approached the chairs at the edge of the bar he stopped and looked up at me.

I don't know what he was thinking, but I grabbed the Led Zeppelin drum stick again and went around to pick him up. This time he stepped up onto it. As I raised him up and walked around the bar he leaned his head up against me.

"Tiwaka buddy. Are you doing OK?" I asked as I lightly stroked his head feathers. He didn't answer, but hopped off at the bar and began walking the length toward the order station there at the end. His head was down the entire time, and I'm sure he wouldn't see any bugs this time.

Marciana had just shown up for the afternoon. She put a fresh pile of bar towels down near the order station. After reaching over to hide her purse under the bar she saw Tiwaka.

"Aloha Tiwaka," her cheerful voice sounding out of place.

Tiwaka stopped to look at her, and then walked over to her pile of towels and put his head down on them.

"Tiwaka," Marciana said, looking up at me for a moment. "What's wrong?"

I shrugged my shoulders when Marciana looked up again. "I don't know, he was just entertaining about a hundred birds a few moments ago, all happy. Then he came back in a funk."

"Oh, Tiwaka, my bird. You go back and rest a while on your perch. Maybe a chocolate nut will help you out, yes?"

I pulled out the bowl of poorly fortified nuts, their armor of chocolate simply a false hope of protection. Tiwaka perked up, lifting his head from the towels when he heard the coconut bowl hit the wood of the bar. It had to be my imagination, but it looked like he sighed, turned and started back slowly. His head was still down.

The bar had just been polished. Maybe he was simply gazing at his magnificence in the reflection? Maybe, but probably not.

Marciana quickly got to work, policing the tables, putting the chairs back properly underneath, and brushing a few leaves away. Tiwaka walked right past the bowl of nuts and with a bit of effort leapt back up to his perch between the liquor bottles.

~~~

The evening was flowing along nicely with a mellow crowd and some great acoustic music from the Kula Cowboys. A fiddle, a six string and one of the best female vocals I had ever heard moved the crowd to sing along. It was Marciana and I only, and Tiwaka for backup. Ma and Pa had gone for the weekend to a party up on the mountain and wouldn't be back until tomorrow.

Sandy had made an airport run to pick someone up. I smiled as I thought of her again. She was back to her old self, bouncy and happy and full of more energy than the ocean. Her cooking had excelled to the point where we actually got a glowing culinary write up in the Maui Weekly. On the three nights a week where I cooked and she tended bar things were hopping as well. The customers loved her and I thought it was only because she was light years better looking than me. That may have been part of it, but we got comment cards like "Best Mai Tai since 1945", "Loved the cocktails, awesome!", and "Tiki Goddess Mixes Love and Adventure in a Glass". She was a such natural in both the arts and entertainment.

Around eight she drove up in the truck. I could hear her laughing all the way from the bar, over the music and clamor of the crowd. Whoever she had picked up at the airport got left in the car and she ran over to tell me.

"You won't believe who is in the car!" she said, half out of breath. "I still can't believe it." Turning to see if they were coming, she ran back.

I could hear her asking a question and then laughing out loud again. This time she walked up arm in arm with a crazy handsome guy about her age.

His dark curly hair framed his brown complexion and hazel eyes like only a Hollywood movie poster could. Carrying only a small suitcase and a guitar backpack, he smiled as he took the stool opposite my station. He looked somehow familiar, but then maybe I had seen the movie already.

Sandy was giddy with excitement, hugging this guy. "Jerry, I just can't believe it is you! After all these years boy!"

"What'll you have Jerry?" I asked quickly. The ride from the airport was famous for making people really thirsty.

"Whatever my sister is having!"

"Wow! You guys...you two are brother sister?" No wonder he looked familiar.

"Sure enough," he said graciously.

"So, you must be from Tahiti too?" I asked.

Jerry looked at me and smiled. "We were both born in Papeete. We must have been, what two or three?" He looked over at Sandy. She nodded. "We moved to Oahu, out to the windward side, Kahalu'u, and then when we were both 18 our parents split up. Dad went to L.A. and I went with him. Mom and Sandy headed back to Tahiti." Jerry gave Sandy a big hug. "Mom said you were on Maui now, and I'm so, so glad I found you!"

"So," I asked. "You're twins?"

"Well," Sandy added. "Fraternal, and I am 45 seconds older." She punched Jerry lightly in the arm. "And, 45 seconds wiser too!"

"Yes, yes you are." Jerry acknowledged. "Here I am, following in your footsteps again girl!"

"Oh!" Sandy exclaimed, so full of energy she couldn't stand still. "Jerry, let me introduce you to the creator of the famous Coco Loco Moco, the best surfer this side of Tahiti and my future husband!"

I stuck my hand out, but he pulled me over for a big hug, across the bar. "You know I have heard a whole lot about you in the half hour from the airport!" Jerry said, smiling broadly.

"And," Sandy interrupted. "There is one more accolade I should mention."

Jerry looked over at her like he was ready for yet another surprise. I leaned onto the bar, head in hand, smiling and waiting on yet another compliment.

Sandy was about to burst! Her eyes were sparkling like sun drenched water falling. The shimmer in her hair and the glow of her skin had me mesmerized as she looked at me and grinned. "I should also say," one hand on Jerry's shoulder and the other hand open toward me. "That he is the father of my children!"

She stood back quickly, thrust both hands high in the air and started hooting and howling and jumping around.

Jerry looked over at me with a great big smile. "Wow! Congratulations!"

I raised up off my hands, my eyebrows up under my hair. Shock and awe had me in its grip. "Did she say..." I asked Jerry. "Did she just say...?"

"Yes," he put his hand on my shoulder. "Father of her children?" He patted my shoulder and sat back down on the stool. "Yes. She did."

I ran over to the ship's bell, with Tiwaka keeping a close eye on me. "Tiwaka! Kids!" I rang the bell several times and ran around the bar to where Sandy was still bouncing around, hands up in the air, and dancing the dance of the New Mama.

She grabbed me around the neck and hugged me tight, still dancing. I tried to follow.

"Oh my god, honey! We're gonna have a baby!" I was trying to keep my tears back, but I felt one splash off her bare shoulder and back onto me.

Sandy just hugged me tighter. I think she was sobbing, but it was hard to tell with all the dancing still in her feet.

"Come on honey, let me offer the bar a toast."

She kept her head down into the crook of my neck, so we walked slowly over to Jerry and Tiwaka.

"I'm just so happy," she whispered. "I just confirmed it today. At the doctors, on the way to get Jerry."

Whispering back into her ear, I let her know the universe was ecstatic too. "Look baby, up at the stars." I pointed up at the clear evening air. "See, they are all blinking, sending messages of congratulations."

She laughed lightly at that, lifting her head a little.

I cupped my ear. "I think I can hear them too." Squeezing her around the waist I kept it going. "They're all saying hallelujah!"

Sandy wiped the tears off her cheeks and looked up a second. "I think they're saying it's about time." She grabbed my face and kissed me hard, pushing my hair out of the way and letting hers cover us both. "It's about...our time."

Applause erupted from the tables and the bar. Tiwaka started squawking and flapping his wings, spilling a couple of beers in the process. Still holding Sandy tight with one arm, I plunged my hand high up into the air, pumping my shaka sign back and forth.

Coming up for air I turned and yelled to the crowd "Next round is on me!" That reinvigorated the applause just as I heard Tiwaka knock something else over.

~~~

Much of the rest of the early evening was a blur of celebration, hugs, kisses, more spilled beer by Tiwaka and of course music. Marciana was busy keeping all the free drink orders straight, but I didn't care all that much. The beer would be free until we ran out as far as I was concerned.

Sandy and I were behind the bar liberating the libations and singing, and dancing. It wasn't work that night, it was fun! My skin was tingling with excitement. I was getting married to God's Gift to Earthlings and having a baby with her! Unbelievable. Really, it was beyond my simple mind's capacity to understand, but it was quite within my heart's. Just barely. At that moment, I will always remember, my heart was full.

I had called Ma and Pa at their party up in Keokea. When Ma answered the phone I hit her with it.

"Is this Grandma?"

Silence for a moment, and then I heard her say "Excuse me? Isn't this..."

"Yes, I was just wondering if I was talking to Grandma," my laugh giving it away.

Screaming followed with "Hey Grandpa, take this call!"

It was the same all night as we made calls to our friends and family. At some point I cornered Sandy up against the cooler and kissed her.

"So, when are we going to make this official?" Before she could possibly answer, or take another breath, I kissed her again.

"How about tonight?" she laughed and kissed me back.

I saw Marciana come back behind the bar to grab the last of the Hinano bottles, wink and move back out into the crowd.

"Sure!" I kissed her neck lightly. "But, we might need more beer."

We both laughed.

"When is the next full moon?" Sandy asked.

"Of course! That would be perfect!" I let her go to turn to the tide calendar above the register.

"I need three more Mai Tais and two Green Geckos!" Marciana yelled above the noise.

"Three weeks baby!" I hollered back to Sandy as I moved to the ice bins and Tiki glasses.

Sandy cocked her hip to the side, tilted her head all sexy like and gave me a big thumbs up.

~~~

Planning a wedding can be stressful if not done correctly. We solved that by planning a huge party, with a wedding in the middle. All we really had to do was get a guest list together. The details followed.

The venue was easy. Ceremony at the ocean cliffs in the field there. Reception, of course, at Tiwaka's Tiki Bar & Grill. Honeymoon in Tahiti, Sandy's first home. Perfect!

Sandy and I were out at the sea cliff hammock taking a break from all the excitement. The trade winds had backed off a bit and were gentle enough to simply nudge the hammock.

My right arm was under Sandy's neck and her left hand was in my left pocket. If we spilled out we would surely both get broken arms.

"Can you feel it yet?" I asked.

Looking at me funny she chided me. "It? You must mean our baby, silly boy."

"Of course, that sweet little baby critter." I moved my hand over to tickle her still flat belly. "If I tickle you will the baby jump?"

"Hey!" She squirmed as I tickled and laughed. "Stop that!" Twisting around she tickled back and sure enough we spilled out of the hammock.

"Must be true," I said, still laughing.

Climbing back up into the hammock, all arms intact, Sandy asked, "What must be true?"

"Angels are indeed ticklish!" Gratuitous compliments were overflowing from me lately. And most of them were true.

"Yeah, buster. Well, keep doing that and this poor kid will be another Seinfeld."

"Ha! How's he gonna get that accent?" Secretly I was thinking I could get front row seats to all his shows...proud Dad and all.

"He? What about she?" Sandy teased. "Girls rock ya know."

"Yes, yes. They rock and guys roll. Now, who are we missing from this list?" I held up our notebook with every name of just about everyone we could think of.

Sandy looked at me and whispered "Coco."

My heart sank again at that. I knew she was not on the list, and I knew why. We had gotten ourselves in trouble surfing and had to be rescued, again. Coco had spent what must have been her last breathes on getting Sandy back to life. Now, I knew it was Coco's generous nature that had jumped in to help us, but now, I knew I had to explain to Sandy what Coco had said.

"I know baby. I know..." I scooted up in the hammock a bit, trying to sit up. "There's something I gotta tell you about Coco. About the day she pulled you out of the water and all."

Sandy didn't say anything. She didn't ask me what or anything. She remained silent, and afraid I think, to hear about the sacrifice.

"You were just reviving and I turned to Coco who had just collapsed. That much you know..." I looked at Sandy but she was looking down at the ground. I had to tell her, even if it was going to be heartbreaking. She had to know what Coco had gone through.

"She insisted she had not saved you," I explained.

"What? You said that she did."

"Yes, of course she did. But she said she didn't save just you. She said she saved two."

I waited for Sandy to figure it out. This was hard for me to even say, much less dwell on.

"She saved me, *and* the baby?" Sandy moaned. "Oh my god. I was pregnant then?"

My voice was about to break, but I held on a moment. "Somehow, Coco knew it and made the effort..." Well, I didn't hold on as well as I had hoped. "...She made sure you got to the beach."

Sandy was thinking, probably doing the math in her head. "The doctor told me I probably conceived that weekend at the Happy Rainbow Sunshine festival. It was only the next day that Coco...how could she know?"

I shook my head in wonder. "I don't know. She was more intuitive than anyone I have ever met."

We both sat silent in the hammock for a while, thinking our own personal thoughts about it all. I could hear Sandy breathing roughly, like she was trying to suppress her tears. My own eyes were far too watery to focus on anything except the blues and whites of the sky above us. After a moment I had to blink them away, hoping they would wash away some of the sadness.

Far above us another big airliner glided higher on its way to the mainland. I wondered if anyone on that plane had a clue about our little lives down here on the sea cliffs. I wondered if they could simply look out their windows right now at our island and get a sense for the miracles that permeated the jungles, the sea and within it all, the people.

"We should name the baby Coco," Sandy finally said. "That would be so..." she had to stop.

"I like that honey," I said, watching the airliner finally disappear. "It's a lot better than Happy, Rainbow, or Sunshine."

~~~

That evening at the bar, things were unusually quiet. A pineapple truck had overturned on Hana highway, which apparently caused a smaller flatbed loaded with papayas to spill its contents. All that sweetness had then attracted several swarms of bees and well, it was a big mess. Being the only road, all traffic was stopped. The coconut wireless of county text messages, radio announcements and aunties calling everyone on the phone sealed the deal: no customers for the most part.

Vic had made it in on his moped and a couple of neighbors had walked over. Jerry was still here, occupying one of the tiny cottages.

Sandy and I had showered and put on our best Aloha wear just for the heck of it. We were going to grieve for Coco, but we were going to be happy too. Coco would scold us otherwise. I knew, deep down in my mystical heart, that Coco was just fine. She, just like every living creature, had other options quite beyond what we find in the mirror every morning.

Jerry had a guitar with him and was tuning it up over by the stage. Sandy walked over and sat with him, talking and touching his shoulder, and laughing.

They must have been quite close as kids. Seeing people come back together after so many years always gave me that perspective of time that I enjoy: the circle of experience always seems to come back around to itself.

I didn't have much to do around the bar, so I picked up Tiwaka on the drum stick and we walked over to where Jerry and Sandy were sitting. Marciana was putting down some pupus and pouring water.

"Sandy," Jerry said. "Do you remember the days when we were younger?"

"Oh yes, sure," Sandy beamed.

"We used to catch 'o'opu in the mountain stream."

"All around the Ko'olau hills we'd ride on horseback," Sandy said, her eyes remembering that very fondly.

"It was so long ago it seems it was a dream," Jerry said, patting his guitar like an old family dog.

Sandy was quiet in thought, as Jerry looked around and then back to her.

"Last night I dreamt I was returning, and my heart called out to you." He looked at her a little sadly. "But I feared you wouldn't be like I left you."

Sandy smiled warmly, nodded and said, "Me ke 'aloha Ku'u Home 'O Kahalu'u."

Jerry smiled broadly and continued his song, his poem. "I remember days when we were wiser."

"When our world was small enough for dreams," Sandy added.

Jerry looked over at me and nodded. He picked up Sandy's hand and held it in his. "You have lingered there my sister, and I no longer can it seems.

"Last night I dreamt I was returning, and my heart called out to you." His face got a little solemn. "But I fear I am not as I left you."

Sandy almost whispered this time, holding both of her hands around Jerry's. "Me ke aloha Ku'u Home 'O Kahalu'u."

"Change is a strange thing. It cannot be denied," Jerry continued.

"No, it can't," Sandy whispered, putting his hands down and wiping a tear.

"It can help you find yourself," Jerry said sadly. "Or make you lose your pride." He put his guitar down and sat back in his chair. "Move with it slowly as on the road we go." He looked to Sandy again. "Please do not hold on to me, we all must go alone."

Sandy nodded, somehow understanding more than I was. Tiwaka was gracious enough to keep his mouth shut while this long separated brother and sister talked of the old days.

Jerry livened up a bit though and kept going. "I remember days when we were smiling."

Sandy joined in again. "When we laughed and sang the whole night long!" She leaned over and hugged Jerry then sat back and added, "I will greet you as I find you, with the sharing of a brand new song."

Jerry was having a tough time keeping it together, but his smile was infectious. "Last night I dreamt I was returning, and my heart called out to you, to please accept me as you'll find me."

Sandy stood up, pulling Jerry to his feet. She looked at him with that love only a sister can show a brother. "Me ke 'aloha Ku'u Home 'O Kahalu'u."

Jerry hugged her and repeated her words, "Me ke 'aloha Ku'u Home 'O Kahalu'u."

~~~

Later that night, after we had all gone to bed, I asked Sandy about Jerry's song.

"All those years in L.A. changed him," she said. "He always wanted to go, see the big city and all. But, the intoxication of it all took something away from him.

"I was never that interested in going off into the world I guess. Sure, maybe Disneyland or something. Moving away from the islands though? How could I? The only way I could leave Tahiti was for Oahu, and the only way I could leave Oahu was for Maui."

We snuggled up and as she drifted off to her own dreams I thought about all those big dreams that people have. We all get presented with opportunities, temptations and mysteries and those things that happen to us. I remember hearing some famous guy say it once: it's not what happens to us that defines us. It's the choices we make when they do.

~ ~ ~

Hawaiian Time Zone

Every bar needs a cat. I don't know why, but they just do. It might be to lend a nice balance to have a ne'er do well, laid back fur ball around. Not that most of our patrons were not laid back, but none of them were ever *that* laid back. It showed us all that despite what friends, family and our employers might think of our self imposed tropical lifestyles, we would never be *that* lazy.

I used to think it was a good idea to have a cat to chase the rodents away. However, this cat, evidently raised by mice, had no interest in them whatsoever.

Yet, there was one thing I could depend on from this cat. It knew when 5 P.M. came around. Give or take 15 minutes, regardless of the time of year, the position of the sun, clouds or rain. Of course, 5 P.M. was when I fed all the various animals around Tiwaka's. The parrot was first, of course. Then the fish in the various tanks around the bar and at the tables. After that the finches, with their happy sing song chirping. Finally, the cat.

Often with bar prep and all I would lose track of time. The cat though would predictably, without battery or electric cord, do a better job than most alarms, jumping up onto the bar and meowing. A clock you could ignore or swear was wrong due to power failure. A meowing cat? No way.

And so it was around the bar and throughout our little slice of jungle, things happened on a rhythm. The ice truck showed up between noon and dark. The customers wandered in when the sun was getting low in the sky. The tiki torches got lit whenever it seemed good to light them. Timing was never precise. It was at best complimentary, fitting in best with the situation.

The problem with this was that you couldn't export it beyond the bar. Show up 15 minutes late at the airport and Hawaiian Airlines would be half way to Honolulu by then. Show up when you felt like it to Ho'okipa and you would miss your heat in the windsurfing contest. But, here at Tiwaka's Tiki Bar & Grill time was accommodating. It flowed easily, eventually everything that needed to happen would happen.

In Hawaii, people live longer than anywhere else in the United States. "Hawaiian Time", evidently, works best toward extending that ultimate measure of time, your own.

~ ~ ~

Ranger Ev

As the time for our full moon wedding approached things around the bar got, well, crowded. People on the invite list, relatively long and all familiar, were beginning to bring things in they thought we might need. Extra tiki torches, new garbage cans, cans of pineapple juice, unfinished bottles of rum and firewood.

Of course, the bar remained open to all who could find it. As piles of goodies accumulated around our feet, our workspace and our storage we managed to keep the magic flowing. The good times rolled out from behind the bar, flowing smoothing across the koa counter and out into the tropical air surrounding our guests.

Sometimes the good times rolled in all on their own. On rare occasions we had new people show up, fortunate souls who were invited guests of the regulars or those with a pirate map that just got lucky. We didn't advertise the bar, we didn't need a growing business. It was already everything we wanted.

A Kihei Rent a Car van inched its way down the gravel path and slowly pulled into the parking area, several people laughing and singing through the open windows. I took a moment to watch them pile out of the car, towels and shoes falling out as the sliding door opened. The driver, a young haole guy with curly hair and an aloha shirt hanging over his white shorts immediately stepped down and back. He extended his hand to the young ladies spilling out of the back. A couple of young local guys laughingly refused the driver's hand and followed the girls closely over toward the bar.

"Hey Tiwaka, I think we got us an instant party coming our way."

The parrot livened up at that and as soon as he saw the girls let out his best cat call whistle.

"Good job dude," I told my best bird and flipped him a small cashew. "We're gonna have some fun with this crowd methinks."

"Yeah boss!" Tiwaka said. "I love you boss!"

Before I could tell Tiwaka anything, one of the girls ran up to the bar, ahead of the others.

"Is this Tiwaka's?" she asked, slightly out of breath. Her long hair flowed around her tube top. She couldn't have been more than 20. "Tiwaka's Tiki Bar and Grill?"

I stood up tall, put my hand over lightly on the parrot's feathers and proudly said "Why yes. It is."

She turned immediately and yelled to her friends, only a few feet away now. "Hey guys! We found it!" Turning back to me she leaned up against the bar, flattening her tube top. "We have been searching for hours." Pushing her hair back off her forehead. "I am sooooo thirsty."

"Well, you have come to the right place!" If I had to guess I would say she couldn't be *that* thirsty, having already had a couple of drinks.

Four other beautiful girls came up to the bar, giggling and laughing and pulling their hair back in preparation for drinking. The guys, three of them, soon moved in with their friends. One of them leaned over and kissed Ms. Tube Top on the cheek, pushing her slightly into the bar again. My focus needed to move elsewhere so I went to get Tiwaka off his perch.

"Tiwaka, please say hello to our thirsty friends here," I looked over at them, to see if they were ready for a show. Tiwaka was already in character, puffing up his feathers and bobbing his head.

"Hey, is that a real parrot?" One of the girls asked, still behind her dark sunglasses.

"Kathy, you really have to get out more often," another answered.

"Of course, who do you think Tiwaka is?" The van driver added.

"No way!" Ms. Tube Top almost screamed. "You told us it was all a myth Ranger!"

"Well, I wasn't sure until we got here actually."

I let Tiwaka down to the bar so he could demonstrate his infinite realness, prancing up and down the bar to the oohs and aahs of the girls.

"What can I get you guys? Beer, wine, Mai Tai, or our in-house concoction a Coco Loco Moco?" I asked, already guessing three beers and five wines.

The three guys quickly huddled, counting their money probably for a moment. The van driver came up to me at the end of the bar.

"How much is everything here?" he asked quietly. "We've been on the road for a week now."

I appreciated a budget as much as the next guy, having avoided them all my life. "No worries dude. First round is on me. After that use this..." I said, sliding a drink list to him discreetly.

He stood up, surprised and smiling. "Wow. Thanks man."

"Where are you guys from?"

"Honolulu. We all work for the airlines, so we are able to get out and party on all the islands every chance we get. We just came out of Hana and fly back tonight." He kept glancing over at one of the girls, who I noticed was returning the favor. Her yellow headband was striking against her black hair, tan complexion and green eyes.

"Hey Ranger," she cooed. "Come on over here and tell me that story about the fire dance again."

"Ranger?" I had to ask.

He laughed and gave his friend the one moment finger. "Yeah, just a nickname I guess. I organize all these outings, so it's Ranger."

A tan arm snaked its way around his chest as a head full of black shiny hair leaned into his neck from behind. "Ranger Ev is our exalted leader and party master," the girl whispered loudly, removing her yellow head band. She put it over Ranger's head. "Without him, we wouldn't be having any fun at all." Her hands were now up under his aloha shirt.

"Let's have seven of those Coco Loco things then," Ranger said, fighting distraction. The head band was now around his neck and being pulled back to the girls barstool.

I quickly looked under the bar and found only three coconuts. We needed more.

"Hey Ranger, I need your help getting some more cocos." I waved him over, grabbed my machete and walked out from around the bar. "Tiwaka, keep an eye on these guys will ya?"

"I love you boss!" Tiwaka announced as loud as I think I have ever heard him.

"He talks!" Ms. Tube Top yelled a little too loudly. "And his feathers are soooo soft and sexy."

I watched her stroking Tiwaka's feathers and making over him like a big teddy bear.

"I love you boss too much!" Tiwaka said again, as all the girls laughed.

Ranger Ev quickly joined me, as well as his yellow head band fan and another girl.

"Great, everyone can carry back two cocos and we'll have plenty." I said, pleased to be leaving the wheelbarrow in the shed.

The other girl had her digital camera out and was taking pictures of everything as we headed out to the coco patch. Several pheasants quickly crossed our path, getting their picture taken as well.

"How long has this bar been around?" The photographer asked, still taking pictures.

I thought about that for a moment. It had certainly been here before I was born, and no doubt some time before that. And then there were the previous version of the bar that had been in Lahaina and before that, Waikiki. I didn't know what to say, so I just went with the first thing that came to mind. "Longer than any of us have been around." It was difficult for most people to think about how the world must have been before them, and so it was impressive to some extent. Funny though, we didn't apply that to people usually. Just places and things.

We soon got to the patch of cocos that I could reach without much effort. My machete came up as I went to cut the first bunch, but the yellow head band girl asked me to wait.

"Can we get a picture of me climbing up to get the coconut? That would make such a good shot."

"Sure, that sounds pretty cool," I said.

"You know," Ranger Ev said. "Originally, coconut pickers had to climb the trees naked, to show their bravery."

I had never heard that, but waited to see what would happen.

"Really?" Yellow head band girl asked.

I think she was considering it.

"Yep, I read about it somewhere." Ranger Ev continued. "Look, we'll get the camera down low here," he said directing the photographer to lay on her back on the ground. "If you put one foot here," he said doing it himself. "And, hold the tree like this," his hands went up to the trunk. "Then we can shoot it tastefully. You know, no da kine, just your legs and back."

"I dunno. Naked?" She was already taking off her shirt. "Are you sure its OK?" Her slippers were off and her dress slid off moments later. It didn't take but about three seconds for that transition.

"Yes, I am sure this will make a great picture. Something you will look at when your 80 and smile. Hell, I'm smiling already!" Ranger Ev was helping her position on the tree just right.

"OK, are we keeping things...private?" he asked the photographer.

"Yes, yes. Swivel her hips slightly to the right. Good, just skin."

"OK, now reach up, stretch and put your fingers on that coconut," he took her hand and placed it on the lowest coco.

I could hear the camera taking multiple shots. Ranger Ev directed it well, and after a minute of so, helped her down. She gave him a big hug before turning to hug the photographer, who gave her back her clothes.

"How did it turn out, let me see."

Still holding her clothes in one hand she watched the digital images rotate through the camera display. "Wait, I can see my ching ching a little there....delete that one!"

The photographer looked at it. "Oops. Yep, deleted."

"This one! This one is perfect!" Yellow head band girl exclaimed, jumping up and down, her dress still in her hand.

"Put on your clothes now," the photographer whispered.

Ranger Ev took the camera and agreed. "Classic tropical beauty, on a tree!"

I had to look as well, and despite what I thought was going to be somewhat pornographic, it was discrete and very well done. Her body was exquisite, and stretched and turned as it was it was easily just a PG rating.

"Let's cut some cocos then!" I said, still a little giddy from being at my first nude model shoot. In a moment everyone had two coconuts in hand and back we went to the bar.

Of course the two girls were holding theirs up to their chest and modeling them. The hoots from their friends at the bar only encouraged more sashaying of their hips and tossing of hair.

I knew just the song for the moment and reached into my pocket for the iPod remote. Dialing it up to song #269 and pushing the volume a couple of notches I watched everyone get up and start to dance. Barstools and coconuts hit the ground.

"Tahiti, Tahiti" by Voyage was just what the doctor, or in this case the bartender, ordered when you had some energy to burn. It was lively, happy and would give me time to make the drinks. My machete got busy and opened seven cocos. I grabbed a bucket of ice and began my task. I kept glancing up at these guys all dancing wild and crazy in the grass, at 11 in the morning, and wondered how much fun that would be. Carefree, on adventure and with a lust for life and each other that broadcast to the world: "We are young!"

Not long after, the guys lost their shirts and the hips were humping. And they hadn't had a Coco Loco Moco yet? This was one wild bunch!

Marciana showed up a little early and jumped in to help me with the order. "Who are these guys?" she asked, incredulous as I was.

"I don't know, Honolulu folks. They sure know how to have a good time don't they?" I thought to myself, what fun it would be to party like this on every island, to travel and party and fly for free. It seemed like a different world.

The song finally ended and something a little less demanding began, letting the sweat soaked dancers move back to the bar. Picking up their barstools and laughing I couldn't help but smile.

"I'm even more thirsty now!" Ms. Tube Top announced.

"Here ya go then!" I said. "The first Coco Loco Moco is yours."

"Yeah baby!" She took it and immediately got the straw in her mouth. I could see her drinking it quickly.

I wanted to warn her that it was strong, but fought the urge to say anything that mundane. She drank heartily and then sat back on her barstool.

"Oh my god!" Her head went back, most of her hair, not sticking to her shoulders and chest, fell back. "That is the BEST drink I have ever had!" She was soaking wet from dancing in the humidity, her tube top changing to a darker color. Pulling some ice from her drink she ran it up her neck and along her chin before letting it fall into the canyon.

"Oh my god!" I thought and moved to grab the next Coco. I handed them out quickly, and for a moment they were all quiet. Marciana went back to the kitchen to make pupus.

Tiwaka whistled in awe. I don't think I had ever made seven Coco Loco Mocos at once. He waited, like a good parrot. Living in a bar gave one a magnificent intuition as to when to interrupt or not.

Ms. Tube Top and Yellow Head Band girl finished first, their faces glowing with the alcohol.

"We better have another," Ms Tube Top said, turning to her friends. "But, if we do, we gotta camp out here."

"What about our flight?" one of the guys reminded.

"Damn, I forgot about that." Turning to me Ms. Tube Top asked "What is in that drink that makes me want to move to Maui?"

I smiled. Success. That was exactly what the Coco Loco Moco was meant to do. "You'll have to ask the parrot."

Tiwaka hearing "parrot" knew we were talking about him. He jumped off his perch again, down to the bar and quickly put his head back while spreading his wings to full glory. He had learned a new trick recently, where he could flutter his wings while they were fully extended.

"My my! You are not afraid of showing your stuff are you?" Yellow Head Band girl exclaimed. "I can do that too!" She stepped back off her barstool, pulled her shirt up and over her head and threw her arms out to the side.

"Ha! Me too!" Ms. Tube Top pulled hers down and threw her arms as wide as she could.

Tiwaka didn't know what to do. These crazy humans were mimicking him, and without feathers no less! He started to squawk, loudly, still holding his wings out. That only got the girls to screaming and the guys to hooting. Now everyone had their shirts off and their arms out, doing the "Tiwaka".

What could I do? I turned up the music.

~~~

Sandy showed up later that afternoon and found seven very tired and half drunk new faces lounging out in the grass. They had towels or hats covering their sleeping faces and rays of sunshine keeping them warm. Marciana and I shooed off a few mynah birds, but other than that they all slept undisturbed for quite a while.

A kiss and a question. "Who are those characters?" Sandy asked causally, putting away the limes and lemons she had picked up at the fruit stand. She smelled delightfully like citrus.

"Tourists, from Honolulu" I told her. "I think they have been pushing the envelope for a week or so. Looks like my Coco Loco Moco took them down."

Marciana was helping me clean glasses and snickered a bit. "Kids these days! Full speed and then full stop." She shook her head a little, then added, "I sure miss that."

"Yeah, you should have seen it! Tiwaka got Tiwaka'd. He spread his wings out and started that new fluttering thing...and they all did the same thing right back."

"Topless, no less!" Marciana added.

Sandy turned to look at the sleeping partiers again. "Those girls?"

I looked out to the lawn again. There was Ms. Tube Top on her back, tube top doing its job. Yellow Head Band girl's head was propped against the photographer girl's hip. The lighting was quite complimentary, or they were all actually bikini models, I wasn't sure.

"Yep," I said. Moving between Marciana and Sandy, so Marciana couldn't see, I pulled Sandy to me snuggly and whispered. "I think yours are actually getting bigger! Is that from the baby?"

Sandy smiled, but knew what I was up to. "Sure, now you say that." She pushed me away playfully and turned around. I could have sworn she wiggled a little at me.

Now, I must add here that I have missed many an obvious clue in my life, but having missed so many I have gotten better at recognizing them. I looked around, the bar was deserted, except for the sleeping Honoluluans. Marciana was quite capable of running the place. And, I had a great idea!

Slapping Sandy on the butt as she tried to run away, I challenged her. "Race you to the hammock!"

~~~

Later that evening, when everyone was revived by either sleep or the magic hammock, I found myself making another seven Coco Loco Mocos. Tiwaka was keeping a close eye on me, and the Honoluluans. I knew one thing, he wouldn't be showing off his magnificence tonight, at least not to them.

The bar was particularly busy, what with a nearly full moon and perfect weather and something else. Something made me suspect that these *Live Life to the Fullest and Then Some* guys and gals from Honolulu had a special talent for attracting a party. Magnets to adventure I guess.

Ranger Ev finally broke away from the girls enamored with a surf story he was telling. It was hilarious to watch. One of the guys had to hold him from falling over as he stuck a surf pose without the benefit of momentum. He caught my eye as I watched him saunter over, fresh from a 40 foot free fall at Waimea, or something like that.

"Yo bartender dude! You rock!" He was pointing at me and grinning from thirty feet but I could hear him easily above the din of the bar.

"Thank you, thank you very much!" I managed to say in a pretty good Elvis imitation. I was a dozen mugs behind in keeping up with Marciana's orders and went immediately back to my suds and towel.

Tiwaka made his way over to where I was, sensing compliments and possibly something covered in milk chocolate. I always wondered if he knew that pure chocolate was actually bad for him. Our bar chocolate was more milk than cocoa, but I wasn't going to explain that to him.

"Tiwaka, right?" Ranger Ev asked of the bird. "You've got it made here at this bar don't you big guy?"

I looked up a moment to see Tiwaka getting his head feathers stroked gently. In his face, this big city Honolulu guy they called the Ranger I saw for a brief moment empathy that I had not expected. It might have been the Coco Loco Moco coloring his facade or the gentle colors of our own setting tropical sun, but I didn't think so.

"So," I asked him. "Are you guys having a good time?" I expected a "Sure!" or a "You betcha!" or something positive. But, when he answered, I put down my soapy mugs and dried my hands.

"I wish I could actually," he practically whispered, pulling himself up onto the barstool.

I looked around to see if I was missing some obvious bummer. His fellow partiers were all dancing in the grass, spilling drinks and flinging their hair far and wide. Ms. Tube Top was getting a lot of attention, but nothing seemed wrong with them. I scanned the bar quickly for something else that might be wrong, but saw only happy people talking and eating and several just watching the action themselves, feet tapping a rhythm we were all sharing.

Finally, I turned my attention fully to the Ranger. His tanned, slightly sunburned face and curly blond hair, spilling across his face hid something. That something met his light smile and blue eyes with a familiarity, a hint of more years than he could possibly have lived.

"I don't get it Ranger, you guys seem to have the world by its tail." I tried not to sound jealous or condescending. They were free humans, doing what they wished. He was surrounded by beautiful women, handsome mates and a tradewind graced evening. What could possibly be wrong?

He shook his head a little. "Ah, you've got a fine place here sir." His hands moved gracefully over to Tiwaka again. "And, a magical bird."

Tiwaka cooed for the first time in years, I had forgotten he could.

I didn't want to psychoanalyze this early in the evening, so I let it play out as he might let it. Tiwaka always came in handy in situations like this, so I pulled out the coconut bowl of chocolate covered cashews.

"Here ya go Ranger. Tiwaka will talk to you about anything. Give him one of these chocolates and ask a question."

Ranger looked up at me like I was kidding. "Seriously, he has solved many a problem." Usually he solved the problem of too many chocolate covered cashews accumulating in the bar, but he had been known to do other amazing things.

"OK, I'll give him a try," Ranger picked out an especially large cashew, the chocolate flowing around it like a frozen waterfall.

Seeing this the parrot moved over in front of his new best friend and leaned his head forward, apparently to hear the question before it was spoken. If he could indeed do that, it must have been to get a jump on a clever answer. I would probably never know.

Ranger Ev turned to look at the Honoluluans out in the yard, still dancing, this time to something from the Castaways. He spun around slowly and looked at Tiwaka closely, head on his hands. "Tiwaka, answer me this: how far can a traveler travel?"

Now that was a perfect question for my feathered co-worker. Almost any random answer would fit. Leaning back against the vodka rack I watched as Tiwaka wound himself up.

First the wings spread out slowly, to a full two feet. Next his foot stomp began, and at this Ranger sat back a little.

"Don't worry, he won't explode!" I crossed my arms like a proud father.

Tiwaka was weaving now, stomping left a step and then back, then again to the right. His wings began that fluttering he had just learned and as he tilted his head back. I plugged my ears.

Ranger Ev looked at me with a big question in his eyes just as Tiwaka let out his signature squawk, some 120+ decibels. I laughed out loud, fingers sticking in my ears watching Ranger fall off the stool in surprise.

From out in the yard, all the Honoluluans looked over and immediately began imitating Tiwaka, as best they could. Like a viral YouTube video the entire bar then began squawking and hooting. Tiwaka couldn't be outdone! He threw his head back and let out a new record squawk, making the vodka bottles sing behind me. I wasn't prepared for that one and got a good dose of ringing in my ears.

Tiwaka and Ranger both looked around at the entire bar, now in full squawking mode. Marciana was parked in a chair laughing hilariously, Ma and Pa came rushing down from the treehouse alarmed and finally Sandy showed up. Her eyebrows were arched like a double rainbow above two pools of beauty.

"What is going on?" She nudged me, as she moved behind me at the bar. "It sounds like a parrot riot!"

"Oh yeah, it's a riot of parrots alright!" I echoed.

Ma and Pa surveyed the craziness and assured it was only bar-related silliness went back to the treehouse.

The Honoluluians finally fell over laughing themselves, unable to keep up the squawking. Ranger Ev climbed back up on his stool. Tiwaka turned to look at me briefly before calming down. He walked a little closer to Ranger, wings tucked in close now and quiet.

"You might need to repeat the question..." I tried to say before Tiwaka interrupted me.

"To the end." Tiwaka said, confident enough in his answer to take his chocolate covered cashew and leap back up to his perch among the vodka bottles.

Ranger Ev looked a little baffled, shaking his head a bit. "How far can a traveler travel?" he repeated to himself quietly.

"To the end, I think he said." I repeated for my parrot.

Ranger looked up at the bird, some appreciation in his eyes. "To the end. Good on ya Tiwaka. To the end. Of course."

Marciana came up with an order for five Crazy Geckos, three Hinano beers and two Mai Tai, save the mint. My focus was pleasantly diverted from the Ranger a moment as I mixed and retrieved her order. Filling orders gave me a moment to think, to gather my inputs if you will, as I robotically grabbed beers and glasses.

I needed a moment as well to think about Tiwaka's clever answer. There was always something valuable in those cryptic answers and I had found many an interesting twist on reality following them.

Sitting out two trays for Marciana, complete with her entire order and some bowls of nuts as well I turned back to the Ranger.

"So, what's with the long face there?"

The Ranger nodded his head a little, as if answering some silent question he had posed to himself. But, he looked up and smiled. "Well, look. We like to party, you can see that. But, what I really love more is the travel, seeing new places, cool places like your Tiwaka's Tiki Bar & Grill."

"Well, thanks! You guys are great customers." They were fun and had run up quite a bill as well. It would pay for the new refrigerator!

He glanced back at his group, still dancing. "We thrive on seeing other slices of reality. You know, seeing how other people make the most of this life, you know, here," he pointed to the counter.

"Maui?" I asked.

"No, no. Not Hawaii either. But everywhere, Earth. Not in a cosmic sense so much as in a human sense. It is fascinating to the point of addiction, this travel bug I have, that we have." He waved his arm back toward the dancers.

"The world is so frickin rich with coolness, with places we have never imagined, and when we stumble onto yet another one, we drink it up. So to speak."

"Well, you guys have been drinking it up alright, and I thank you for that!" I beamed.

He smiled broadly. "Yeah, we have a bit of a habit of doing that. It kind of helps us integrate into the scene a little easier. Otherwise, we might seem like documentary-film types or anthropologists."

That somehow made me look up at Ms. Tube Top. As she spun and bounced on her bare feet I had difficulty making the anthropologist connection. She was holding onto Kimo, one of our musicians as they both moved to the deepness of a Tiki Jazz beat.

"Anthropologists? I don't get it Ranger." I shook the confusion from my head a little. I never felt shy about admitting I didn't understand what the hell someone was talking about. You learn that in a bar.

"Well, it's like this my bartender friend. We aren't here just to get liquored up and act silly. All of us, me especially, thrive on being somewhere different, with different people we meet. We study people because we find it fun, engrossing.

"Look, here," he spread his arms out to encompass the bar. "Your slice of reality here, separate from mine back on Oahu, is wonderful! I would never have had the chance to experience this if I didn't travel here to this little point of jungle on a neighboring island. My reality is enhanced by yours, and I thank you!"

"Well, that deserves a free drink," I said, sliding a frosty Hinano to him. Sandy slid up behind me after finishing some fried marlin pupus in the kitchen. Her arms wrapped around me from behind and her cheek leaned against my shoulder.

"Thanks. Our, or rather my problem with all of this is pretty simple." He took a long drink of the cold Tahitian lager and let the liquid move down gently before he continued. "The bummer is that despite our constant drive to see more of the world, we are beginning to feel the pull of making our place in the world. Of no longer just observing other people, but of being a part of a place.

"Every time I return home, to a wonderful little beach shack, I find myself thinking about when the next trip is." He took another drink of the Hinano, almost finishing it. "Except lately. Lately, I wonder if maybe instead of simply seeing what the world is like, maybe I should stay where I am."

Sandy was listening intently, quiet in her intense observation. She squeezed my hand a little and asked him, "What are you afraid of?"

I thought she might qualify that question a little, to give him a polite way to answer, but she left it open.

The Ranger shook his head a little, while looking down at his bare feet propped on the bottom rung. After a rather long pause, he looked up at both of us, Sandy first, then me, and answered. "I'm afraid," he paused a moment. "I'm afraid I will miss all of this," sweeping his arms through the air. "My infinitesimally small slice of reality, no matter how cool, never could offer the adventure we find on the road.

"Life is a big coconut creme pie, and my slice," he sounded a little sad, "is such a tiny slice."

Sandy squeezed my hand again, in a silent signal that she found something poignant, and I expect painfully true. She had traveled with the pro surfer crowd around the world, seen a good deal of the tropic oceans and no doubt missed parts of that life.

I felt a little of what they were feeling, and knew again the familiar loss inherent in life choices. My hands instinctively went to Sandy, reaching around her magical waist, now the home of another being. Kissing her lightly on the cheek I turned to look at Tiwaka, then back to the Ranger.

"You know," I said, thinking out loud. "Our little tiny slice, here on Maui, with Sandy, and Tiwaka and the bar..." I paused and looked around. Ma and Pa were back out, enjoying the small crowd and talking with some visiting friends. The musicians were on yet another break, and had found their way into the okolehau stash. Don Ho had rotated around again on the playlist somehow mixing in perfectly with the light warm breeze. A momentary whiff of plumeria flowers moved in for just a second, and then danced away again. "You know Ranger, that tiny slice will be so much richer..." I squeezed Sandy again, tightly. "...so much sweeter when you taste it every morning. When you see it in your sleep, smell it on your hands and drink it in deeply with your eyes closed."

~ ~ ~

A Hawaiian Wedding Song

The full moon was only three days away and the wedding preparations were, well, not done. To complicate things only a little people were arriving from far away places and had to be picked up, escorted or talked to on the phone. Not a bad problem of course, but more workload.

The Tiki crew from Facebook had all left from Salina Cruz, Mexico on some kind of a tramp steamer and had spent almost a week making their way to Maui's northern harbor.

Tiki Chris Pinto had managed to get a satellite text message out two days ago, but evidently had a limit on the number of characters he could transmit. All I got was: "2 days more. Rum, Rum, Rum."

I knew Sunshine Tiki and Brad Beach were with him and anxious to visit Tiwaka's after reading about it for months on Facebook. Our fan page had well over a few thousand thirsty, cold and far off customers still waiting on their first Coco Loco Moco.

Tramp steamers are not known for their predictable arrivals and so it was 2 in the rainy morning when I got the call from the police station in Paia. It was Officer Ka'ahuamanu, on old Kula High classmate.

"Sorry to call so early, but I've three suspicious characters here claiming to know you. Found them walking through the cane fields near the harbor, said they were headed for Tiwaka's Tiki Bar and Grill."

I had to try two or three times before I figured out I was awake and actually talking to someone. Finally, I muttered something. "Hey Creighton, what did you say? Three whats?"

"Bruddha, three *friends* of yours. Had to pick them up before they hurt themselves in the dark. You know anyone that calls themselves Tiki Chris, or Sunshine? Oh, and a Mr. Beach?"

I laughed myself awake at that. "Sure! I know those characters. I'll be right down. Mahalo!"

"Good," Officer Ka'ahumanu said. "You might keep the bar open, these guys look real thirsty."

~~~

Sandy had a plane load of relatives and friends coming up from Papeete and Mo'orea. The flight from Tahiti only held 302 passengers and 250 of them knew Sandy and her family. Smaller planes from Kauai and Oahu brought in more of her extended crew. Every bed and breakfast on our side of the island was speaking French, Tahitian or excited English.

Most of my connections were on Maui, but some came from Molokai. Ma and Pa had friends that were riding the ferry from Lanai as well. Fortunately, it was slow season at the hotels and there were plenty of rooms. As much as I wanted to host everyone close by, most people honestly wanted to stay at the beaches. Jungle sea cliffs weren't for everyone.

There was a lot to do to get ready, yet the bar was still open. Mornings were productive, but by noon, the tops of the bar stools were all being warmed up. All the early arrivals for the wedding filled the place for breakfast, lunch and stayed for dinner. Marciana brought in a new helper who looked disarmingly familiar. I just couldn't figure out how I might know her. I probably didn't but she had to at least be related to someone I knew. Anyhow, we needed the help and Wailani worked like she already knew the place. Thank goodness!

The three 'boat people' were lined up at the bar, faithfully soaking it all up. They had taken up residence in a large bamboo A-frame in the next valley, unpacked from their arduous journey across the sea and already been to the waterfalls to refresh.

Tiki Chris Pinto, slightly hidden behind a light brown Panama hat was still shaking his head at their 'little boat ride' as he had put it.

"I don't think we told you this, especially not in front of Officer whatever his name was." He looked up at his compatriots and then down at the tall Mai Tai in lead crystal sweating nicely on the bar. "We had to damn near mutiny to get off that Tramp in Maui." He pushed back the panama with the tops of his fingers and looked at me briefly. "Captain said he was going to Singapore first!" Tiki Chris chased that thought back with a full taste of what was to be the first of many. "Can't go to Singapore. I'm a wanted man in that god-awful port."

A couple of young exotic dancers, friends of someone from California, were already hovering over his broad shoulders. These women seemed drawn like bees to his black Hawaiian print shirt with green and gold flowers, accented nicely under an impeccably white suit.

"Mr. T.C." one of the girls cooed. "I could use a dance honey." Her hands played with his arm.

"Baby!" he turned and lightly scolded the blonde beauty. "Please don't touch my drinking arm." Looking up at me with a broad smile he added, "Spilling but one drop would be a crime against all that is natural and exotic." Slapping her on her hibiscus decorated bottom he told her to go warm up without him. "Dames! What you gonna do?"

I couldn't answer that, not having any idea whatsoever, so I nodded like any good bartender might.

Sunshine Tiki turned to watch the two girls run out to the middle of the dance, swinging their hips in perfect time. Glancing over at Tiki Chris I noticed him frowning a little. He looked over at Tiwaka and hunched his shoulders. "Look at that choreography Tiwaka!" Sunshine exclaimed. "Have you ever seen such glorious timing?"

Spinning around on his stool, and now getting our attention as well, we all watched the girls move in intoxicating interpretations of the deep jungle beat. I had to admit, I had never seen a hibiscus move that way. They had a grace and fitness only professional dancers could possibly possess. Tiki Chris seemed to enjoy the show from afar, nodding his head slightly as both of them looked over to him.

"You see gentlemen," he said while turning to retrieve his drink. "There is nothin' you can name that is anythin' like a dame."

Sunshine Tiki perked up at that. "I know that line…South Pacific, the musical I believe."

"Exactly, my sunlit friend. They know it, and I know it. It's all a play, right here on the stage of my imagination baby!"

This guy, I thought, had that something some guys just seem to inherit. Some genetic link to Frank Sinatra sitting in a dark Jazz Bar. It was an aura of power and mystery that was irresistible to many on the prettier side of humanity.

"Imagination!" Tiwaka squawked while sauntering down the bar with a little more wiggle in his tail feathers than usual. My favorite parrot had been on patrol for over an hour, checking out the guests at the bar one by one. This time he stopped in front of Brad Beach, another of the Tramp castaways.

Tiwaka may have been admiring Brad's bright orange camp shirt, or the cascading bird-of-paradise print flowing down either shoulder. I knew the bird was attracted to bright colors, but I knew it wasn't the artist in him. Tiwaka saw it as competition, something attempting to rival his own talents at bending sunlight into fabulous tones.

Brad got a hint of this and backed away a bit, setting his barstool to the side. He reached into his cargo shorts pulling out a handful of seashells.

"Here you go Tiwaka," he offered. "Please accept this most colorful cowrie shell as a token." Brad moved back to his barstool as Tiwaka focused on the iridescent reflections. "A token of my," he turned and looked at the other castaways, "at our appreciation for your hospitality."

I watched to see if he might try and crack the shell, thinking it was something to eat, but he didn't. He pushed it along the bar like a toy, round and round.

"Here, let's try this..." Brad said, reaching into another deep cargo pocket. He pulled out a small amount of leather string.

"Tiwaka, may I?" He reached over to the cowrie shell and gently took it into his hands, with the parrot watching him very closely. Threading the thin leather through a hole already drilled he pushed the shell to the center of the three or four inch length.

"May I?"

"Sure, if you can get him to go for it." I answered, moving in a little closer in case I had to pull a beak off a finger.

"Here, Tiwaka," Brad offered moving slowly. "This will surely attract all birds and chicks, as it were, to your magnificence!" Brad had the necklace up and around Tiwaka's neck so quickly that the bird had no time to complain. With a quick twist and a tie, it hung perfectly against his chest.

The drums in the music were really thumping now and while expecting Tiwaka to try and remove the adornment, he simply began tapping his feet to the beat.

Brad sat back to admire his work. "Perfect Tiwaka. It fits you well."

Tiwaka bent his head down to check it out, fluffed his wings a bit and squawked loudly, and I assume proudly. Suddenly, he leapt up onto Brad's right shoulder, nearly knocking off Tiki Chris' panama.

"Well, well, you must like it eh?" Brad asked.

"Mahalo. Mahalo plenty." Tiwaka whispered and then proceeded to preen Brad's sun-bleached blond hair.

I mixed up another Mojito for Mr. Beach and slid it over. "It looks like you've made a new friend Brad." Tiwaka continued to rummage around in the blond hair.

This was beyond amusing to everyone at the bar and the cat-calls began. "What's that bird looking for?" "The chocolates are under the counter!" "Hope he doesn't find anything to eat..."

Brad was laughing out loud just as I saw a hand move through his hair from behind. The brightly adorned finger nails hinted at an exoticness that was soon followed in fact.

"So, Brad, who is this in your hair?" She said leaning in close to kiss his ear.

I tried not to stare, but lost. Tiki Chris was whistling a low appreciation and Sunshine Tiki was admiring what a bronze tan can do for a sheer, brightly colored beach dress.

"Oh, that's just a happy parrot honey," Brad said, turning into her and a full hug and what looked like a kiss From Here to Eternity. At least it seemed to last that long.

Breaking away, I freshened everyone's drinks. Tiwaka had moved back down the bar toward a group of beer drinkers, wings in full spread. His shell necklace was eliciting comments all the way across the bar.

After a moment Brad came up for air to introduce us. "Guys, this is my lovely Latin wife Loli. Loli, this is Tiki Chris and Sunshine Tiki," tipping his Mojito to his right and then left. "And, this of course," pointing to me, "is the groom!"

I nodded and smiled and wondered just how many extraordinarily beautiful women God had made. Apparently, quite a few.

"How was your flight baby?" Brad asked turning back to Loli.

"Long and hard for ten hours!" Pulling him to his feet, she demanded. "Come, dance with me!" She was pulling him by his belt, as he reached into yet another deep cargo pants pocket and pulled out what appeared to be a huge shark tooth necklace.

Tiki Chris immediately got up and started toward his two hibiscus ladies. Seeing him finally pay them some real attention they ran over, each grabbing a hand and soon blended into the seething mass of music, color and bodies.

"OMG and WTF!" Sunshine Tiki proclaimed. "What's a guy gotta do around here to get a dance?"

It took me a brief moment to remember what those acronyms meant which allowed him quite enough time to grab the conch shell and leap up onto the bar. At least he was barefoot, which was the official requirement for dancing on the bar. He tilted back his head, put the conch shell up to his lips and with some surprising amount of expertise blew a few opening notes from Charge of the Light Brigade.

It was difficult to outplay the drums and the music but he did an excellent job of interjecting the conch right into the flow of sound. Looking over to me briefly I gave him a two thumbs up and he threw his head back again, almost like Tiwaka would, and blew a long steady tone. His classic green tapa patterned bark cloth shirt and khaki cargo shorts shimmered under an oversized puka shell necklace. People were now taking his picture and pointing. He was indeed a sight, one that was irresistible to quite a few admirers now, grabbing at his bare feet.

"Come dance with us Conch Man!" they shouted, guy and gal alike. One more rendition of the Charge and turning to toss me the conch he grinned and laughed out loud. Grabbing his Mai Tai, extra big garnish still afloat he literally leapt off the bar and into the carpet of grass, almost falling but was caught by ten pairs of hands. He never spilled a drop, God bless him.

The music was almost deafening now. The intensity would have been too much if not for the perfect compliment of all the dancers out in the grass. In fact, as I looked around it was only me missing. Marciana and Wailani were twisting and turning as well! Even Tiwaka was atop Brad Beach's head again, wings spread wide and head back in avian ecstasy.

I gathered up the *empty* glasses from the castaways, a point of pride to any bartender, threw my bar towel over the bamboo rack and ran out into the fresh air, full of the moment.

~~~

I dreamed of Coco that night. As I turned away from the growing moon in my window and pulled my covers with me I saw her. Walking on the beach, carrying her mumu over her arm. Her skin was that of the sea turtle but her face, and hair, were all Coco.

She walked toward me, in this dream, caution on her face. I didn't need to hear her tell me, but she was extremely concerned about something. I raised my eyebrows in silent question, what could it be?

The beach where we must have been was awash in waves, rushing up the steep slope and falling back almost as fast. I found myself having trouble standing as I sank into the wet and loose sand. Coco looked down at my feet. I did too and now saw my legs covered in the large pattern scales of the Honu. Looking back up to Coco in a state of confused happiness she looked back in horror. I could see her mouthing the word 'no' and shaking her head. Waving wildly with her hands she raised her voice to the sky and screamed 'NO!'

That woke me up immediately. The moon was almost high enough now to stay out of my window. I sat up and saw movement outside, but it was only a pueo flying low over the garden looking for mice. I tried to stretch a bit and took a good long drink out of my bedside water bottle. That felt better, for a moment.

If the spirits were going to visit me in my sleep, I figured, then I would try and invite some in that were more cheerful. I concentrated hard, as I let my head fall back to the pillows, on those happy little voices I had met in the hammock.

~~~

I didn't sleep long that next morning, getting up a little before sunrise. Climbing up into the lookout platform of the treehouse, I looked toward Unknowns for any sign of surf. Nothing, the horizon was dark and unbroken with any hint of swell or whitewater. I turned to check out the summit of Haleakala where the sun was already decorating her house. Glancing down toward the bar I thought I could see overturned chairs out in the grass. Several cars were still hiding silently under the coconut grove.

I looked back out to the distant Hana airport, where the beacon light was faithfully turning even if there wasn't a plane for hours. In the opposite direction the West Maui mountains were just now getting lit and in the far distance, Molokai kept to her shadows.

As I walked over to descend the ladder I glanced again at something catching my eye out to sea. There, just to top off the perfect morning view was a thin line of whitewater rolling in at Unknowns. It must have been pretty small, but it was there! Longboards were the call I thought as I suddenly felt awake, calculating how much time I might surf before bar and wedding chores captured me.

As I made my way down to the second floor and finally to the bar level I heard some noise in the kitchen. Maybe a mongoose I thought, as I slowly made my way to investigate, a convenient if under used broom in hand. Of course, few mongoose could turn on a light or make the sweet smells of fresh coffee, so I relaxed a little. Still I made my way silently into the kitchen just as she turned and screamed.

At least it was only a small *I'm scared but not going to feint* scream. It was enough though to make me bring the broom up as a shield, my Shield of Straw.

"Wailani! Sorry, I was just..." my words came to a halt as I saw her eyes suddenly widen and water up, looking exactly like Coco's had on a few occasions. It was certainly early, and I was just only awake but it looked like she had the sea turtle eyes like Coco.

"Oh, it's you!" She quickly looked down, to hide herself then thoughtfully turned back to the sink. Her hands came up to her face for a moment, rubbing. "You startled me," she said softly, still looking away.

I had to work hard at finding my composure enough to answer. "I thought there was...a mongoose." I was stuttering for a comfortable word. "A mongoose, you know, in the kitchen." I glanced down as well, in some subconscious effort to give her a chance to change.   To change...her eyes back.

"Wailani," I attempted to speak, but my voice was breaking a little. I cleared my throat, but my voice still shivered. "Wailani, are you...did you know...Coco?" I swallowed hard and tried again. "Did you know Coco?"

She didn't look up. She didn't say anything. I noticed her hands wringing a dish towel over and over, in nervousness. She looked so young, maybe it was just so vulnerable, but as I stared at her from the side I began to see something familiar in her again. I couldn't quite place it entirely, but her hair was one thing for sure. It was that long black fullness, shiny black hair all the way down to her waist. The kind of hair that looked even better in the ocean where each strand could swim alone. Alone, but with the millions of others, reflecting the tropical sunlight like wet jade.

Finally, after what was probably becoming a very awkward moment, I turned to leave.

"You startled me," she whispered as I made for the door.

Turning back to apologize I saw her watching me and recognized then who she was. Who she reminded me of, who she must surely be. Her eyes were still a little watery, but normal now. Yet, there seemed to be a depth to them that spoke of a shy wisdom, of a modest omniscience.

My heart was racing now, and for a brief moment I tried to check my emotions with the hammer of logic. I must be tired I offered myself, or still dreaming, or having a bout of the predawn crazies. My imagination had been allowed to run amok for so long that it might now be taking me on another Alice in Wonderland spin.

I found myself staring at my feet as she softly asked "Are you OK?"

Looking back up to her youthfulness, to her bright eyes and smile I felt myself almost cry in utter relief. It was her, it had to be. She had returned from the sea. Somehow. She was here, right in front of me. Younger, but her.

My mouth could barely pronounce her name. "Coco?"

She moved a few steps toward me, smiling. Her eyes briefly nodded, but returned to me. "Wailani," she whispered, but with some music in her voice.

I was still frozen in my steps as she came even closer. My eyes were tearing up in happiness. I couldn't look at her, even as she came up to hug me.

"Thank you," I said into her ear now as she embraced me. "Thank you so much." I couldn't help but sob but caught myself at just one. "You saved Sandy, and...our baby...I was so worried about you."

"It's a wonderful life you have." Her body felt as warm as the mid day beach. "Now you can share it," she squeezed me a bit, took a step back and held onto my hands.

My eyes blinked away enough for me to see again. She smiled and waited for me to gather myself together. It took a moment, but I cowboy'd up as best I could.

"Tiwaka sent the birds to find me you know." She gripped my hands tightly.

"Tiwaka?" I asked, not really understanding. Then I remembered his gathering of the jungle birds and the song he sang to them.

"Your friend Tiwaka is a special, special creature. So much love with him." She let my hands lower and lightened her hold.

Her eyebrow went up in question as she emphasized her name. "Wailani?"

I knew what she required of course, and repeated it. "Wailani."

"Wailani," she nodded and let me hands gently go. "The surf is small today, go and have some fun." Turning away from me to return to the sink I felt her allowing me a graceful exit.

I stared at her for just a moment longer.

~~~

Throughout my life, when I had to figure something out, of a vast and mystical nature, I found surfing a conduit for solutions. Something about being in the ocean, the playful sea clear and warm reflecting a blue sky, did wonders for problem solving. And, a problem solved did wonders for your mind.

Sometimes just getting to the water could be therapeutic. Maui, like all the Hawaiian islands surrounded its surf spots with unparalleled beauty. Unknowns, nestled in an almost hidden cove, down a wild banana plantation lined dirt path, had one of the finer entries.

I had left the kitchen and Wailani only minutes ago when I found my favorite 9 foot long board tucked under the deck of the bar. It had been quite some time since it had tasted the salt. Dusted heavily with red dirt, gecko droppings and other unsavory textures it would require a baptism at the shoreline. My secret stash of coconut scented Sex-Wax became one bar less and finding a relatively clean towel hanging on the railing I turned to make my way down the path.

Just as I my toes made their first foray into the soft wet mud of the path, my nose picked up the sweetness of plumeria and my mind began its drift into daydream.

Then, I heard my name shouted. At first I honestly wondered if it was real, until I caught the accent.

"Yo bro! Wait up!"

I turned to look back up the path. Waving wildly and unsuccessfully avoiding a patch of overripe fallen guavas were Yo Vinny and Paden, carrying long boards as well.

"Howzit!" I half heartedly called back. My problem solving would have to wait I supposed. Distraction, I knew well, was the bad mistress of progress.

"Can we get a ticket to ride dude?" Paden asked. Everyone knew Unknowns was a so-called secret spot and it was impolite to just show up. I stopped walking and turned toward both of them, setting my board down on its tail and letting it balance against my shoulder.

"OK, sure." Their big grins made me feel a little more gregarious than I might have.

They walked up to me like a couple of little kids getting invited to Grandma's Cookie Bake Off, totally stoked to have lucked into such fortune. Standing tall and backs straight, they knew the routine, boards under their left arms, right hand held up to swear secrecy.

"OK, repeat after me," I said.

"Right," Yo Vinny said.

Paden nodded, eager to get in the water.

"I Yo Vinny and Paden," the words sprang from my memory like a childhood rhyme.

"I Yo Vinny..." merged with "I Paden..."

"Double, triple swear super secret allegiance..."

"Double, triple swear super secret allegiance..." they repeated.

"To keep Unknowns true to its name, forever and ever," I added.

"To keep Unknowns true to its name, forever and ever," they faithfully said.

"Amen." I gave them that stern look that I figured helped a little.

"Amen dude," Yo Vinny echoed.

"Amen already, let's get wet!" Paden yelled pumping his fist into the air like Tiger Woods in the early days.

"Cool," I felt better now. A couple of good friends to catch some mellow longboard waves with would be better than trying to solve the problems of space and time, and turtle people.

We walked down to the where the banana patches began dominating the scenery before anyone talked.

"Hey, where's Sandy?" Yo Vinny asked.

My smile broadened at the mere mention of her name. In the brief instant before I answered, I thought about how lucky I was to be with her. "She is all sequestered with her Tahiti tribe in the next valley. Preparing and such."

"Nah! She got any cousins, sisters or … " Paden was asking.

"Geez Paden," Yo Vinny scolded. "You know I got first dibs on any Tahitian beauties. We drew straws!"

I looked at both of my friends in amazement. They drew straws?

"Yeah, well, there might be more than one you know," I had to tell them. The valley next to us was filled with dozens of gorgeous Tahitian cousins, aunties and a unrelated friends who could afford the plane tickets.

That stopped Yo Vinny in his tracks and Paden as well. They both hooted and threw high fives at each other, chanting "Yeah Baby!"

"Don't worry guys," I advised, looking over at two relatively good looking guys. "With your American accents and longboards, you'll be a hit for sure."

Both of them contemplated that for another few minutes as we approached the beach. The wind had held off nicely, which was critical for such small surf. I could see probably waist high waves rolling in slowly. The sun was picking up steam, cresting the southern cliffs and the water was clear enough to pretend it wasn't even there.

None of us talked. We had surfed perfect waves before, especially back in our Mokuleia days, and knew the routine. Words, exclamations, even the breath of amazement couldn't describe the feeling. Silent gratitude was the call, and we paddled out completely stoked, yet again, with our incredible opportunity to embrace the magnificence of the sea.

Yo Vinny was racing ahead of us to try and catch the first one. Paden and I kept pace behind, watching a small set line up off the left reef. He would probably catch the second wave, a sweet little shoulder high peeler.

I took a moment to look down into the clearness before focusing on the waves. There, ten feet down or so were the sea turtles, gliding ever so elegantly above the coral heads. One of them looked up. Instantly I felt Wailani's presence, Coco's legacy. It was funny, but at that moment, after so many years living here I finally figured it out. They, the sea turtles, the Honu were my 'amuakua, my protector of sorts. The Hawaiians had assigned deity to animals or places they felt were kind to them, that protected their families. Some worshiped their 'amuakua, but I didn't feel that need. Glancing down once more before I raced Paden for the next wave, I felt only a desire to thank them. Worship, for me, was better manifested in enjoying what nature was offering at the moment.

So, that in mind, I managed to catch the next wave. Paden lined up with the wave behind me and Yo Vinny was paddling back out to catch his next one. The scene was idyllic, to the point of being ridiculous. How could we have possibly managed to be in this perfect place with perfect little waves?

My wave held up just as I might have asked it to. Turn after smooth turn and I flowed along the glassy surface finally into the deep water, good friends hooting and hollering now. The tingles in my scalp were telling me, once again, that this was the apotheosis of existence.

I remember telling Ma once, back when she asked me why I didn't attend church services anymore, why I didn't feel the need. It was this, surfing. Nothing brought me closer. Closer, no, not closer, actually embedded within the very soul of it all. Church services, with their speeches and their stories were awesome no doubt. But, nothing approached actually dancing with God on the waves.

~~~

Three hours later, tired and thirsty and a little bit sunburned we decided to paddle in. It had been another of those classic surf sessions that we would remember decades later.

"Hey, who's that on the beach?" Yo Vinny asked as we made our way through the center of the bay toward the sand.

Looking closely at what must have been a dozen or so people I finally made out Sandy standing feet in the water, pointing at us. I had to laugh out loud.

"Hey guys! You're in for a treat." I looked over at both of them and their eyes were growing bigger, anticipation flooding their faces. "That's Sandy and her Tahitian crew."

Paden whistled low.

"Oh my god! Are you kidding?" Yo Vinny exclaimed.

I started paddling hard, in a race to get to Sandy. "You'll have to make your own introductions guys!"

Paden and Yo Vinny raced as well, not to be left behind. We were young, healthy men, and knew that if we paddled hard, we would be nice and pumped up for the ladies when we got there.

"Yo Vinny, I think we're outnumbered. I count ten honeys." Paden noted.

Yo Vinny was pulling hard through the water, but managed to console his friend. "No worries bro, I'll leave you one."

I made it in only a few seconds ahead of the guys, jumping up and giving Sandy a big wet hug. Even as I did, I could hear the excited voices of her crew.

"Hi baby!" Sandy whispered in my ear. "Missed you plenty!" She took a chance and pulled me real close. "I really missed you…"

Being the shy guy I sometimes was, I had to agree, but made an excuse to do introductions. But, first I had to make a date. "Hammock in an hour?"

She pinched my butt with a yes and turned to her crew. "Mesdames, ceci est mon fiancé!"

They all clapped, so I felt compelled to bow a little. Turning to the guys still standing in ankle deep water, boards under their arms and muscles flexed and dripping, I added, "And, here are my friends, Yo Vinny…" Yo Vinny raised his hand to the ladies.

"And, Paden."

"Mesdames!" Paden announced. "Merci, j'ai le plaisir de vous rencontrer."

Yo Vinny turned to Paden. "Where the hell did you learn French?"

Paden grinned and leaned over to Yo Vinny. "An old girl friend. Don't worry dude, I'll leave you one."

~~~

Sandy was a few moments late for her date, but the hammock and I were in no hurry. Cut mangos and bananas decorated a small bowl I had brought up from the kitchen. Two glass bottles of our own purified rain water sat on the same small table close by.

My feet were propped up comfortably already, hands behind my head. I watched Sandy running over from the surrounding jungle, down the little path through waist high groovy-grass. She was beaming! It was like a slow motion sequence as I turned toward her, something I would replay in my mind forever ~ as a dream come true.

In fact, as her long black hair literally shimmered in the sun and her cotton dress flowed behind I felt like some lucky observer who had found himself in just such a movie of dreams.

She was laughing lightly, throwing her head back a little and her arms out to her sides, waving like a happy little girl. Like a happy little boy I stood up, pushed back the hair from my face and grinned.

"Honey girl!" I said loudly, arms open now. She was running fast right at me, and I was glad to have my hammock, my safety net right behind me.

"Oh..." she grabbed me as we both fell back. Her kisses captured my mouth as we fit together from shoulders to toes. We were like a couple of Lego blocks - and we still had our clothes on!

"Too long..." I managed to breath between kisses.

"Oui, mon amour…" then she laughed right into my face, pulled back a couple of inches. "Yes, my love. Sorry, too much Français over in that valley."

She was laying on top of me and watching my eyes. I could feel them watching her right back, and I wondered if she could read my mind at this moment. Just in case she couldn't I decided to tell her.

"Sandy, you are the most beautiful creature I have ever, ever, and I mean *ever* seen!" It was true and not just because she had me pinned to the hammock either.

"Lucky you," she smiled and kissed me deeply again.

Funny, it was like when she kissed me it turned off all the world. All I could sense was her and the wind. Both were warm.

Suddenly she pulled back, looked at me and sat up.

"What honey?" I asked. She looked worried. I instinctively wanted to check for food stuck between my teeth.

"Tomorrow. We get married tomorrow. I just…"

Nervous I thought. "It's OK baby, no worries. Everyone gets nervous…"

Turning to me she smiled. "No, silly. I'm not nervous. I just don't know if your Aloha shirt is going to match my wedding dress."

She was serious. Well, if that was all there was to worry about, we were good to go. I was a bit mystified though.

"Don't Aloha shirts match everything?" Then I thought about someone I had seen in Waikiki. "Except maybe Aloha pants?"

Sandy stood up and went for the plate of mango and cut banana, her sun dress flirting with me and the breeze. The bright sun behind her made no bones about telling me everything else about her. I tried to focus back onto the conversation.

"Look," I offered. "I have a closet full of Aloha shirts. Why don't you go through and pick out the one that works best. I'll wear anything in there."

Turning to me with the plate, her fingers delicately picking up a cube of mango and moving it luxuriously up to her lips, she licked it first before letting her mouth engulf the sweet fruit. Focus was becoming difficult again.

"Well, you'll be wearing a Cook Island Maile lei," she said, thinking about the colors. "That is usually light green." She looked thoughtfully at me. "Do you have something with dark green, or red?" A slice of banana took the same path as the mango and I lost my thought train again. In cases like this I had learned a long time ago to just nod my head yes.

"Good," she said. "That's all I had to figure out." She walked over and sat back down on the hammock next to me, plate on her lap. "Did you want a piece?"

"Sure!" I laughed before she got the joke and slapped my shoulder playfully. "Mango would be fine," I admitted.

She looked down at the plate and picked out a nice succulent cube of what had to be the world's absolute best tasting fruit. Holding it up to my lips, she drew it back right before I opened my mouth.

"With this mango, I do thee wed. Tomorrow," she whispered lovingly. She watched me closely. I tried not to blink.

I opened up as she placed it in my mouth.

She went back to the plate and picked out a banana slice. "With this banana I place my trust, my heart, my unborn children with you my love, my friend. My man."

I nodded and smiled, enjoying the fruit and this special moment. This women, this beautiful loving woman was trusting me to love her. To help raise her children, our children. That was an incredible gig for sure. Since I still wasn't sure she could read my mind I had to tell her.

"I love you Sandy. Forever baby."

The last thing I remember before the world turned off all around me again, was the sound of the fruit bowl hitting the ground.

~~~

The morning of our wedding was a flurry of activity around the bar and the ceremony site out by the ocean cliffs. Vendors hired to cater the food, deliver and setup the flowers and décor and of course to play music were all showing up. Tables and chairs had been rented, a dance floor too, hanging lanterns and even more Tiki torches. Lawn furniture was showing up and I hoped it was waterproof, since we got a little rain every day.

Sandy had just shown up, having spent some time with her Mom in the valley next door. Her Tahitian friends were already all working hard at helping. Yo Vinny and Paden were doing a great job of assisting the Tahitians.

The castaways from the Tramp Steamer were sleeping in, no doubt to recharge for a full night of revelry. I had left them well entrenched at the bar around 10pm, surrounded by admiring ladies, and Tiwaka. My guess is that they had greeted the dawn.

I was finally able to get Ma off to herself at the bar for a question that had been on my mind since surprising Wailani. She went straight for the refrigerator and the glass ice tea container.

"Ma," I asked. "Remember last year, when I told you I almost drowned out at the bay, and how a turtle had helped me into the beach?"

She looked up at me with some degree of recognition, but I wasn't sure if it was based on having heard the story, or something else. "Yes, I remember." She moved her eyes back to the lime tray to cut slices.

"Well, remember when Sandy had that bad wipeout recently, how she almost..." I couldn't bare to even say the words.

"Yes, son. I remember that very well." She was watching me closely now, waiting on me to hit her with something she had been expecting for some time now.

I looked at her for a moment, and saw that she already knew. "Turtles saved us then," I glanced down at my hands. "Again."

Nothing was spoken now between us for what seemed like a long time. So, I had to tell her. "That's when Coco...when she went missing." Catching my breath, trying to keep my composure and continue was getting difficult.

Ma was looking at me. Looking at me with that depth of compassion, of love that only a mother can have.

"It was Coco that saved Sandy..." I lost it there, but after a few seconds managed to get my voice to behave. "Then, she disappeared...with the turtles."

"Yes," Ma replied softly.

I looked up at her. She did know something. So I kept going. "Now, Wailani...she...she seems to be a lot like Coco. A lot."

Ma poured me a tall glass of her famous southern ice tea, dropped a lime slice in and smiled. "Don't you remember Sunday school any?" she chided lightly.

I shrugged and smiled back. Not much, I thought.

She looked at me for a long moment, no doubt wondering how much goodness had flowed my way, and perhaps for what unknown but wonderful reasons. "Angels, son. Angels." Looking down at my untouched glass she added, "Now, have some ice tea."

Out in the yard a bit of a commotion broke the spell. I kissed Ma and walked to check it out.

Suddenly the Tahitian girls all ran up the driveway as I heard a small truck rearranging the gravel there. Last time I had seen anything like that happen was with an ice cream truck in a hot Lahaina neighborhood.

The brightly painted Sprinter van pulled around the corner, announcing to all the world that our florist had arrived. A young handsome man was driving and pulled up under the plumeria trees. Another darker haired young man jumped out of the passenger seat and immediately went back to open the sliding door.

There an absolutely gorgeous brown hair girl, about 14 or so, climbed down and behind her the famous Della of Dellables Wedding Design and Florals. She was an elegantly approachable Sicilian woman with a big smile already on her face. The three young people with her must have been her kids. A thought flashed across my mind briefly...their Dad must have been a real looker too.

It seemed a little strange to hire a florist when we were surrounded by flowers here in the jungle. At least to me, but not to Sandy and certainly not to Ma & Pa. They had insisted on Dellables, claiming her to be a genius, a Picasso. But, it was especially due to a 5 star rating from Tami Redes Roberts.

"Tami Redes Roberts?" I had to ask. I know I didn't get out much, so I was used to asking for clarification on most of what the rest of the world evidently was quite familiar with.

"Yes, silly jungle boy!" Sandy laughed. "Consultant to the Stars ring a bell?"

"Well..." I paused, feeling like a guess would make me look worse. "No, not really."

"Son," Ma said, shaking her head a little. "Son, you really do need to go to the mainland at least once a decade!" Ma teased me knowing it had been about that long. "Tami Redes Roberts is like the most influential reviewer on the West Coast of all things Beautiful and Elegant."

"I think that's her logo isn't it?" Sandy asked. "All Things Beautiful and Elegant?"

Ma nodded. "She recommended Dellables on her website and her cable show. She even featured Dellables on her magazine cover a few months ago. Top notch."

"She's the best honey!" Sandy added, anxious to run over and greet them. "She does things with flowers that makes nature proud." Immediately she ran over to the van, screaming.

I turned to look at the floral crew begin to unload some of their equipment, ladders and such. Della turned to give Sandy a big hug, even as Sandy was jumping up and down. Inside the van I could see what appeared to be a rainbow of textures and colors sprinkled with jewels and beads.

Sandy turned and waved me over, so I took Ma's hand and we walked over. The three teenagers with Della stopped their work as she waved them over to meet everyone.

"Honey, let me introduce you to Della!" Sandy almost sang.

I looked into some of the happiest, friendliest eyes I have had seen. Standing there with her three children I also saw quite a bit of pride in her face.

My hand went out to shake but she pulled me in for a hug. "I am so happy to be a part of your big day." She gave me a light kiss and pulled back.

"Here, let me introduce you to the rest of my crew, my wonderful children. Michael, come here...

"This is Michael Angelo Kilakila O Haleakala, my oldest."

I did shake his hand and felt the firm grip of a powerful personality. He was one of the most handsome men I have ever seen, brown eyes of considerable depth, short cropped hair waiting to curl in its next inch of growth, and tall. Easily 6 feet he was an imposing figure, fierce intelligence sparkling from deep inside.

"And, Matthew here," Della said pulling the darker hair teenager over. "Matthew Crews Kuahiwanani Waialeale is my designer in residence. He helps us fashion all the fantastic arrangements with his engineering ideas." She leaned over and gave him a big kiss, embarrassing him a little.

His hand was strong and he caught my eye with a glint of artistic light.

"And finally, but certainly not least is my daughter Angela Marie Ohialehua O Kaala. She has been singing at events and does a beautiful hula."

I took the young Angela's hand and kissed it as if she were nobility, which she appeared to be just under the surface of her surfer girl smile.

It was impressive to see such a family team all project such confidence and talent. I immediately had a sense that whoever this Tami Redes Roberts was, she was on to something with her understanding of what really was beautiful and elegant. I took note of her most excellent recommendation and filed away a little thought how I had met, early on, the heir apparent to Ms. Oprah.

~~~

It was still pretty early in the morning, but Sandy and her bridesmaids finally retreated back to the valley to get ready. Yo Vinny and Paden reluctantly remained behind, but apparently not without having impressed the Tahitians.

"You know Paden," Yo Vinny remarked as they both turned and walked back to the bar. "I gotta admit, that story about you riding on the back of a grizzly bear impressed those island girls."

Paden nodded and smiled. "Yeah, I think they liked that. But, hey! that tale you told about scuba diving with piranhas had 'em hanging on to your every word."

I listened to them from the bar, where I had found a few moments of peace from the hectic pace everywhere else. Besides, Tiwaka needed some company. Their voices stirred the bird into a little activity, jumping down from his perch to the bar top.

"Hey guys," I asked from the shadows. "Any luck with the girls?"

Both of them laughed. "Well, not really. Two of them were zoologists..." Paden was saying.

"Yeah and one was an oceanographer!" Yo Vinny complained. "Now they *all* know we're liars!"

"Well," I offered. "At least they know you're good storytellers."

The way I figured it the Tahitian girls probably appreciated the bravado and attention, if not the accuracy.

That thought was interrupted with the low pass of an airplane, right over the roof! We all ran out to check it and saw a Cessna 150 climbing back up over the ocean, then turning tight to dive at us again.

Paden seemed to know who is was. "Yo Vinny, do you think that's..."

Just as the plane was over us again, it dropped its wing so we could see inside. A very white butt was pushed up against the glass.

"Yep," Yo Vinny confirmed. "It's the Claw."

After this pass the plane flew back over the ocean and began a slow circular climb, straining to push through the cloud scattered tropical air.

Paden came up to me and asked how many Grolsch beers I had in stock.

"Probably a dozen or so with the flip tops," I remembered. It was one of my personal favorites.

"Good," Yo Vinny added.

"And," I remembered. "I have 1.5 liter giant as well, somewhere."

"Perfect!" Paden said. "You're gonna need all of them. Come on, lets get out to the ceremony site. They'll have to land there for sure."

I ran out from behind the bar again after ensuring the 1.5 liter was indeed cold. "Land?" I exclaimed.

"Oh yeah, we forgot to tell you," Paden said, looking over at Yo Vinny. "But, we have to now, I guess."

"Sure," Yo Vinny nodded. "We got some skydivers scheduled, for the party."

"You mean the wedding..." Paden corrected.

"Oh yeah, the wedding." Yo Vinny laughed. "Smack dab in the middle of the party."

"Every party needs a theme," Paden said slapping Yo Vinny on the shoulder. "And this one is a wedding!"

The three of us practically ran the few hundred feet to the cliffs and into the large field there. We could hear the plane's engine still struggling to climb, but not like it might fail. It was more like the little engine that could, working hard at doing what it knew it could.

We finally got to the field and tried to pick out the tiny dot that might be the plane. Just staring up into the sky that high was breathtaking.

"There it is!" Paden yelled. "Just south of straight up."

"Got it," Yo Vinny confirmed just as my eyes caught the barely perceptible movement of a black dot against the deep blues of space.

Just about then the engine noise stopped and a few seconds later one smaller dot emerged from the plane, and then a moment later another.

"I count two," Paden said, shielding his eyes from the brightness.

"Wait, there's another!" Yo Vinny added, a third tiny dot exiting the plane as it suddenly turned off its jump run and headed to the north of the skydivers.

"Three." Paden confirmed.

We watched fascinated as the three dots came together. They seemed to be playing some kind of game, a game of tag. They broke away from each other, came back toward each other, but then flew past their buddies. A moment later they came back together and stuck again. They then began to spin right, then left and after what must have been almost a minute they all split apart.

I could almost hear the rock and roll guitar riffs I might play along to this action, maybe *Pipeline Sequence* by Honk! As their chutes popped open, loud and multicolored we could hear them hooting and hollering.

The trades were blowing lightly from the east and they followed them until they got what seemed like just a few dozen feet above us. Immediately, in single file they turned into the wind and with the grace of a perfect landing, made a few tiny adjustments and swept through the grass to their feet.

We couldn't help but run over to them, thrilled to be a part of this. I could feel my face trapped in a big grin and fought the urge to pull it back.

The three skydivers were gathering their parachutes into big bundles under their arms and walking toward us with the jauntiness of a cowboy who could carry his own horse.

"Aloha!" the red headed beauty announced, waving at us.

"Hey Claw!" Paden yelled.

The guy they must be calling Claw had his arm around the red headed girl next to him, looking all the more a pirate with his booty.

"Howzit!" Claw returned. His curly brown hair did little to hide his sailor look or his extremely satisfied demur. I guessed every skydiver looked like that upon landing softly.

"Nice butt shot on the fly by Claw!" Yo Vinny joked.

"That fine derriere was, I'm afraid, too perfect to have been mine. Obviously it must have been the Irish Woman's!" Claw said, giving her a big hug.

"No way!" she complained. "Didn't you see all the hair on it?"

I could hear her slap his butt from where I was.

"Ouch baby!" Claw looked over at their third partner. "This here is Smilin' Mike folks. If you've ever been trapped in a remote African village, you've most likely been rescued by him."

Smilin' Mike waved at us, and true to his name gave us a big grinning hello.

"We needed to check out the landing zone before we bring in the troops this afternoon," the Irish Woman started to tell us.

"Gotta a couple of virgins in the group," Claw said, shaking his head.

"Virgins?" I had to ask.

Claw looked up and smiled a big 'I knew I could get you to ask' smile. "Yeah, virgins! Like in *never jumped into a field next to a cliff* virgins."

"We'll make sure they wear their swimsuits," Smilin' Mike said. "In case they miss."

My face must have registered more horror than my nervous laugh could disguise. "No worries," the Irish Woman conceded. "This was Claw's first time!"

Claw walked up to me, put his arm around my shoulders and whispered "It felt great too!"

"Now," he said quite a bit louder. "Where would be a few Grolsches?"

~~~

If I die young, I always said, I wanted to go during a party, a big blow out of a party. No one would probably notice until the next day, but I wouldn't care at that point. The advantage would be that I had gone out in the midst of a big time, when the world seemed to cater to us. The bonfires, the dancing, the camaraderie, the promise of adventure. And, I would miss the hangover as well.

Strangely enough, I thought of this while taking another few moments to sequester myself during the final hectic wedding preparations. My jitters had been under control for most of the morning until the preacher showed up with a parrot on her shoulder. She explained to me that the parrot and her were a team, that they would be singing during the ceremony and that I was fortunate to have her during this busy wedding season.

I just had not known, honestly, that I was actually *that* lucky. This was no time to get all particular about such details so I had decided to take a few moments to relax, up in the treehouse, above the fray.

My life, in and around a bar, was always a bit unpredictable, there was no doubt. But, today, this day, the day I was going to get married, was multiple times more so. I could handle it, I knew I could. It would just take a few extra deep breathes.

Paden had just found me hiding up in the tree and was calling up. "Yo dude!"

I couldn't hide much longer. People might think I had cold feet, which of course I didn't. I just needed a moment to let all the chaos sort itself out into a song. Noise into music.

"Hey!" Paden continued. "I heard the skydivers are going to jump in naked!"

~~~

It was only an hour left to ceremony time and I was just climbing out of the bamboo lined shower. I had shaved, stopped the bleeding, and combed my hair too. My closet door was open and one of my dark green Aloha shirts was hanging on the door knob with a note.

You'll look great in this one,
Love Sandy
p.s. You'll look great out of it too!

I chose a rare set of pants, a pair of Elvis-white slacks that looked great with bare feet. They fit loose enough to warrant a belt, so I chose my rope belt with gold buckle, but let my Aloha shirt hang out anyhow.

Walking over to my little treasure chest next to the bed, I opened it up for probably the first time in months. There, inside, were all my favorite tokens and memories from past adventures. I picked out a large 50 franc Tahitian coin, putting it in my right pocket. Then a large prehistoric shark tooth went into my left. A Captain Crunch plastic sailor from a long ago McDonalds visit joined the Polynesian francs as well as a eucalyptus seed and a Boston subway token. A few puka shells from Niihau joined the shark tooth and I was ready.

Turning to look in the mirror I studied my face. I watched my eyes, looking closely at my heart. I tried to find a moment there when I felt like I was transitioning to a new life. I just couldn't. I guess I had already done so.

I made my way out the door and down the ladder to the bar. Paden, Yo Vinny and Pa were there waiting on me. We all smiled and with a round of hugs set off for the ocean cliffs. I did notice one thing in particular though. The air was especially sweet and the grass tickled my feet.

Looking up at the palms trying so hard to decorate the sky behind them I laughed out loud. Maybe I did feel something different, something I had subconsciously been trying so long and so hard to do.

Pa came up to me, his arm around me lovingly. "How ya doing son?"

I turned to him, gave him a kiss on the cheek and remarked, "I guess I'm all grown up now Dad. Thanks."

~~~

The first thing I noticed were the flowers. They were everywhere. Pomanders were hanging from the trees, lei were strung from coconut to coconut. Pillars graced the path, decorated with countless orchid sprigs. The chairs, lined up like faithful menehune sported roses and bear grass. A flower petal path flowed like red lava up to two huge bamboo poles waving strand upon strand of purple and white orchids, all moving in the breeze like flags.

"Here, here! Wait one moment please!" Della the florist was rushing over with something in her hands. Angela was right with her holding boutonnieres as well.

"Hold still just a moment..." She pinned a large white orchid, surrounded by red berries onto my shirt. Angela pinned orange roses onto Paden and Yo Vinny. Pa got an orange cymbidium orchid with green coconut bark.

We all got a kiss on the cheek and an 'atta' boy as we continued up to the altar. Yo Vinny and Paden went first, stopping just a moment to get kisses from the Tahitian girls lining the inside aisles. Pa went next, shaking hands along the way and turning occasionally to see if I was following.

I was, until I saw Tiwaka. He was alone on a chair in the back row, watching me. No one sat next to him. His feet were nervously stomping, morse coding his fear. A fear that he would be left behind, a fear that my new love Sandy would take me out of his life slowly.

Tiwaka was like my little brother, there was nothing I could do about my new life, but there was one thing I could do for him. I gently bent over to him, picked him up and put him on my shoulder. We walked the rest of the way together, like we had always been, like we would always be.

I felt him rummaging around in my long curls, trying to make way to my ear, where he whispered as quietly as he could.

"I love you boss too much."

We moved along the red rose petal path slowly, people reaching over to touch Tiwaka's feathers and my Aloha shirt. It was Big Island silk afterall.

Ahead of Tiwaka and I was the Preacher Lady and her own parrot, both watching us very, very closely from the rising ground of the altar. Her dark green haku lei accented her white hair and ruddy complexion well. I wasn't so sure about the purple mumu though.

I could hear her humming a song now, moving her hands slowly up and out, and then the parrot started up too! It matched her note for note, but a couple of octaves higher. When its wings opened and spread out just like Preacher Lady's arms I had to look over at Tiwaka.

He was just turning to look at me, mouth slightly agape and eyes about as big as possible this side of the taxidermist. Just who was that parrot we both thought to ourselves?

Preacher Lady took our minds off that question though, as she now began to swing her expansive hips to the rhythm of the light drumming, and clapping her hands. I had to look twice just to be sure I saw what I thought I saw and yes, her head was back and her eyes closed in trance. Her parrot then, in perfect timing, began to make a hands clapping sound in tune with her.

I could feel Tiwaka getting a little agitated on my shoulder. He was picking up his feet and switching his full weight to one side, then repeated that on the other.

Reaching the bamboo poles and lining up next to Pa and the guys I looked out at the crowd and couldn't help by smile. Wow, they were beautiful! Everyone was full of color, flowers adorned every head or ear or shoulder.

The castaways had huge white hibiscus flowers in their right ears as well as bright purple lei around their necks. Tiki Chris Pinto's fedora even had a feather lei hat band. Sunshine Tiki actually had two white hibiscus flowers, one in each ear. Brad Beach and the striking Loli had something I had never seen before, a very large single lei that went around both of them.

Ma was in the front row, shimmering in her elegance and pearls. She was crying a little, so I gave her my best macho two thumbs up right as my eyes filled as well.

I tried to blink away the tears, but they fell out onto my cheeks anyhow. Trying to look around a bit to gain my composure I got a moment to take in the view. Haleakala was clear from the sea to the summit, the expansive green of the jungle rising up dramatically from where we stood. The tropical blue radiated through the sunshine wearing her own white pearls in the few little clouds hanging out for the show. It was stunning.

Or so I thought. Until I saw Sandy. Her entourage came around the corner of ti leaf bushes with an impact that hit me hard right in the chest.

It might have been the now heavy drums that heralded her entrance or it might have been my absolute amazement but I had to consciously take a breath. Her bridesmaids were wearing short grass skirts, ankle adornments of yellow flowers and oversized thick lei that almost covered their otherwise bare chests. I think I heard Yo Vinny mutter 'oh my god', again. Their haku head lei were bright red and each had two flowers woven into the very ends of their long black hair. The four of them glided through my vision, a lost sailor's water deprived hallucination. They were too exotic to be real.

Sandy soon moved into my vision, drawing my eyes to her with perfect clarity. Half expecting something exotic as well, I was forced to blink twice. A stunning hand sewn and perfectly New England whale bone white dress offset her glowing tanned skin with every bit of elegance the universe could afford.

We caught each others eyes from 20 meters. I knew our big smiles were reflections in a mirror, each of us taking our turns over these last many months as the glass. We complimented each other, encouraged the other and often felt perfectly content showing the other their own beauty.

The small crowd watching her approach had gasped a little at the bridesmaids, but fell into a burst of applause when they saw Sandy. I heard later, years later in fact, that everyone still thought she was the most extraordinarily beautiful bride they had ever seen. Hands down.

No longer a thirsty sailor I now stood tall, and proud. Proud of my queen. Mostly though, I was dumbfounded. I simply stared, my jaw falling to gravity. Still watching me she gave me a wink. That brought me out of my trance, always the princess at heart.

Vic met her at the beginning of the pathway, took her arm and looked over at me. He was impeccably dressed in his best khakis topped with one of my rainbow splashed Aloha shirts, polished coconut buttons and all.

I gave him a double thumbs up and they began to walk toward me. The drums quickly ceased. It was then that I noticed the four big tenors standing on either side of the bamboo poles, slightly behind me. Dressed in many yards of colorful cloth I recognized the opening in those 'deep in the coconut jungle village' voices from the old Blue Hawaii movie;

"*Ko a-lo-ha ma-ka-mea e i-po.*"

I had thought they might just play a recording of Elvis' Hawaiian Wedding Song, but I was wrong. Very, very wrong.

The next line of the song, sung by Elvis in the movie, came from behind me, as if the man had never left the building.

"This is the moment," the Preacher Lady crooned.

I turned immediately to her, not believing my ears. She was spot on Elvis!

Her parrot echoed her in Hawaiian, *"ma-ka-mea."* The big tenors had the parrot backed uped as well.

"I've waited for", the tenors echoing softly in Hawaiian.

I turned around to look at Sandy again, my expression of surprise mixing right in with my fascination with my Bride.

"I can hear my heart singing"

"Soon bells will be ringing"

The tenors echoed with *"ring...ring...ring...ring"*

Vic and Sandy walked slowly, one step at a time, in a gentle rhythm to music. The guests soon began a slow sway back and forth as well. Sunshine Tiki had both of his white hibiscus flowers in his hands held high, swaying like lighters at a concert. The Tahitian girls turned toward Sandy, their hands doing a welcoming hula.

I had to turn back to the Preacher Lady to see if this was actually happening, the best Elvis I had ever heard. Her eyes avoided mine as she continued.

"This is the moment"

"Love's sweet Aloha"

She stepped forward a little, her arms outstretching to the crowd, her parrot faithfully holding on.

"I will love you longer than forever"

"Promise me that you will leave me never"

Her parrot was swaying with the music too, head tilted back quietly mouthing the words herself. Tiwaka, still on my shoulder, was busy keeping an eye on this other parrot as well, maybe both eyes.

My eyes though, went back to the center of the universe, walking up the aisle now, beaming like the sun herself. My heart was in the full grip of her tractor beam and suddenly I found the words coming from me as well.

"Here and now dear"

"All my love I vow dear"

Preacher Lady was hitting the low notes sweetly making my voice sound a lot better than it might have. I glanced over at Vic, still holding Sandy's arm as they moved toward me. His cheeks were streaked all the way to his proud chin. He was mouthing the words as well.

"Promise me that you will leave me never"

"I will love you longer than forever"

At this point everyone joined in for the Hawaiian chorus, thankfully having practiced it for weeks. This was so much better than I had expected. My arms rose on their own, embracing the scene before me.

"U-a, si-la"

"Pa-a ia me o-e"

"Ko a-lo-ha ma-ka-mea e i-po"

"Ka-'u ia e le-i a-e ne-i la"

Sandy joined in with me now, stepping up and taking my arm.

"Now that we are one"

"Clouds won't hide the sun"

Preacher Lady threw out her chest and bellowed, her head shaking a little as she sang,

"Blue skies of Hawaii smile"

"On this, our wedding day"

I said to Sandy, now standing very close to me, and she repeated it right back at me, smiling with a laughter at our big production.

"I do"

"love you"

"with all my heart"

Vic reached up to shake my hand and then stepped back. The song was over and everyone was wildly clapping. One of the musicians began drawing a violin stick over his specially tuned ukulele, playing softly one of the sweetest sounds I have ever heard.

The crowd took their seats as Preacher Lady and her parrot moved forward to speak, the ukulele violin sweetly decorating the background breezes.

"No Keia La, No Keia Po, A Mau Loa," Her voice had suddenly found that tonal quality which matched her better, an older heavy set lady. Elvis, I realized, had now left the building.

"From this day, from this night, forever more," she continued. "We have gathered here, in this most special of places, to greet God and his two children and welcome them into holy matrimony."

Tiwaka was still on my shoulder, but as I turned to Sandy and went to hold her hands, he fluttered off. I couldn't see where he went, but Sandy laughed a little while looking at the Preacher Lady. Looking too, I saw that Tiwaka was now on the other shoulder of Preacher Lady. She didn't seem to mind at all, actually I think she liked it twice as much. The two parrots sure seemed to enjoy it.

As I turned back to Sandy, I thought I heard him try and whisper to the other parrot, "Howzit..."

~~~

The skies graced us with a very light sprinkling of rain that had moved down from the upper valleys, but lasted only a minute. As it moved out to sea the sun caught it just right and we got ourselves a full rainbow. I've seen 10,000 rainbows. Every one of them rocked.

The vows were done, and the reception music had begun, even as we stayed between the bamboo poles. I looked down at our rings, glinting in the light and wondered at how momentous this was. Sandy and I were now married! Deep inside somewhere I felt awestruck.

She was hugging her Mom and I took a moment. A moment to turn and look out to the ocean. I knew it couldn't really show favorites but I looked into its deep cobalt blues and sparkling whites and felt it smile back.

People were lining up to congratulate us now. Preacher Lady, now with both parrots had us sign the official Maui County Wedding Certificate and then retreated back into the crowd. Tiwaka gave me a very stoked look and I winked at him. Good luck dude...

I looked around the crowd and finally found Wailani, standing in the very back, at some distance, standing by herself. Her eyes were that now familiar large round watery affirmation of who she really was. A large yellow sunhat shaded her well, but I think she wanted me to see, see her now.

There was something in her face, satisfaction perhaps, or maybe it was simply accomplishment. Whatever it was it felt like history and the future itself had been tweaked for Sandy and I, for some very good reason.

Wailani nodded slightly to me, reached into her purse and retrieved a pair of large sunglasses. Putting them on she then moved into the receiving line with all the others.

Sandy was squeezing me as we both said our mahalos to our guests. Auntie Lois was several feet behind the last guest we shook hands with so I took the time to turn to Sandy. Looking deeply into her eyes, and seeing mine reflected there I deftly moved my hand up to her stomach and knew right then ~ our very good reason.

She moved in to kiss me. The last thing I remember before the world turned off all around me again, was the sound of cheering and in the not very far distance the sounds of extremely cheerful little children.

~~~

Invisible Shadows

It had been a couple of months since Sandy and I had returned from our honeymoon in Tahiti. I was just about recovered, but still felt my feet start tapping when I heard heavy drums.

I saw Ranger Ev again, on my way through Makawao for some upcountry produce. He said he was back again, not alone, but without the "Honoluluans". Indeed he was.

She had olive skin with reflective black hair, eyes too deep to show color and a smile that rivaled any. They were headed up to the summit of Haleakala, for an overnight hike through the crater.

"Well, it's a big ol' full moon," I volunteered, trying not to ask if he had ever done that before and if he was prepared.

"Gotta be the 20th time or so that I've done it," he added, solving my problem as well.

"It's my first!" The Italian beauty told me, proudly. "Ranger Ev here said I will do just fine."

He looked down at her with admiration for a long moment. "We both might get a little sore, but it'll be worth the effort."

I wasn't often envious of anyone, but here I was thinking it would be fun to have less chores. I thought about my being tied so closely to the bar, and how much fun it might be to float the planet like the Ranger. But I knew... knew I had a baby on the way. And I also knew I had a good job, lived in one of the few perfect spots on Earth and had found an angel, Sandy, to surf with and to love. And surf, geez, the surf! I almost neglected the obvious! But, I had to ask him, as soon as his friend went for a Tejava.

"Ranger, I need to ask your advice. A question."

He looked at me with a moment of hesitation or seriousness, I wasn't sure which. "Sure dude, no worries. Ask away."

I looked over his shoulder, she was still shopping. "Look, how do you manage? You know, to always be on adventure, footloose and fancy free? I want...I need to get back to that, those days. Somehow.

"But, you see," I turned my head around, as if I were in the middle of Tiwaka's and not on a sidewalk ten miles away. "I got a good gig going on here, maybe better than I could expect anywhere else. I got a baby on the way! And Sandy! A wife who digs me. You see? See what I mean? Man, my crayon is bright, but I've got to stay inside the lines."

Ranger kind of nodded and smiled as if he had asked that question. "That's funny. I always thought of you, and the people like you that I run across, as the ones to be envious of. I feel like I'm a foreigner. An alien tourist coming to Earth to see the best of the best. And, when I stop at one of this planet's most pristine places, or most intimate cities or even a jungle bar, I feel like I am only a ticket holder to see the show. That I don't belong, nor can stay very long. But, you! You guys are the actors, the ones who really get to live it, to be it."

He looked at me with a quick intensity for a brief second or two, and then withdrew, his feet having never moved.

"I understand though, I get it," he continued. "No one really knows that they have perfection until they venture out and see imperfection. How could you know? You can't. You, my friend, are one of those lucky ones. You know it, somewhere deep inside." He tapped his heart lightly and then brought the same hand up smoothly to touch his forehead. "You know."

He was right, I knew. I had traveled years earlier. But, I wasn't traveling anymore.

"Yeah, thanks. But, I'm still anchored here. What do you do, after you've traveled, after you've seen the adventure in far away places?"

A burst of wind moved through the hundred year old stores on Makawao Avenue, catching his long curls as he considered an answer. It appeared, at least to me right then and there, that the traveling angels were already trying to move him along. For just a brief second, I saw the Ranger as a lost soul, trapped in wanderlust. A prisoner of his own curiosity for the world.

He seemed to mentally brush those angels away and root himself for at least a moment. This man's clock was obviously ticking, and he was trying to enjoy the precious seconds he had in any one place.

I watched his face closely, watched him fashion an answer that I expected to placate my imprisonment, albeit on Maui. Kind words, as it were, to offer the caged peacock.

"If you are indeed anchored then you are invested in a place you *must* like, right? Or else you would pull anchor and sail away! Of course." He threw his arms out again to emphasize his point. "Believe me, the world has many perfect patches to settle in, and they all have their boundaries. Those boundaries might be visible from time to time.

314

That's OK." For a moment he paused and then with his eyes more focused than I could almost stand to watch he added, "Stay inside the lines - just draw them wider."

His arms were moving around like he might actually hug the sky. "Look," he added. "Look around. This is you, this island, this entire feeling. It's your reality, no doubt about it."

He looked around again, just like a tourist might trying to soak it all in. "Me? Mine? My reality is different. But, it's no less real, certainly no *more* real than yours. We have ... we live in ... separate realities. For a few days, ours have overlapped, and for that I feel fortunate indeed." He slapped me lightly on the shoulder and grinned.

The Italian Beauty was returning, her arms full of bottled water from far away places, cheese and crackers from closer by. The Ranger caught my eye catching hers. He turned to see and went to help.

I watched them embrace as they traded away her fullness for his emptiness. I smelled love too, somehow. I say smell because it was a sense, just not one of the five famous ones. He walked back over for a brief moment.

"The mountain beckons dude. The moon will soon tell me stories I haven't yet heard." He glanced over at his companion, then looked me straight in the eyes. "What did we do right?"

He lost me there. "What?"

Laughing a little he explained. "What did we do so damn well, before, to get a chance at Earth? To be human?" He said it all a little too loudly.

I hunched my shoulders and thought about that.

"Dude," he added, pointing up to the purples in the late afternoon sky. "Something out there loves us bigtime!" He walked away with the Italian beauty, but didn't get far, just out of voice range when he turned back to me.

Taking a long baguette in each hand he slowly drew out a big circle all around him and mouthed the words I would remember forever. "Draw them wider."

~ ~ ~

It must have been a month later, when it happened, as I was driving the truck back from town with supplies. I circled around the airport back road to beat some of the traffic and hoping to have a widebody swoop over me. Two hundred feet between you and a landing spaceship was always entertaining. I looked east toward their typical downwind leg to see if any planes might be in the pattern to land at Kahului.

There, one of Hawaiian Air's older 767s glided against a backdrop of the rising slopes of Haleakala. The sun was at my back and painting the colors of the aircraft vividly. Immediately, it began a shallow turn toward me and my thoughts.

As it dropped lower and lower it moved right through the light cloud cover mid way down the mountain. It was fascinating to watch it move so gracefully through such an intoxicating sky, full of depth and texture.

The thin clouds that rung the mountain were spread out toward the airport and I. They seemed to point the way for the pilots inside the flight deck of the massive flying machine. Inside the flight attendants no doubt having been here a million times looked forward to a quick ocean dip and an early night. Couples planning on beach weddings held each others hands as they craned their necks to see the green expanse of sugar cane fields below. New lovers entwined their feet as they imagined a long night of exploration. Dozens of Northwesterners and Canadians were probably plotting out their Costco run before rushing out to their Kihei condos, in time to make the sunset from their balconies.

Everyone had an adventure, wherever they were. I thought of mine so far, and what I might be fortunate enough to have tomorrow and the next day, and the next decade.

The plane moved a little lower yet, sparkling in the bright afternoon sun when suddenly it's colors softened. The glare off the polished wings faded to detail and beautiful lines. In another moment it left the shadow and moved back into the brilliance.

Suddenly, something made sense deep inside my imagination. There it was. The invisible nature of miracles. I could always sense it, but now I knew why I could never quite see it. It took something else to show it to you, like the airplane showing me the shadow. The shadow was always there, you just couldn't see it unless something moved through it.

A lot of things came together then, how all the wonder in my surroundings here on this little island were just different ways of showing me something that was already there. The magnificent mountains, the unresting ocean, the winds and the waterfalls. And the people, the fascinating and extraordinary qualities in all of them. They were all like that airplane, manifesting the invisible. The invisible nature of God I suppose.

~~~

I continued to day dream a bit as the plane finally flew right overhead, the wing tips creating those ripping vortex sounds that followed a couple of hundred feet behind all that aluminum. A van full of kids had stopped to watch as well. It was a big event even if it was repeated a hundred times a week.

I could sense the excitement. The plane was no doubt full of excited people, anxious to dive into the reality of their tropical dreams. And the Island, subtle as always, couldn't hide her excitement either, despite her quiet majesty in trying. It was a symbiotic love between a place overflowing with magic and those hoping to find some.

I had to get on back, to Sandy, the parrot and the bar. A lucky soul or two on that airplane might actually find their way to Tiwaka's tonight. A Coco Loco Moco might already be on their minds. Glancing one last time at the airplane now kissing the runway I wondered if they all knew how fortunate they were.

~~~

As I pulled back onto a now empty road and headed toward Paia and the jungle, the full moon quietly moved into view. Soft but determined clouds moved toward me on the tradewinds, racing ahead of each other ~ all of them obviously trying to be the first to give up their own little magic to someone here ~ on the little island of Maui, in the middle of the third planet's most wonderful of oceans.

~ ~

INSPIRATIONS

~ the clean drug: music

~ Ku`u Home O Kahalu`u, by Jerry Santos and Olomana

~ old dogs that don't bark

~ cats that follow you on a walk, like a dog

~ spontaneous parties

~ cookouts that clean out the refrigerator

~ little kids that look up at me and squint

~ birds that will eat out of my hand

~ volcanic sunsets

~ my son Michael's awesome musical discoveries on iTunes

~ rainbow dreams ~ thanks Matthew, my other cool son!

~ my daughter Angela's text messages that say: I love you!

~ Della, my wonderful wife and her patience in educating me
  about what is beautiful and wonderful when I don't see it
  the first time.

~ warm surf on a sunny morning

~ the sequence of events that got me this far

~~

* Tiki Drink Recipes *
Tiki Chris Pinto

proprietor of TikiLoungeTalk.com and Facebook Tiki Pioneer

The Tiki Galore

1 oz. Amaretto
1 oz. Dark Rum
1/2 oz. Triple Sec
2 oz. Orange Juice
1/2 tspn powdered sugar

Pour everything into a shaker with shaved ice, shake, and strain over ice cubes in a tiki glass. Garnish with everything tropical-looking you can find. You can make it a little more tart by squeezing in some lemon, a little sweeter with more sugar.

~

Cap't Mack's Pirate Grog

1 oz Sailor Jerry Rum
1 oz Malibu Coconut Rum
1 oz Dark Rum (I prefer Meyer's)
3 drops bitters
1/4 teaspoon vanilla
sprinkle of nutmeg
Coke
Lime

Start with a shaker of ice, add the three rums, bitter, and vanilla. Shake it up, baby. Strain into a large Tiki mug filled with ice. Liquor should fill mug about half way. Fill with Coke, squeeze in juice of 1/4 lime, and two shakes of nutmeg, stir. Top with a little more nutmeg and lime wedge. Damned good grog! IF you like it sweet, add a little pineapple juice to taste. Avast!

Sunshine Tiki

proprietor of ZenTikiLounge.com and Facebook Tiki Pioneer

Coral Beauty

1 oz Canton Ginger Liquor
1 oz Cruzan Aged Silver Rum
2 oz Fresh Grapefruit Juice (Yellow)
1/2 oz Ginger Sour Syrup*
1/2 oz Coruba Dark Rum float
Combine all but dark rum in shaker with ice. Shake well to combine citrus and rum. Pour into brandy snifter filled with crushed ice. Garnish with 1/3 grapefruit wheel and 2 maraschino cherries.

*Ginger Sour Syrup: To 1 cup 151 Rum, add 1 cup fresh chopped and peeled ginger, zest of two ruby red grapefruits, 40 allspice berries crushed. Let it sit covered overnight. In another jar, mix 2 cup sugar, the juice of 2 pink grapefruits and juice of 3 lemons till the sugar is dissolved. Carefully strain solids out of rum mixture with coffee filter or cheese cloth. Strain juice mixture through filter as well to remove pulp. Combine both mixtures in a larger jar or bottle. Chill. Stores for about 90 days. Great in cocktails, iced tea and club soda.

~

Tiki In Love

2 oz pineapple juice
1 oz passion fruit juice
1 oz orange juice
1 oz passion fruit vodka
1 oz amber rum (Mt. Gay works well)
Squeeze of lemon juice

Toss everything in your shaker with ice. Shake. Pour into tiki mug filled with crushed ice. Garnish with pineapple spear. Also makes a great punch when made in large quantities. Float an ice ring in the punch bowl to prevent too much dilution.

Those are two of my favorites and guests always ask for another. Safe bets.

Brad Beach

proprietor of BeachOutpost.com and Facebook Tiki Pioneer

Blue Coco Mojo

The infused syrup adds an exotic kick to this tall rum concoction.
Makes 1 drink

Ingredients:
1/4 oz blue Curaçao
1-1/2 oz Cruzan Estate Light Rum
1-1/2 oz CocoMint Syrup (recipe follows)
1 oz fresh lime juice
2 oz chilled seltzer water

For garnishing:
Fresh mint and/or cilantro sprigs
Shaved coconut (optional)

Directions:
1. Fill a tall glass with ice. Measure in the Curaçao, rum, syrup, lime juice, and fizzy seltzer water. Stir with a bar spoon.
2. Garnish with fresh mint and/or cilantro and a sprinkling of shaved coconut, if using.

~

CocoMint Syrup

Makes 3 cups, enough for about 16 drinks

Ingredients:
1 cup shredded sweetened coconut
1/4 teaspoon red pepper flakes
1 bunch fresh mint, torn
12 large sprigs fresh cilantro
2 cups sugar
2 cups water

Directions:
1. Combine the ingredients in a medium saucepan and bring to a boil. Boil for 2 to 3 minutes. Remove from heat and let steep for 1 hour.
2. Strain, pressing out as much liquid as possible, then discard the solids.
3. Let cool to room temperature. If not using immediately, cover and refrigerate, for up to 1 month, until needed. Remix before using.

Stacey Smith

owner of Maui Bars Are Us .com

LAVATINI

Vodka, Passion Juice, Guava Juice and Strawberry liquer shaken and poured into a Martini glass, with Strawberry Puree, streaming down the inside of the glass like MOLTEN LAVA!

YAHOO!!

~ drink responsibly, mahalo ~

~~

ALOHA KAKOU

~~

Made in the USA
Lexington, KY
05 August 2012